AMERICAN ROMANTIC

ALSO BY WARD JUST

AMERICAN ROMANTIC

Ward Just

Houghton Mifflin Harcourt
BOSTON   NEW YORK

For information about permission to reproduce selections from this book,
write to Permissions, Houghton Mifflin Harcourt Publishing Company,
215 Park Avenue South, New York, New York 10003.

www.hmhco.com

Library of Congress Cataloging-in-Publication Data
Just, Ward S.
American romantic / Ward Just.
pages cm
ISBN 978-0-544-19637-7
I. Title.
PS3560.U75A86 2014
813'.54—dc23
2013026310

Printed in the United States of America
DOC 10 9 8 7 6 5 4

To Sarah

PRELUDE

THESE EVENTS HAPPENED a while back, when the war was not quite a war, more a prelude to a war. Their army was called a guerrilla force. Our army was called a Military Assistance Command. The war is the least of the story that follows. It cast its own shadow, and to live within it was to live within a sphere of strained silence and self-reliance.

Foreign service officer Harry Sanders was visiting river villages in one of the southern provinces. He traveled by boat with a helmsman and a bodyguard, a lethargic army sergeant who sat in the stern, a carbine in his lap, his eyes invisible behind army-issue sunglasses. Foliage along the edges of the river was thick and, where the channel narrowed, so close that the leaves touched the boat's hull. The helmsman throttled back, explaining that he was disoriented by the river water, dead still and reflective as a mirror. Stare at it long enough and it was hard to tell up from down.

The Americans were there to inspect projects in five villages, a schoolhouse in one, wells in two others, a guardhouse in the fourth, a clinic in the fifth. The clinic was Harry's particular interest, certainly the most troubling, completed only the week before. Construction delays were chronic. The idea was to verify that the work had been done and that the projects were fully operational and useful to the inhabitants. There were always complaints and Harry

3

was there to listen to the complaints—the leaking roofs, the lack of proper medicines, the strange noise the well made. In each village the headman would take Harry to the project, whatever it was, and explain the difficulty, and Harry wrote the complaints in a notebook and promised action, though not right away. The sergeant always stood a little apart, holding his carbine while he scrutinized the surroundings. The first three villages were empty of people, always a bad sign. Asked about that, the headman would say the people were in the fields, harvesting. But they were nowhere in sight. The villages were the soul of silence. Nothing moved in the damp heat. Even the insects had disappeared. Asked about the security situation, the headman smiled vaguely and said there had been no change. The villages were exposed. Why, only the other day a platoon of the enemy had arrived at dusk and harangued them for an hour or more. There were threats. Finally they took what they wanted and departed. What did they want? They wanted food and volunteers and went away with the food and three teenage boys. The headman was small of stature, middle-aged, with a wispy beard that fell to his chest. His eyes were hooded and he never looked directly at Harry.

We should go now, the sergeant said.

What do you see?

Nothing. That's the trouble.

Harry thanked the headman and gave him some money and he and the sergeant walked slowly down the path to the boat. When Harry looked back, the headman had vanished. He wondered how they did it, disappear into thin air like Ali Baba. He thought that somehow they dwelled in a parallel universe, one of their own making. The American presence covered them the way a shroud covered a grave. No hint of the shape of things beneath the shroud. The shroud was opaque. Anything could be under it, a corpse or a bomb or a pygmy elephant or a naked woman. And if the shroud were suddenly ripped away—well, perhaps one would find nothing at all. Harry supposed that someday a native of the region would

4

write a poem describing the parallel universe, its weather and dimensions, its values, what it loved and what it loathed, its aspirations. Why were foreigners hated so? Not only Americans but everyone else. And the poem would be translated into an English filled with obscure allusions, dry as dust but something seething beneath the surface.

They motored on to Village Number Four, mostly unoccupied, though the word that came to mind was abandoned. The guardhouse looked unoccupied. The headman stood impassively to greet him, two small children hanging on his legs. Harry took the presence of the children as a hopeful sign. They were the only hopeful sign, and as he looked about him at the stilted houses and the gray concrete guardhouse he thought that a splash of color would improve the look of things. He often summoned optimistic images when in the sullen countryside and what he conjured now was a newspaper kiosk, the sort of cheerful amenity found on Paris boulevards. Perhaps a café with red awnings and a white-aproned waiter balancing a drinks tray on the tips of his fingers. Somewhere nearby music floated from an open window, French cabaret, horns and violins and Piaf's raw throat. Girls in short skirts, a boulevardier walking his dog . . . The mirage was unsuccessful. Perhaps next time, something more durable, the Hoover Dam or a Mayan pyramid. Stonehenge. Harry shook hands with the headman, who avoided looking him in the eye. They stood a moment talking of the security situation, the weather, his family. The weather was normal, the security situation in flux, his wife was ill. Harry said, Your village appears deserted. Where is everyone? The headman moved his arms as if to indicate they were elsewhere, in the fields, round and about, parts unknown.

Harry nodded as if he sympathized. He always wondered how the villagers got on from day to day. He had difficulty imagining ordinary life in this settlement that looked so sour and bereft and fantastic at the same time—as if somewhere in the knotted jungle was a great golden temple with flourishing gardens and still

5

ponds. The stilted houses seemed to float unmoored above the earth. There were just six houses and the guardhouse. Of course these were observations from Western eyes, fundamentally doubtful. Certainly life in this village was as dense as life anywhere, subtle rules and ordinances, unusual understandings, civic mysteries, all of it crowded by the ghosts of ancestors. It was said that native people wanted what everyone everywhere wanted, a roof over their heads, three meals a day, a doctor's care when they were sick, a more prosperous life generally; the rule of law would come in there somewhere. Surely all this was true but there was much more besides, a way of life that was in some measure unique, a life that honored the past and spoke to the spirit. In any case, in this village intruders were tolerated but not welcome. There had been many intruders over the centuries and what they had brought was grief. Harry and the headman walked to the guardhouse, the headman silent. He had exhausted his English and so they stood mute before the building. This was yet another difficulty. The language was complex and not easily mastered, a tongue of indirection and metaphor, untimely laughter as punctuation. Perhaps that was how remote societies protected themselves, presenting a masked face to the world, a face so blank that anything could be read into it.

Guardhouse roof leaks, the headman said.

Ah, Harry said.

Three leaks.

Three?

I have put pots on the floor.

For the leaks?

Yes, for the leaks.

Harry looked in and saw the pots in the corner, and where the washstand was meant to be there was a television set, its antenna coiled uselessly beside it.

I'll see to the leaks, Harry said. No prisoners, I see.

We are a peaceable village, the headman said.

All this time, Sergeant Orono had been looking at his watch

6

while he snapped gum. Harry smiled at the headman and the headman smiled back.

They returned to the boat and continued downriver to the fifth village, the one with the clinic that lacked medicine and a competent doctor. The river meandered, its slow current weary in the afternoon heat. The river widened and the sergeant seemed to relax. Then he lit a cigarette, all the while staring into the vegetation, reeds and light green bushes. He stared now to port, now to starboard, watching for movement, but there was no movement nor any breath of air. No birds. The helmsman suddenly throttled back. He nudged Harry, took a deep breath, and pointed at his nose. The air was different. Decaying vegetation and the silty smell of water yielded to something else.

Smoke, Sergeant Orono said.

Ahead, the helmsman said.

Our village, the sergeant said. This is not good news. We should abort.

Full ahead, Harry said to the helmsman.

The goddamn village is burning, the sergeant said.

We will keep on, Harry said.

You are not *armed*, the sergeant said.

Nevertheless, Harry said, I have orders.

Smell it now, the helmsman said. I think the sergeant's right.

I've been here before, Harry said. It's an ordinary village. No better, no worse than the last one.

So have I, said the sergeant. I've taken fire from this village. It's a shit village, enemy village.

Slow ahead, Harry said.

The helmsman decreased speed a fraction, steering the boat to midriver. The surface was glassy and the reflections of the trees made it difficult to tell up from down. A Janus-faced river, Harry thought. But the river was safer than inland, where line of sight was nil. Smoke was visible now, rising in a gray cloud and dispersing. Harry tried to remember the name of the village but could not. He always thought of it as Village Number Five, the last on the list. He had the name in his notebook but had no wish to consult the notebook now. Dead slow, Harry told the helmsman, and the boat commenced to drift, carried by the invisible current. The channel narrowed again and when they swung around a lazy bend they saw two small boats disappear downriver, away from the village. The settlement came slowly into view. The houses were built on stilts owing to storms during the rainy season, the river filling and overflowing its banks. The sky above the clearing opened up, pale blue that seemed to go on forever. In the sky nothing moved. What a terrible place to live, Harry thought, and then remembered his last visit and his admiration for the simple construction of the houses, so austere in the clearing. They looked as if they had been occupied for a hundred years. Maybe more. Maybe since the coming of Christ, village life unchanged for two millennia. Births, life, death.

The helmsman settled the boat to the dock and waited. Smoke rose from a building at the far edge of the village. The clinic. The building looked destroyed within. Harry remembered the clinic's file, a dozen inch-thick folders describing the community and its importance to the region. That was guesswork. The village had some religious significance, but no one knew precisely the nature of the significance; it was said that a holy man had lived there in the previous century, an ascetic admired for his literary works. The village surely deserved a proper clinic. Three years of deliberation before authorization, the Parthenon itself probably received less scrutiny. The file was a masterwork of the bureaucratic art, due diligence run amok, the dimensions of the clinic and exactly where it was to be located. The materials. The shape of the windows and the door. Its height. Its cost. And who would build it? The army offered support but the army had its own procedures and methods. No one thought to consult the villagers, who had scant knowledge of the methods and procedures. Due diligence was not in their repertoire, and certainly the province chief was on board; he himself would see to the materials. And when the clinic was completed at last, it became the centerpiece of a congratulatory hearing before a subcommittee of the United States House of Representatives, lavish praise from the chairman. The ambassador himself journeyed to the village for a look-around and a meeting with notables of the province. Of course all this was before the money spigot was in full flow, millions following millions, more than enough to buy the train to haul the coals to Newcastle, procedures and methods be damned. But now the clinic was finished, erased by the arsonist's match.

Harry stepped off the boat and secured the line, Sergeant Orono behind him, his carbine at port arms. The helmsman said he would remain with the boat and then thought better of the idea, and the three of them advanced in the silence of the afternoon, passing one vacant house after another. The smell of smoke grew sharper, acrid, sour to the taste. In the windless afternoon nothing moved. He could have been looking at a vast canvas in a gallery, an oil in nine shades of blue, no focus to it, blurred at the edges. There was no sign of life but Harry believed he was being watched.

We've seen enough, the sergeant said. The helmsman nodded agreement.

Go back to the boat, Harry said. I want to look at the clinic close-up. I'll join you in five minutes.

Harry walked on alone. The dirt surround was immaculate, free of litter, not so much as a gum wrapper or cigarette stub. This was not normal. When he reached the clinic he called out but received no answer. He waited a moment, then stepped back when a figure appeared at the door. The light was failing but he recognized the village headman, a cloth bundle in his arms. He was filthy and the bundle was filthy. The headman stared straight ahead and if he noticed Harry he gave no sign. He moved his head and the cloth fell away to reveal a young girl. She was emaciated, skin drawn tight over her face and limbs. She was rigid in the headman's arms, her mouth agape. Harry asked if he could help but the headman said nothing. Perhaps he hadn't heard. He seemed to be in another realm altogether, a place of unassailable privacy. Harry took another step

9

back, understanding now that he was not looking at a young girl but a middle-aged woman. The headman carried her as if she were light as a doll. He swayed, appearing to lose his footing, and suddenly sat on the top step of the clinic's verandah. And still he did not speak. The woman moved her fingers, searching for something. Her eyes were large and black as a doll's, without expression. She was surely near death. Harry was reminded of photographs of Nazi death camps and also of photographs from Hiroshima and Nagasaki, not at the time of the explosions but many months later, burned and radiated survivors cared for by their families or left to die alone. A shortage of beds. Never enough morphine. A photograph always put the viewer at a remove, present but not present. A photograph was only a piece of film paper, the result of a shutter's click from an invisible hand, though the most poignant did remain in the memory of anyone who saw it. Harry took another step back. He had no business there, yet he was drawn to the woman as if she were somehow kin. But they were not kin. They were mysteries to each other and he was an intruder, a minor official of the American government unable to offer anything of value, unless compassion had value and he doubted that it did. Compassion was only personal. He heard the sergeant call his name, the voice abrupt in the stillness of the moment. The clinic continued to smolder, almost extinguished now; he had no idea if others were inside. Harry had the thought that he was witnessing an event from the deep past, decades past, centuries, and he himself the unwelcome guest, uninvited, a voyeur come to observe the suffering, a simple bystander unable to supply even the most meager assistance—and then he stepped forward to ask the question, What happened here? But the headman paid him no attention and the woman closed her eyes. Her body shivered and seemed to wither, her limbs drooping as if made of putty. Harry had never watched someone die. She made no sound. The headman pulled a flask from the pocket of his jacket and put it to her mouth, still agape, the water spilling over her chin and falling to her chest, darkening the cloth tunic. The flask was empty and still the headman did not move in his observance of what surely was the last sacrament.

Harry! the sergeant called, his voice urgent. Then, softly, Get out of there now.

He stood quietly a minute longer, then stepped back once more. From the interior of the clinic a soldier in fatigues appeared, followed by three more. They wore forage caps that looked to be of U.S. Army issue and their faces were camouflaged with soot. They ignored the headman and the dead woman in his arms, indeed seemed as weary as soldiers anywhere after a long march. Their fatigues were filthy, torn in places. Their carbines were slung carelessly over their shoulders. They were young and three of the four wore wire-rim spectacles, giving them the appearance of students, except for the carbines, now unslung as one of them pointed his at Harry, standing alone twenty paces away. Harry thought they looked at him with curiosity, this tall American in khaki trousers and a blue polo shirt, as if he had just come from the terrace of some suburban country club. They wore no badges of rank, but the oldest, perhaps he was thirty years old, seemed to be the one in charge. The other three were looking at the headman and the dead woman without interest. Harry felt his left leg begin to twitch, the usual sign of nerves. He took one more step backward, his arms at his sides. The elder soldier had locked eyes with him, a frank challenge, daring him to make some move. Either that or something else. All this time in-country and he had never before seen the face of the enemy. This was in the hands of God, Harry thought. He was a believer but thought God was often distracted and careless, not someone to count on. God went His own way — certainly great, but cryptic also. Now the soldier raised his hand in warning but Harry paid no attention, taking a step backward once again. The soldier shouted something and raised his carbine but Harry paid no attention to that, either. He turned his back and walked slowly to the boat, his leg fluttering now like a butterfly wing. The soldier fired just once, the bullet whistling high overhead.

Jesus Christ, you idiot, the sergeant said when Harry reached the boat.

What are they doing now? Harry had his back to the village. The boat was under way.

I can't see them, the sergeant said. Crazy goddamned stunt you pulled. Get us all killed, you.

They weren't interested, Harry said. They had other things on their minds. I think it was a long day for them, too.

Yeah? How could you know that?

I knew it.

Even so —

Fuck you, Sergeant.

They motored west from Village Number Five. Harry stood in the stern, watching the village disappear, dusk coming on. In a few minutes they were around the bend in the river and the helmsman throttled back until they reached the point where the river narrowed sharply. Then he gave the little engine all the speed it could manage. The river opened up again but the helmsman did not slow the boat; and then it was dark except for the gibbous moon, lazy in the night sky. When the boat began to tremble and visibility went to pieces the helmsman throttled back once again. Harry saw flashes off the starboard side and realized someone was firing on them. But the distance was too great and the bullets went astray. He said nothing to the others, concentrating on the riverbanks ahead. Harry cupped his hands and lit a cigarette. He knew he would remember that village forever, the headman and his burden, the smoldering clinic, the nine shades of blue and his own disarray. His surprise when the soldiers appeared without warning, dirty faces, torn fatigues, carbines, wire-rim eyeglasses. He had the idea they were not skilled with weapons, and the carbine was about as low grade as weapons came. He himself had been in another realm, calm except for the twitch in his leg. And all that time the headman had not moved, seemed lost in reverie or grief. In this, Harry seemed to be the odd man out. His tour of duty in the war zone had one year to go and he supposed that, in good time, his heart would harden. A hard heart was evidence of maturity, a hard-won stoic ideal. The ability to put yourself at a remove was better still in the chore of getting on from day to day. Women were not immune, though their lack of immunity took a different form. Visiting one of the army hospitals one day with the ambassador, Harry watched a nurse lose her temper and scream at a patient, a middle-aged civilian caught in crossfire somewhere. A friend had smuggled him a can of beer and he was drinking it without bothering to conceal the can. He had a distant look in his eyes, the look of the convalescent alone in an unfamiliar situation, and as a civilian he was entitled to write his own rules. His head was bandaged and his back wrapped in a heavy poultice. All around him were badly wounded American soldiers, many of them unconscious, several of them amputees. The nurse was very pretty and looked scarcely older than a schoolgirl, except for her mouth, twisted in a snarl. *Who do you think you are?* she screamed. *You asshole. You moron. There are sick people here. You will not drink beer in my ward!* The startled civilian was unable to reply. His eyes welled with tears and he looked away as the nurse seized the beer can and threw it into a hamper before running from the room.

They motored on, Harry gazing at the humpbacked moon as he continued to fix Village Number Five in his mind's eye. He wanted very badly to remember it whole, the burned-out clinic, the old man, and the dying woman. He tried without success to remember the village's actual name. Much later he learned that it had been evacuated, as if it were contaminated or cursed.

PART I

One

THE NEXT MORNING, Sunday, Harry went to Mass at the church near the harbor, Église St.-Sylvestre, the one with the yellow wood walls and ungainly spire, cane chairs in the nave, and Christ on his cross behind the altar. The church was built in the late nineteenth century, a spiritual souvenir of the colonial power. There were many Roman Catholics among the well-to-do element of the capital. Missionaries in the countryside had also been energetic, though the soul of the nation was said to be Buddhist. Buddhism took many forms in the countries where it was practiced, and in this one the salient feature was intransigence, a failure to get on the team. Street demonstrations were common. Monks were known to set themselves alight in support of the demonstrations, confounding officials of the Military Assistance Command and the American embassy. Something perverse about it, this failure to help out. A newspaper photograph of a monk burning in the street was not at all helpful, and they knew it wasn't helpful. But all that was remote from the formal atmosphere of Église St.-Sylvestre. The single spark of color in the church was the stained-glass window in the east wall of the nave, a recent gift from wealthy Connecticut families who wished to show solidarity in the struggle against communism. One of their number was an important publisher and he solicited funds from friends in the neighborhood.

Finely etched in the glass was a fragment of poetry from the hand of Cardinal Newman, a puzzling choice in the circumstances but the publisher insisted. Harry knew two of the Connecticut families, friends of his parents who often came to lunch at their place in the hill country near Salisbury. Harry's father was asked to join the window subscription but declined, sending a check instead to the Boy Scouts. Harry Sanders Sr. did not approve of the war, being an isolationist Republican of the old school. He always asked himself, What would Bob Taft have done? Surely Bob Taft would never have gone to war in a country so remote, so without promise, a country that would remain on the periphery of things for generations, probably centuries.

Harry was an infrequent communicant at Église St.-Sylvestre. Now he sat alone in the rear and did not participate in the singing of hymns or the recitation of prayers. He did not choose to receive communion that day. He was remembering the village, the headman and the dead woman, the sour odor of smoke in the air, the desolation of it. He said a private prayer for their safekeeping and also a thought for God, neither careless nor distracted, at least where Harry's life was concerned. He did believe that it was selfish to asks for God's aid except in the most trying circumstances.

The priest was voluble, his sermon lasting the better part of an hour. He pleaded for an end to the insurgency. He asked God's blessing in that undertaking. God was not indifferent to the suffering of the people, and neither was He indifferent to the many sins of the communist enemy, communism a heathen ideology ill suited to their ancient land, the soil of their ancestors. The communists wished only the death of God, His eradication. But God would never yield. God would aid the good people in their virtuous efforts to vanquish the heathen. God's spirit was with the ordeal of the good people. We have suffered much, he said, and we must bear much more. We will bear whatever we are given to bear because our faith is mighty and our cause is just. We must remember that

God walks with us on our long twilight journey. Two rows ahead, an American army colonel in dress uniform bent his head in prayer.

The congregation stirred, restive as time passed. The priest was small of stature and, for those in the front seats, invisible behind the high altar. He spoke in a reedy voice, his tiny hands outstretched. Harry wondered how many in the church sympathized with the revolution. No more than half, he reckoned; probably less. Perhaps about the same number as adulterers in his family's church in Connecticut, where the priest was worldly and not particular about the sins he absolved. Murder and blasphemy would be exceptions. Murder or blasphemy in that church would be similar to Marxism in this one. The priest's voice faded and was lost altogether as Harry reprised Connecticut and then the events of the day before, motoring back to base, the helmsman mindful of navigation. He had steered the vessel in the middle of the river, and a good thing, too, for a mile downstream they took fire from the mangroves to starboard. The shooters were not marksmen, the bullets falling far astern. When they rounded a bend all was quiet once again. The sergeant fetched three cans of beer from the cooler and handed them around, a reward for their unsuccessful afternoon. Harry sipped beer as night came on, back now in his family's summer place near Salisbury. There was always a crowd for Sunday lunch, spirited conversation, gossip mostly of Washington with detours to horseracing and real estate. Sometimes the local congresswoman and her doctor husband dropped by, everyone pleased to have them at Sunday lunch. Mrs. Finch, as politician and horseplayer, always had something to add. She was a great raconteur. His father maintained that she was the only woman he had ever met who knew how to tell a story, beginning, middle, and end. She was also an accomplished mimic. Her specialties were Connecticut squires and tidewater Virginians and also the president and the speaker of the House, everyone laughing, and at the end of the story the doctor husband exclaiming again and again, Isn't she wonderful? Whereupon the congresswoman smiled and patted his wrist, there, there. The bourgeois life, Harry thought, often a battle in the trenches but never on Sundays, a fine meal served on a three-part Regency table that seated sixteen, Chippendale chairs, a low vase of flowers dead center, decanters of Bordeaux that never ran dry. A wide window looking out on a disheveled English garden, hollyhocks and gladioli, here and there a rosebush. His mother thought the table much too grand for a country house but his father insisted. It had been in the family for a hundred years. Why, the young Winston Churchill had sat at it, drinking everything in sight and reminiscing about the Boer War, rum show. A Marsden Hartley landscape on one wall, an Alfred Munnings stallion on the wall opposite, a wee Homer next to that. Kilim rugs on the floor, not so out of place as you might think. A martini or two before the meal and a walk in the fields after it, a stroll accompanied by the Labrador retrievers, Pat and Dick. There were firearms, too, in case anyone wanted to shoot a pheasant. More Washington, more horseracing and real estate, and an agreement to get together again soon, in Connecticut or the city. Harry was attracted to this life, its iron routine and American naturalness. He could have done with more conversation concerning the world, foreign affairs, but the world was far away on Sunday afternoons. He wondered then if the girl he had been seeing would take to Sunday lunch in Connecticut. She was German, her name Sieglinde Hechler, a technician from the hospital ship docked these past months in the harbor on the river. He had no idea; the life of the squires was an acquired taste. It took some getting used to. Sieglinde was game but it took more than gameness. Gameness took you only so far around the Regency table and its revolving decanters.

Connecticut. He remembered how in late-afternoon darkness gathered in the corners of the high ceiling and over the yellow hills curling west toward the Hudson and, beyond the Hudson, all of the American interior. The dying sun gave the landscape a golden glow, even the lichen-topped tumbledown stone wall with the dogs' graves behind it, four generations of Labrador retrievers. Prime time was mid-October, the air so crisp you could break it in your fingers. Everyone turned to look out the big windows at the autumn light show. Conversation softened and became intimate, as if a stranger might be nearby and listening in. Soon enough the westering sun was forgotten, an object on the edge of their vision. They were indoor people, most comfortable at a crowded table; indoor air, indoor vistas. The Candlesses, old Mr. Wilson who did something in the energy sector, the widow Born who looked after diamonds at one of the Fifth Avenue shops, the brothers Green who ran a private concern on Wall Street, Congresswoman Finch and her doctor—all content. Harry's father once remarked that he preferred Marsden Hartley's landscape to the one in front of his eyes out the window, a thought his mother found baffling. Look at the way it catches the light, his father said. As it happened, the old man preferred his own horse to Alfred Munnings's horse, but that seemed to matter less.

That afternoon two years past: Someone asked Harry about the war, the true situation, where things were and how they might develop. Harry was silent a moment, wondering where to begin and, once begun, where to go. Wasn't it all a matter of stamina? the doctor asked. Yes, Harry said, that was true enough and should give us pause. He commenced with what diplomats called an appreciation of the situation, meaning the long view, the macro-estimate of the state of security upcountry and down, which provinces were secure and which were not; well, most of them were not. The degrees of difference were important. Harry talked about the war until the expressions around the table grew slack and then impatient. Old Jimmy Candless at the end of the table poured a glass of wine and stared into it as if it were a fortuneteller's crystal ball. He had been an airborne brigadier general in the war in Europe, a war of easily described measurements. The boats landed at Omaha and Utah and Sword, and the troops drove east to Berlin. That was essentially it, although his old army comrades—now very senior generals—said that was not essentially it in this war. It was hard to grasp. It was a damned enigma. *It*—well, *it* was a kind of riddle.

Harry explained that the war could be grasped only in its many details, and the details continued to accumulate until the congresswoman intervened to tell a story about her encounter, years back, with General Marshall, the general ill at ease in her presence even though she was the ranking member of the House Foreign Affairs Committee. Perhaps his discomfort was for that very reason. At any event, she let him off the hook. He so obviously preferred the company of men. His great probity and sincerity, his military courtesy, made him sympathetic. When he offered her a cigarette, she took it, and as he lit it she leaned forward, touched his hand to steady the match, and winked. A blush ensued. Everyone at the table laughed, and the doctor most of all. One story followed another and Harry's war was discreetly put to one side. He did not blame them for their inattention, his awkward sentences summoning a house of cards built on quicksand, one fact after another and so many of them counterfeit. He felt he had let them down—his father was gazing at the Marsden Hartley and his mother had begun to collect the plates—but the war fit no known precedent or pattern in American history with the possible exception of the Revolutionary War. It was sui generis and unspeakably tedious unless you were engaged with it day by day. When you were there, the war was your entire life, as seductive as the sun now disappearing over the western hills, their outlines becoming indistinct. Coffee arrived and his father stepped to the sideboard to organize the cognac. Everyone except the doctor lit cigarettes, the smoke rising and hanging in the still air of the dining room. His father once said that Marsden Hartley reminded him of Vuillard, the one drawn to the outdoors and the other drawn to the in. Vuillard, the master of enclosed spaces, bedrooms, sitting rooms, dining rooms. Meticulous Vuillard, nothing beneath his notice, no piece of bric-a-brac or vase of flowers or the oval mirror on the wall. Sunday lunch in Connecticut ended in a drawn-out sigh, everyone rising slowly from the Regency table stifling yawns, tipsy.

The priest wound down at last, exhausted by his oration and perhaps by the demands of his faith, concluding with a toss of his head and a long fingernail pointing at the stained-glass window—it was known by the American community as the Connecticut Window—so the congregation could read for itself Cardinal Newman's prophetic words:

The night is dark, and I am far from home.
Lead Thou me on!

Harry was first out the door, emerging into the naked street, the familiar restaurant close at hand. Only a few of its sidewalk tables were occupied. He stood irresolute, wondering if a drink in the shade would help the afternoon along. The day was very warm and the heat came at him in a rush. He felt sweat gather on his forehead, the curse of the tropics; and then he remembered lunch. A colleague was giving lunch at his villa nearby, an open house in honor of an important guest from Washington, in-country for a look-around with a confidential report to the Secretary later, Eyes Only. It was necessary that the civilians get to him before the generals did, damned generals with their bogus coherence. Bogus charts, bogus bar graphs, with a young lieutenant fresh from Princeton to supply commentary. A military briefing was an art form that hovered somewhere between German Expressionism and the Innocenti of the Italian Renaissance. By contrast, the civilians drew cartoons. Tell our guest about your clinic, Harry. What gives? But Harry thought better of the open house and decided to go home, have a bite of lunch, read something. He could take a book to the silk-string hammock under the spreading ficus tree, a pitcher of iced tea at his side. Something on the phonograph. But then he felt a hand on his arm and turned to find Sieglinde, the technician from the hospital ship. He did not expect to see her. She had hinted she was going away, perhaps for good and perhaps not for good. But he was awfully happy to see her now. The street was crowded and he could hear the last rumbles of the organ inside the church. Sieglinde's hair was wet and he supposed she had gone for a swim at the Sportif. She was dressed plainly in a short skirt and white blouse, espadrilles on her feet. She said nothing for a moment, only looked at him with a slight smile.

You, he said.

Me, she answered.

They had known each other only a week, the beginning of something. Two nights before, she had come to his villa for dinner and stayed on, still asleep when the alarm sounded at five a.m. He had explained about the clinic at Village Number Five and the installations at the other villages, a day's chore. She did not hear the alarm and slept on peacefully as if the bed were her own. He had carefully pulled the sheet over her and slipped away after a soft kiss, the sergeant's jeep already idling in the driveway.

Sieglinde took his hand and smiled, remarking on his sweaty brow and evident weariness. She said he did not look well. Was everything all right? What happened at the clinic? Harry said that everything was fine and he would explain about the clinic later. She said she had errands to run but after the errands she was free for dinner. We can go out or I can come to you. She said, I'll cook. I'm a good cook. I'll cook you schnitzel if I can find veal.

Come to the villa, Harry said.

Poor Harry, she said. You look tired.

Interminable sermon, he said.

Do you go often?

Couple of times a month, I suppose. More or less.

The ship's captain and I went a few weeks ago. Ugly church. That hideous window.

You don't like the Connecticut Window?

Is that what they call it? What does Connecticut mean?

It's an American state. Like Bavaria.

There is nothing like Bavaria in America.

I'll take you there sometime. You'll like it.

Bavaria? I've been to Bavaria.

Connecticut, he said. Wonderful ocean scenery.

There is no ocean near Bavaria, she said.

You have me there, he said.

I'll see you at seven, she said, and walked off.

Don't be late, Harry called after her.

Why would I be late? she called back.

Are you listening?

I'm listening.

I don't think you are. What was I saying?

Humbug. You were telling me about Humbug.

I'm through with Hamburg.

That's what you said all right. Adieu Humbug. Adieu Neustadt and Binnenalster. Adieu Elbe. Goodbye to German men of the big blond type, arms the size of anvils. After that I lost track. You've worn me out.

Move your foot.

Why?

Your toenail is scratching my thigh. You've drawn blood, I think.

Sorry. Unintentional.

You must keep your feet away from tender places. Also, this hammock is not—suitable.

We've invented a new use, that's true. The instructions from the manufacturer made no mention of sex in their hammock. Still, sex was not specifically prohibited. I can hear the click of your bracelets, the ones you bought in the market. They sound like castanets. What are you doing?

Wiping away the blood. And speak softly, please.

I don't see any blood. And no one can hear us.

There was a toenail's worth of blood.

That much? Do you really hate the hammock?

I like the open air, and the hammock allows us to be in the open air, so I suppose I approve of the hammock.

I'm happy you found me. I saw the ship in the harbor but I wasn't sure you were on it. I was afraid you'd gone away, as you said you might do. And I had no idea where that might be.

The boat will be leaving soon, I think. That's the shipboard rumor. The crew is excited. The officers, too. They hate it here. Everyone complains. Shore leave is tightly supervised because they are so concerned about an incident. We had one last weekend but it was covered up. We have already overstayed our time by one month, and each day there are more patients, so many of them children. They are a resilient people. Built of barbed wire, one of our doctors likes to say. It is unnatural for a ship to be tied to a dock like a tethered bird for months and months.

What incident?

The usual thing. One of the orderlies and a bargirl. The orderly was rough with her and she complained and the matter died there. They gave her some money and she went away.

And you? What about you?

I don't know. I may remain. I may jump ship. By the time they realize I am missing, the ship will be miles and miles away. The captain and I are friends. I can get a pass any time I want one. I will leave a note for them explaining what I have done and why. Perhaps not why. Why is none of their concern. I have no desire to return to Hamburg. Hamburg has no meaning for me. I have no affection for the ship. You have complicated things for me. I did not expect someone like you.

It's the same with me.

So we are both complicated with each other.

Seems so. If you stay here, what will you do?

I can do something. I don't know what.

I can find you something at the embassy. Can you type?

Of course I can type. I also take dictation. And operate an x-ray, if you have x-rays at your embassy.

I'll fix it up. But we'll have to make up a story.

What story?

I can't tell them that you've jumped ship and need a job. That would not do. You have to be here for a reason.

I am my own reason. I am a tourist. I am here for tourism.

This is a war zone.

Is tourism illegal? Where does it say that one cannot be a tourist if one wishes to be a tourist? Tourism is a human right. Do not laugh, I am serious.

I can see that. I'll fix it up.

That would be good. So, then. If I remain, can I stay with you?

Of course.

Such a big house you have.

We'll have to keep it quiet. You here.

They don't like you living with tourists, your government?

They are not against tourists. They are against communists.

I am not a communist.

Exactly. So you have nothing to fear from my government. You should give this a moment's thought. This place is finished. You have no future here. It is not dangerous now but it will get dangerous.

The war has nothing to do with me.

The war doesn't know that. The war is closely focused, indifferent to anything outside its sphere. It's remorseless. It works according to its own logic, its context. There will be no end of it.

Everything has an end, Harry.

But you don't have to wait for it.

As it happens, she said, I prefer beginnings.

They stared at the stars through the leaves of the ficus tree, the leaves pendulous in the heavy air. When he first arrived in-country, Harry spent many evenings in the silk-string hammock searching for the Southern Cross, until he learned that the Southern Cross was visible only much farther south. Its anchor was Antarctica. He had read about the Southern Cross in Conrad's books, a mystical constellation, if you could call four lonely stars a constellation. Ancient mariners swore by it. He asked her if she had ever wanted to see the Southern Cross and she replied that she had, on the voyage from Hamburg. The ship's captain told her all about it and also about celestial navigation, but she was so caught up with the stars she hadn't listened carefully. He nodded, thinking about the Southern Cross and listening to her bracelets click as she ran a pianist's riff on his belly. He was unable to fathom how he and Sieglinde had found each other, beyond the prosaic facts of the matter. She had asked him for directions to the post office and he was walking in that direction, and after she had mailed her postcards they had coffee in a café and made a rendezvous for that evening, and now he had what he thought of as a normal life, one of discovery, fresh and erotic, a life apart from the war. Well, the war didn't have anything to do with it. Anyone could have two selves, a daytime self and a nighttime self, a sort of yin and yang. He could keep the damned war to himself and at night he could go home like any ordinary businessman, forgetting the office. He wondered if Marx, at the conclusion of a raucous sexual encounter with his faithful Jenny, muttered something about each according to his needs . . . He did not. Harry hoped the time would come when he could separate who he was from what he did, except that in America it was always the salient question, the one whose answer spoke volumes. In Britain the same question was deemed intrusive, none of your damned business; if you didn't know, don't ask. The ambassador once referred to him as a model government man, a Fed through and through, good at following instructions, very good at reading the opposition. Harry took the remark as a compliment. He supposed he had the manner, coming mostly from his childhood around the Regency table at Sunday lunch. When he was a schoolboy he was often called upon for memory tricks: the states and their capitals, the captive nations that constituted the Soviet bloc. And then he was encouraged to sit and listen while the adults spoke. There was often someone from the government, usually retired and working for a bank or a law firm in the city, and he was the one asked to clarify the awkward questions of the day, the personalities of the men in the Kremlin or the reliability of the French and, later on, the criminal regimes in Cuba and Red China. The former government official, often a diplomat or Defense Department specialist, less often a White House assistant, usually spoke soberly, one question always leading to another, each more difficult than the last, with a reference somewhere to "holding the line." There were very many lines. Something glamorous about it, Harry thought, being at the center of events, always at or near the top table. He did pay close attention to the demeanor of the former officials, the way they fell silent at a certain point, eyes far away and stunned as if struck by a sudden blow. But they were only remembering that which could not be said, a secret still secret, information that, if known, would alter the agreed-upon landscape. The ambassador said that the government was excellent preparation for life because in the nature of things you devoted your days to weighing and measuring—what you said and who you said it to and why and the objective, cards always close to the vest. And when you turned one over, sometimes with reluctance, sometimes with nonchalance, you got something for it. The way things were in the world, your queen nearly always trumped your opponent's king. That was because you held the American card. When to play the card and what you expected to get for it was the essence of the diplomatic art. And you did this every day and the result was: an examined life.

Sieglinde said, I like your villa. It's spacious, nicely arranged. I like it here under the stars with you.

Look, he said. I'd like you to stay. You know that. No question about that, is there? But after a while you won't like it because there's no future here.

But I do like it. I like the tropics. I like the heat and the pace of life, the scurry. A siesta in the heat of the afternoon. Afternoons last forever in the tropics, don't you think? It's from another century, this country. And since I don't care much for this century I've decided to choose another, especially the afternoons. I know the war is here but I pay no attention to it. Why should I? The war is not my concern. What time is it?

Around three, Harry said. In the morning.

Listen now, Sieglinde said. Not a sound. Not a breath of air. The air has a weight of its own, the scent of your garden and the trees. Can't you feel the dew falling? That's why I don't like Hamburg, its burdens. Clamor. Cold and wind. Rain from the north. You say it's dead here but it's not dead, it's indifferent. You can bend this country but you will never break it. The people have old souls and their patience is infinite. They don't even think of it as patience. I'm sure they have another word for it in their infernal language that you can't understand. Germans have patience, too, but we call it thoroughness. Hamburg nights are glum. There's a glare. The truth is, Germany is badly oversized. There's too much of it. And I will not stay here forever because German people make bad colonists and that includes me. But I will stay for a while.

They do?

Not one of our colonies prospered. Not one.

What about France?

Ha-ha. Ha.

Sorry. Irresistible, Harry said, realizing he had played a queen and gotten nothing for it.

The French did not want it badly enough.

Want what?

Their country, Sieglinde said. They didn't want it badly enough to fight for it. Or maybe they wanted something else. Maybe they were tired of the life they had and wanted a new one. They were halfhearted.

I think it's fair to say they were very badly generaled. And they were overwhelmed, superior force, superior weapons. Soldiers with fight in their blood.

30

Always the Third Reich, Sieglinde said. The war is over for years and years and our Third Reich is still with us. Probably it will never go away in my lifetime. My grandparents and my father died in it. And I will say something more. It doesn't seem like yesterday. When you mention the Third Reich I think about my mother, always. These thoughts are not good thoughts—

Sorry, Sieglinde.

When something is irresistible you should resist it, Harry. There is nothing you can tell me about the Third Reich that I do not already know. I think you do not study your surroundings. Also you do not listen with care. Always your own thoughts. I think your war is always inside your head. Don't bother to deny it. I know it's true, every minute of the day. You're like a pianist with a head full of musical notes except your head is filled with the war. No, I do not care to have you kiss me. Kissing avoids the issue. This stupid war of yours. It's a stupid thing to have in your head at all times.

You, Harry said. I think about you.

You must understand I have nothing to do with the Third Reich.

I know that, he said.

It's an accident of nationality.

I know that, too.

I have a photograph of my father the day he went away to the war. He was roughly the age that I am now. He wore a wool uniform with corporal's stripes. His face was full of hope, I would almost say of rapture, as if he were leaving to join a religious order, its specific rituals, chants and choirs, meditations, observances, discipline. The four last things: death, judgment, heaven, hell. He was slender but very strong, a marksman, and so handsome, with a loop of hair that fell over his forehead. Freckles, too, and a mustache that made him look older. He stood not at attention but in a kind of slouch, his rifle held butt-down as a farm boy might hold a pitchfork. My father was a hell-raiser and now he was going east, the Russian front. My mother held the camera and my father was smiling into it, a brilliant smile, the one that was full of hope. I was so young, I thought his uniform was a costume, a clown's suit or a knight's armor. My father didn't last the week, but we did not know that right away. We didn't know for months and all that time my mother was writing letters to a dead man.

Harry was silent now, listening to the rise and fall of Sieglinde's voice, its urgency and melancholy. This was the first he had heard of the war's progress from the other side, the civilian side, the enemy side. She spoke slowly, her attention fixed not on him but on some distant point in the night sky. He remembered one of his university professors described the American victory as a mixed blessing. Its unambiguous result did not encourage introspection. The victory was total. After Hiroshima and Nagasaki, the worm of triumphalism began its laborious crawl—though things would look otherwise to a marine waiting in Okinawa for the invasion of Japan. Harry doubted the professor's sour complaint. He seemed to ask for too much. Yet it was true that a colossus had been born. A colossus was heedless, difficult to manage, so many irons in so very many fires. Three wars in twenty-five years and at last the colossus was forced to look inward. Now it faced an enemy whose will and cunning seemed without limit. The Chinese adage, preposterous when applied to the Military Assistance Command, fit snugly in the mind of the guerrilla force: "To gain, you must yield; to grasp, let go; to win, lose." He realized that Sieglinde had fallen silent.

Are you listening to me?

Yes, Harry said.

I can stop if you want.

I don't want you to stop.

You want me to shut my mouth.

No, I do not, Harry said. Believe me.

My father, she said, was an auto mechanic. A good one apparently. The official notification of his death stated that he died bravely. He did his duty. My mother was bitter and, young as I was, I remember her asking if he died fixing a tank's engine or the flywheel of a staff car and how many others died with him. Perhaps it was a bomb that fell from nowhere, an unseen aircraft in the night sky. So, Sieglinde went on, our house was never the same. My mother was often absent, foraging. She became a forager for food. We lived in a small town east of Hamburg and when the firebombing came we could see the flicker of lights in the sky and later the west wind blew smoke and debris over our little town. The smell of it was horrible. And in the morning we saw ash on our lawn and the sidewalks, the streets, too. Oh yes, also we heard the explosions, a kind of rolling thunder that went on and on. I am only looking for a place of repose, not so much to ask.

Sieglinde, Harry began.

I have never told that story to anyone, she said.

It's safe with me, Harry said.

My mother died in the last year of the war, Sieglinde said. It was so cold that winter, the coldest in decades, they said. They told me she died of pneumonia. They did not say where. Her body was not recovered. Perhaps it was pneumonia and perhaps it was something else. I have always thought she just went away to a place of no return. I would not be surprised if she were still alive. So I went to live with my aunt in Lübeck. She didn't want me. She didn't know how to feed me. She had barely enough for herself. But we managed. I went to school and later I learned about the x-ray and so I have made a life for myself thanks to my knowledge of the x-ray. I am looking for repose and that is why I came here on the ship.

As you say, Harry said, not so much to ask.

No, not so much. Hard to find.

Maybe this is your place after all, Harry said.

I shall have to see for myself.

You are welcome to stay with me. More than welcome. As you can see, I have plenty of room. Of course you would have to jump ship.

I can do that.

What's stopping you?

I have not made up my mind.

33

You would be perfectly safe here. The shooting war is elsewhere, in the countryside. Out of sight, really. I suppose this house could be a place of repose. It's quiet. I have one servant who keeps to himself. The library is quite good. Do you read French? The house belonged to a French businessman and his wife. A year ago they sensibly decided to return to France.

So it wasn't a place of repose for them.

Evidently, Harry said. I believe they were between the lines, playing a double game. They say the French are good at that, but they aren't any better than anyone else. It's exhausting. The family had been here for three generations and now they've gone home, some village in the north near Arras. They went there in the summers and now they live there. I met them before they left, a charming couple. They hated leaving. They loved the villa. Among other things, they liked the food here. Accomplished cooks, both of them.

And you?

Repose is not in my repertoire. But I have no objection to it.

She was silent. Then, after a moment, Sieglinde said, I may be an emigrant my whole life. Before she died, my mother said she hoped I would find a place in the world. And now I suppose I have, like it or not.

A rolling stone, he said, an attempt at a joke.

Perhaps a rolling stone, she said. You like it here. I know that.

I like my job and my job's here.

You don't miss America?

Not yet, he said.

I wonder why, Sieglinde said.

The time was now four in the morning. They were lying toes-to-head, head-to-toes, in the silk-string hammock. The night was very warm, their bodies slick with sweat. Harry's toenails were thick and ragged, Sieglinde's tiny, painted pink, bright thimbles of color at Harry's ear. The hammock moved but slightly and the heavy leaves of the trees overhead did not move at all and at that moment, dawn far away, even the rotation of the earth seemed to slacken, a use-less castaway lariat. Sieglinde's eyes were closed, her hands curled up under her chin. She was lovely in the moonlight, her skin the color of alabaster. There were emigrants all over the world, fugitives from oppression or famine, disease, revolution, heartbreak, simple boredom, bad memories. He did not like to think of her as one of those now here, now there, always far from home. At first when she began to tell her story, he believed she was laden with guilt, feeling that she was somehow responsible for the calamity in her family. But it wasn't guilt. She was furious at the turn of events in her early life. Furious at the war, the struggles, the deaths. He remembered a story the ambassador told him. The ambassador had visited the Jewish cemetery in Warsaw with an old friend, a worldly Jew. His friend took care to examine the gravestones, everyone dying in 1939, 1940, 1941, 1942, 1943, 1944, 1945 — and when he came upon a grave marked 1952 he gave a little strangled laugh and said, At last, someone dead of natural causes.

Harry was looking at Sieglinde and thinking about nationality and responsibility, always different in the old world than the new. Except for Native Americans, everyone in the United States came from somewhere else. All the nations of the world were represented in America. Homogeneous nations had a tighter fix on responsibility when things went wrong, and the result was either bloodshed or a sullen quietus with subterranean thoughts of revenge because there had been a stab in the back. Nothing had ever gone so wrong in America with the exception of the Civil War, and President Lincoln, dead from an assassin's bullet, became the nation's most revered figure. Harry held the thought, thinking that it needed refining. Sieglinde stirred, muttering something, and curled her hands more firmly at her throat. She said, What are you thinking about? You're so quiet.

He said, You.

The streetlight at the end of the long driveway cast a wan glow. Now and again in the street, heard faintly but not seen beyond the high hedge, were bicyclists, announced by the splash of rubber tires. The police, perhaps, or workmen on their way to the early shift. Harry took no notice. He believed himself secure in the world, the silk-string hammock as invulnerable as golden-armored Orion high above in the summer sky, light years away. Sieglinde stirred once more and Harry thought of her freckle-faced father, off to the war, less than a week to live, posing for her mother's camera. She had called him a hell-raiser, and what did she mean by that? He was good with engines. Liked to clown for the camera. None of Harry's own family had gone to war, neither the Great War nor the one after that. He was the closest anyone in his family had come, if you call a few random and ill-aimed shots near a no-name river at dusk being "under fire." During World War II it seemed to him that his parents went to a funeral every other week, though it was surely much less than that. He had not thought to ask Sieglinde about her childhood. He supposed it was misplaced tact that caused his reticence, and they had known each other only one week. Now he knew her memories were not happy, her father dead, her mother absent, a diminished life in a defeated nation. She seemed to be on the run from all that. Sieglinde had not thought to ask him either, so she was spared descriptions of Connecticut, the clapboard houses and their swimming pools, the cocktail hour, the yellow hills rolling off to the mysterious interior. Political talk at table on Sundays, a self-conscious yet sincere effort to be engaged in the affairs of the nation, civic responsibility. Would these memories, his and hers, speak to each other? They would not. A German childhood of the twentieth century would be a grueling experience, most strenuous, one could say a burden or nemesis—both justice and retribution, the irreconcilable tension between remembering and forgetting. Certainly there would have been good times in the early days following 1932, things returning to normal, patriotism rekindled, community gatherings around towering bonfires with inspiring speeches and song, the nation rising once again, fresh confidence, industrial production up, inflation in check, an audacious ambition that resulted in peaceful coexistence at last with the ominous Soviet Union, a miracle of diplomacy worthy of the Iron Chancellor himself. In less than a decade, all of it in ruins.

Sieglinde had not mentioned her childhood until this evening, her wordy coda to five hours of more or less constant lovemaking. It had been a while for him and, he suspected (probably the better word was hoped), for her, too. The silk-string hammock took some getting used to, so for a while they were a kind of ménage à trois, afloat and then not afloat. The hours became minutes and the minutes seconds, until they were both outside of time altogether, slick and overheated; and when they gave themselves over to it, he found another, happier self, an assured self, one he had not known existed. Her eyes were closed, her face rosy, and she was smiling. This went on and on in a circle of abandon, time expanding, time diminishing, time uncrowded, and in a moment of drowsy delight he proposed that they remain in the hammock forever, or anyway until they were too old for lovemaking, and even then there were ways and means, and if the ways and means failed they had memories enough from just this one flawless night—and what did she think of that idea? Her answer was another arpeggio on his thigh. He dozed, half asleep and half not, conjuring a meeting between her memories and his, not only this night but from their childhoods, a sort of symposium without a moderator. Her father was in a dark corner of the room drinking schnapps. His father was explaining Marsden Hartley to her mother, a startlingly pretty woman who wore thick glasses and a white silk ascot. Then his mother interrupted to mention the Regency table, unsuitable for informal gatherings, which this certainly was. She abruptly switched to German but the effort was unsuccessful, and Mrs. Hechler nodded in agreement and asked if there was anything to eat. General Marshall was gazing out the window, distraught at the number of Germans in the room. Who brought them? Why were they here? Congresswoman Finch asked the general for a light and he lit a match, his fingers trembling slightly. He said softly, I don't understand a word of their damned language. Mrs. Finch smiled grimly and said, I know. Sieglinde offered to translate but the offer was not taken up. From the dark corner, Corporal Hechler was polishing the buckle on his infantryman's belt and humming the overture to *Tannhäuser*. Finally, at a loss, everyone fell silent. Harry slept.

A little later, Harry extracted himself from the hammock and stepped across the lawn to the villa. He fetched a bottle of lager from the fridge and stood in the kitchen looking across the tree shadows to the hammock and the high hedge beyond. Sieglinde was invisible but the hammock looked full, motionless in the still night air. The neighbor's cat, black with white paws, scuttled up the ficus tree and sat on the low branch. Harry lit a cigarette and walked back outside, as contented as he had ever been. More than content. He had the idea that he could snap his fingers and summon an orchestra or a black-tied waiter with a tray full of champagne. The grass was wet underfoot, cool to the touch. It took a moment to resettle in the hammock, cigarette in one hand and the bottle of lager in the other. Sieglinde took one long pull on the cigarette and another from the bottle of lager and closed her eyes again, settling her head on his shoulder. In a growly sort of voice, Harry began to tell her about the clinic and Village Number Five, the headman with the bundle in his arms. The settlement was immaculate, not even a gum wrapper or cigarette stub, his own silence in the face of it all. He stopped there, the experience so strange in retrospect he was unable to describe it with precision—and he realized then that he would have this story for the rest of his life and in time it would become as shopworn as a much-used passport, the visa stamps smudged, illegible dates, illegible signatures, the hodgepodge of a traveler's life. His own photograph was anonymous, not a good likeness; his signature was undecipherable. What had been crisp was now blurred. The bare bones of a well-told story required coherence, ironic asides, and a plot as well knit and tied together as a jigsaw puzzle and somewhere in it a detail as provocative as a cat in a tree.

Go on, Sieglinde said.

I'm thinking, Harry replied. What he meant was, I'm trying to get the sequence of things straight in my own mind. The exact time of day. The precise shape of the headman's bundle. The dimensions of the clinic; well, he had those. But he could not summon an account of his own emotions—not fright, something other than fright. The clinic was smoldering, he said to Sieglinde, and the scene before him seemed like a relic from the century before, an eternal tableau vivant. It was as if he were witnessing an event from history, something written about in books and puzzled upon—the fall of Carthage, the construction of the Great Wall of China. Hamlet's soul. The headman looked through him as if he were made of glass, superfluous in any case. He had the idea that an invisible hand was in charge, a manifestation of fate itself, implacable, not to be denied, not to be understood most of all. This small corner of the world, he said to Sieglinde, was not my business. I felt I had no right to be there. I was an interference. My presence was an offense. More than an offense, a provocation. I had arrived unannounced and uninvited, as if I had every right to be there, almost an obligation—to open the door without knocking and be welcomed without question. My clinic, my *laissez-passer.* The bundle moved and I saw that it was a woman, at first I thought a child, and then I knew she was old. The headman carried her easily, as if she were weightless. Harry said to Sieglinde, And when the woman died at last, I took one step back. When the sergeant called to me from the boat, I could hear the fear in his voice, a kind of stutter, his desire to be quit of village life. I hesitated only a little while before walking away in order to leave them in peace, the last two inhabitants. They were lost as surely as if they had been in a death camp or on the *Titanic.* The headman remained still as stone on the top step of the clinic stairs, smoke misting around him. When I turned at last to go I saw four soldiers emerge from the clinic looking dazed. They were filthy and obviously disoriented and almost at once one of them saw me and unslung his carbine and said something, I had no idea what. *I do not have the language,* and so we were strangers to one another. But his meaning was not difficult to imagine. *Stop! Who are you? What are you doing here?* I decided to ignore him and walk away. I pretended to myself that he was not present. That he was not armed. And that is what I did, and when I reached our boat he remained where he was, now with a look of—I would call it disgust. The sergeant told me later he had fired one round, but I did not hear it and doubted the sergeant's word. Later, when we took fire from the shore, I knew somehow that we would not be harmed. The shooting was a farewell. Adieu. Don't come back. And we motored on without incident. Early this morning I attempted to write a report of the affair. We call it a "report for the file." But it wouldn't write. It was a sentence fragment, you see. So I went to Mass and listened to the songs and the interminable sermon at the end, all the while looking at the light falling through the Connecticut Window and thinking of Cardinal Newman's directive. Thinking about it, I concluded that my fate was to witness events I didn't understand and would never understand. The way of the world. I did believe that the invisible hand had shown its cards, a specific prophecy, perhaps a warning—and what that warning was, I cannot say.

Nothing good, Harry concluded.

Sieglinde yawned. She said, I don't believe in invisible hands.

Harry said, You should. You don't know what you're missing.

I think you are an American romantic, Harry.

I've been told that before.

I think also that you love the war. I think you have found your life in the war. Everything else is an interlude.

That's not true, Harry protested, and even as he said it he knew that Sieglinde was on to something. A partial truth, certainly: not the whole truth, but still a useful truth, though not to Harry.

Why did you tell me that story?

It was on my mind. Who else would I tell it to? I had the feeling you might see something in it that I didn't. Or couldn't.

She said, Maybe I did.

He said, I had to tell it to someone.

Did it bother you, your afternoon in the village? What did you call it? Village Number Five?

Bother? Bother would not be the word.

No, she said, I suppose not.

But believe me, the invisible hand was real enough.

Oh, she said dismissively, that again.

Fireflies gathered in the crown of the tree, a kind of celestial starburst or halo. Dawn came softly, silky pink and then crimson. Exposed in the daylight, their Garden of Eden stark in the glare, their emotions were disconnected. They might have been strangers. Harry wished he had never brought up the village, the headman and the dead woman, or the invisible hand. A busted flush, it turned out. He supposed Sieglinde was uncomfortable with enigma. That would be the German in her. Germans were uncomfortable with enigma generally, even Nietzsche. "God is dead." But Harry did not appreciate her silence now, nor the stubborn expression that went with it. They carefully disentangled themselves from the hammock and stood together, swaying a little. Then her hand flew to her mouth and she gave a sharp cry, stumbling backward, losing her balance. Harry looked up and saw the cat in the tree, its back arched, yawning, its slender tail coiled around its legs.

My God, she said. It's a cat. I didn't know what it was—

Only a cat, Harry said.

I thought it was a snake, she said.

They walked the few steps to the villa. She allowed him to take her hand but did not seem happy about it. He fetched two robes from the bedroom and gave one to her in the unlikely event the houseman, Chau, showed himself. Harry made a pot of coffee and they sat side by side at the kitchen table without speaking. Sieglinde looked uncomfortable in the robe, as if by accepting it she had assumed an obligation. Harry watched the sunlight gather. Somewhere far off he heard the thumpa-thumpa of a helicopter and a car's horn in the street. It seemed the morning did not belong exclusively to them, Sieglinde and him. She pulled the robe tightly around her and bent over the coffee cup, the coffee too hot to drink. How did they reach this point of discord? Harry knew it was something he said or something he failed to say. He had been misunderstood, certainly. He looked out the window at the limp silk-string hammock and remembered a conversation he overheard years before between his father and his father's oldest friend. The friend had recently separated from his wife and was explaining that they, he and the wife, could not agree on the definition of "virtue" and once they understood that, the fundamentals of it, the disagreement seemed to illuminate everything else. All their disputes over how a life should be lived, including who was responsible for what in the household. A great relief, really. Once they discovered their irreconcilable views on the subject of virtue, the marriage was ended, case closed. Harry remembered a long uncomfortable silence and then his father clearing his throat and giving a wan laugh. Virtue? You can't be serious. Never more, the friend said.

Harry said, I've offended you.

Yes, I think you have. You didn't mean to. Perhaps that's worse.

Can we forget it?

It's better forgotten, she said with a slight smile.

We can come back to it later, Harry said.

Or not at all, Sieglinde said.

When we know each other better.

Sieglinde did not reply to that.

It's my job, Harry said. It's what I do. I'm assigned somewhere and I go. Today it's the war, and if you're a foreign service officer and want to get ahead, that's where you must be. The war is in first position. You could be somewhere else, New Zealand or Portugal, but what would be the point? Or back at the State Department in Washington, moving pieces of paper from the in box to the out box and back again. That's part of the drill, too, tedious but necessary.

That's where I'll be in a year, Washington. But right now it's important to understand what's wrong here. And much is, and the end is not in sight. The war is the interlude, Sieglinde.

She said, What kind of war is it that we can devote six hours to screwing in a hammock?

He said, I think there was some of that even in the Great War. Even in the trenches.

She was silent a moment, idly stirring sugar into her coffee. She said, My grandfather was in the Great War. He never spoke of it. Not one word. But he left behind a diary, a day-by-day account of his life. A thick diary, ninety-two pages. He began with full paragraphs, often accompanied by drawings. He was a competent draftsman. And ended with two- and three-word entries and one word repeated: *Shrecklichkeit*. Frightfulness. My feeling was that the sense of life, the pulse of it, had been drained from him. He was a shell. A husk of a man. And he lived to great age, perhaps because there was so little of him to be kept alive. I do not think there was sex in the trenches, Harry. Not at Verdun. Not on the Somme. I have discussed this with the ship's doctor and we agreed that Herr Freud was wrong, perhaps because he led a sheltered life. Sex is not the primal instinct. Survival is. I have to say that my other grandfather was the lucky one. He was killed in 1916 and did not bother to keep a diary. His experiences died with him. The one who lived, quite frankly, frightened me. I think he frightened himself.

Harry watched her carefully all this time, her voice a monotone, the voice of a sleepwalker. If her voice had been a musical instrument he would have called it an oboe. She spoke with tremendous conviction.

Sieglinde rose, stepped to the counter, and poured a fresh cup of coffee. She stood quietly looking at the appliances, the refrigerator and the range, ovens side by side, the dishwasher, a toaster, an electric coffeepot. She had never seen a kitchen like it except in advertisements in *Der Spiegel* and *Paris Match*. She peeked inside an oven and was not surprised to find it pristine. She ran her hand

43

over the counter, smooth as glass, similarly spotless. She had heard that Americans made a fetish of cleanliness. The open shelves were filled with canned goods, beans and tomatoes and condensed milk and chicken soup and *lychees au sirop* and English tea and artichoke hearts, enough to feed a family for a week or more. During World War II such a hoard would last a month. More than a month. Sieglinde shook her head and began to laugh.

What's funny?

Your kitchen. There's so much of it.

It's an ordinary American kitchen, Harry said.

Yes, I suppose it is.

You don't like it?

It's a splendid kitchen. Do you actually cook in it?

A wartime kitchen, Harry said with a smile.

A fine wartime kitchen, she said.

Harry said, I know I've brought up memories for you. Memories you'd rather not be reminded of. I'm sorry about that. I wish I hadn't done it. I wasn't thinking. Our past lives are so different.

And present ones, she said.

Yes, he agreed.

I'm not complaining, she said. You're a darling.

You too, he said.

So, she said. Two darlings.

It's forgotten then?

A momentary thing, Sieglinde said.

Can we make plans for the evening?

Dinner out, she said. I know the place.

I don't want to lose you, Harry said.

I'm not lost, Sieglinde said.

She said she had to put in an appearance at the ship, to let them know she had not wandered off or been kidnapped, mugged or murdered, dismembered by communist thugs in a back alley somewhere. The ship's captain had a vivid imagination, believing that the capital crawled with agents provocateurs, including pirates. And you, she

44

said, don't you have to go to work? Make your report for the file? They walked up the stairs to his bedroom where their clothes were. She showered for a long time and then he watched her dress, bikini bottoms the size of a handkerchief, a Gernreich bra. A prim plum-colored skirt and a white shirt, espadrilles on her feet, a blue ascot at her throat, aviator glasses with yellow lenses. She was combing her hair and whistling some tune when Harry went to shower and shave, already thinking of his leave, due next month, a two-week leave. He had plenty of money saved. They could take a trip somewhere close by, put in at one of the ancient ports with a grand old hotel that had a swimming pool and tennis courts, a view of the sea, a dining room with twelve-foot-high ceilings, the perfume of flowers, elderly waiters in tuxedos. He wondered if she played tennis. She looked as if she could, rangy of build, graceful of manner. She moved in a shuffle-walk. In one of the ancient-port hotels they could talk about anything in the world except the war — Expressionist painters, trends in architecture, cats versus dogs, the Baltic at sunset, Connecticut in winter, New York on New Year's Eve, the sort of life she envisioned for herself, city or country, crowded or quiet. What that life was he had no idea, but the finding out would be thrilling. She came with baggage but everyone did. He would fill her in on the routine of the American foreign service, more agreeable than she might think. Much more agreeable abroad in an embassy — unless the embassy was in a West African jungle or one of the Stalinist utopias, and even then there were exotic sights to discover, a new language, a fresh culture well away from the Washington bureaucracy, tedious at all times unless you had rank. Washington itself had charm, surely more charm than glum Hamburg. Georgetown was quaint. Harry realized then that his life had turned on a dime. He lived in the present and had done for two years. Now the present was elastic and stretched as far as he could see. It stretched to twilight.

Harry was a long time showering and shaving. His skin was chafed everywhere. When he looked in the mirror the face he saw was not in all respects his own. This face he saw was possibly the face of a brother, an older, wiser brother, an experienced brother who had gone ten rounds with Aphrodite and when the bell rang was still on his feet. Congratulations from the referee. He took a long look in the mirror—a look, it had to be admitted, of no little self-regard. And then he laughed and waved his thumb at the brother in the mirror, rosy-cheeked, damp hair, bloodshot eyes, but in fine shape all in all. All in all in exceptional spirits. All in all looking forward to the morning, something he rarely did. Harry was an afternoon and evening man. Twilight and darkness were his friends, and now he had someone to share them with. Wasn't she something? He patted his stomach, taut as a bowline. Harry did not think of himself as vain but thought now that a revision might be in order. Was that a side effect of losing your heart? Did lovemaking lead to megalomania? He carefully combed his hair. Then he put a styptic pencil on a tiny razor cut near his left ear. Deodorant under his arms. He told the face in the mirror that he would spend time with the German classics, Goethe, Fontane, Musil, Brecht. He would reacquaint himself with Dürer.

When Harry stepped into the bedroom, already talking about resort hotels in the ancient ports, Sieglinde had vanished. Her shoulder bag was gone. Only her jasmine scent remained. For a moment Harry did not move. The room was barren without her, and she had not thought even to say goodbye. Not so much as a tap on the bathroom door. He looked for a note but there was no note. Then, from downstairs, he heard piano music, a waltz, or not quite a waltz. A melancholy nocturne. Harry descended the stairs barefoot, making no sound, and paused at the landing, watching Sieglinde at the piano. Her fingers moved light as feathers. Morning sun streamed through the big window, the edge of it touching the piano. She was playing a Chopin adagio, a familiar piece he could not name. It had the melody and tempo of old Europe, nineteenth-century Europe, Europe before the fall. Harry listened without moving for the longest time, watching her, watching her head slide left

46

and right, watching her fingers, and when she looked up at last, seeing him at the bannister, she tossed her head, gave a brilliant smile, and winked.

They planned a rendezvous for that night at a restaurant near the harbor, a twenty-minute walk from the embassy. Harry spent the day in his office finishing up the report, a bare-bones affair minus enigma. Enigma was nowhere to be found. Instead, there was clarity, cause and effect, troublesome enigma trampled under the goose-stepping feet of one fact after another. He did his best to make a story of it, a beginning, middle, and end. He had difficulty making the atmosphere of Village Number Five credible, though at some level he understood that the report would likely not be read. At most, skimmed. Now and again he laughed out loud, though the material was not humorous. Harry was not bothered except by the ambassador's secretary, who looked in to say that the old man wanted to see him in the morning, ten sharp—and added, with a strange look, that he seemed in especially good spirits. It's good to see you—so cheerful, Harry.

We've been worried about you.

No need, Harry said airily. All's right with the world.

No, it isn't, the secretary said, and walked away.

The report concluded, Harry straightened his desk and disposed of the usual memos, wondering all the while what the ambassador wanted. A one-on-one with the boss, and that was what the secretary implied, was unusual. He wrote a letter to his parents, the first in weeks. He told them everything about his life except for the events at Village Number Five and his romance—that was how he described it to himself, a romance—with Sieglinde. That left a dry observation on the course of the war and one or two thoughtful comments about the disarray of the government at Washington and about the weather, hot all day long and into the evening. He said his health was good aside from a rash on his thigh. Now and again he looked up from the letter, thinking about the romance and what the ambassador wanted. Whatever it was, he hoped it would not interfere with his two-week leave. He hauled out the atlas to look up the precise location of the ancient ports so he could discuss plans with Sieglinde.

At five he went around the corner for a drink with his office mate Ed Coyle, who said he was much missed at Sunday lunch. The Washington supremo wanted to hear about the events in the village, already the subject of lurid gossip, thanks to Sergeant Orono. Sergeant said you got shot at, Ed said. Sergeant said you were a block of ice under fire. That true? Harry told him a little of what happened, the smoldering clinic, the headman and his dead wife—if that was who she was. Harry asked, What did the supremo have to say? How proud they are of us here, Ed said, our hardships and hard times and hard knocks and the rest of it. You'll be glad to know that hazardous-duty pay's going up. More staff here. More troops in the field, *many* more troops, and many more ships at sea. We're in for the long haul. Whatever it takes, according to the supremo. Ed went on to give specific numbers and dates but Harry did not listen closely. He was preoccupied by the clock on the wall. The café began to fill up, mostly Americans from the embassy and the USAID mission nearby, but there were other nationalities too, mainly Middle Eastern and European traders in search of contracts. The atmosphere was one of feral low-stakes conspiracy.

Harry was at Café Celine most evenings, usually with Ed. They had become friends with the owner, a belligerent Algerian named Yves. Yves had the latest gossip concerning the government and the Americans, who was up and who was down at the presidential palace, and if there had been an atrocity or other incident the previous evening he knew about that also and was eager to share his knowledge. Yves was said to be a valued member of French intelligence and perhaps that was so, despite his frequent and public denunciations of the French government. But then again, he would, wouldn't he? I heard you had an ugly time the other day, he said to Harry on their arrival. Could have been worse, Harry said, and Yves raised

48

his eyebrows a fraction and made the first round on the house. Yves said quietly, I'll bet you don't know that the bastards burned that village, every house. A dozen casualties that we know about. So I think you were lucky. When he saw the expression on Harry's face he nodded and said, Sorry.

They drank up and Ed returned to the embassy. Harry strolled through streets crowded with tiny cars, mobile soup kitchens, and sidewalk vendors. He saw a pretty scarf for sale and bought it for Sieglinde. The streets were alive with conversation and music, American pop and French yé-yé. Harry was early for their date at the restaurant and decided to meet Sieglinde as she got off the hospital ship. There was commotion on the dock, one freighter arriving and the other leaving. The one arriving was of Nigerian registry but the skipper was yelling in Italian. Stevedores were everywhere, and here and there a police car with turning blue lights, policemen lounging inside. There were prostitutes and panhandlers and crippled veterans on crutches. Harry sat on a bench and watched the show, thinking about the village and what had been done to it. He supposed the headman was one of the dead. The place would be swarming with press conducting interviews amid the ruins. All the villages in the vicinity would be up-to-date: the assault, who died and by what means, and the significance. News traveled fast in the countryside, helped along by the enemy tom-toms. The significance was that the villages were fundamentally unprotected, abandoned by their own army and forgotten by the Americans. Villages were burning all over the country. Not that there were any disturbances in the capital. Nor grief, to the extent that grief could be identified.

Harry watched a scuffle, two teenage boys pushing each other around. There was so much movement and noise that it took Harry a moment to understand what was in front of his eyes. The freighter had taken the berth of the hospital ship. The ship was gone. He hurried to the edge of the quay but there was no sign of it upstream or down. Harry stood there wondering if somehow the ship was tethered at another berth. That was unlikely. Impossible, really, because of the size of her. He remained a few minutes longer and then asked one of the policemen what happened to the German hospital ship. It took him three tries to make himself understood, and finally the policeman shook his head and said, Di-di, gone, gone away. When Harry asked where, the policeman shrugged. Harry thanked him and hurried to the restaurant but Sieglinde was not there and had left no message. Harry sat at an outside table under the awning and ordered a drink. In fifteen minutes he ordered another and by nine p.m. he had ordered three more, all the time watching the street. He pretended nonchalance, a lone American drinking gin in a rough part of town. He saw no Americans or other foreigners. Local girls came up to him offering companionship but when he shook his head they left him alone, muttering what sounded like a curse. It had been some time since he had sat alone at a restaurant table, chain-smoking cigarettes, ill at ease, with the expression of an insomniac counting sheep. The street grew quiet, only a few furtive strollers here and there. They kept to the shadows.

You want girl?

A face was at his elbow. Harry said, No.

Nice girl. Young girl.

No, Harry said again.

Ten-dollar girl.

Go away, Harry said.

You give me money.

Harry gave him some money and the pimp went away.

In due course Harry paid the bill, hailed a cab, and returned to his villa. She was not there either, but he had not expected she would be. He sat uncomfortably in the silk-string hammock and imagined her at the rail of the hospital ship watching the countryside disappear to port. The ship would be ablaze with light although the moon was full. All hands on deck drinking and saying goodbye to the war. Goodbye and good luck. Goodbye and good riddance. The open ocean would be but a few nautical miles distant. The night was warm. He pictured Sieglinde sitting with the captain, inquiring about the route home. How many days? Were there any ports of call?

He went inside and made a gin and tonic, peeking into the living room to see if she were somehow at the piano. She was not at the piano. He wondered if it was something he said, some ill-judged remark that irritated her. Infuriated her. Harry went back to the hammock and sat quietly sipping his drink, at a loss to explain her disappearance. He reached for a cigarette but the pack was empty and he crumpled it and threw it away. He imagined her at the ship's rail, looking skyward, counting stars. Harry looked up and found what he thought was the Little Dipper but might have been mistaken. He was all in. His eyes were filled with gin. He had no idea of the time but supposed it was near midnight. In the darkness he could not read his wristwatch. He had no certain idea of the vessel's immediate destination. Sooner or later she would put in at Hamburg and there Sieglinde would remain, unless she jumped ship at an earlier port. She was a resourceful woman and would get on one way or another. She hated Hamburg, though. Probably she would find an earlier port, Singapore or Columbo. Who the hell would want to visit Columbo? As she said, she was not lost. She was gone.

Two

HARRY AWOKE AT six a.m., thick-tongued, vision impaired. He lay still, coming into consciousness, patient about it, listening to the unfamiliar sound of drizzle in the trees. The cat was asleep at the foot of the bed. Harry threw on a robe and crept downstairs, hearing Chopin. But the piano was unaccompanied. He continued on into the kitchen, where he plugged in the coffeemaker and watched the rain fall. The silk-string hammock was damp with rain leaking through the ficus. He thought about cooking an egg, then decided against it. Two aspirin made more sense and he took those with a glass of orange juice, filthy-tasting army-issue concentrate. The orange juice worked its way down, sluggish as glue, metallic, altogether foul. He put his forehead against the windowpane and tried to remember the dream he'd had. Nothing came to him except bright colors. They said all memories were stored in the brain, even dreams. The key to the door was somewhere. But nothing presented itself except the bright colors. He believed his headache was retreating, thanks to the cool window glass against his forehead. He smelled coffee but made no move to pour some. Instead, he poured milk into a saucer for the cat rubbing up against his shin. Time was out of joint. Rain was an anomaly at this time of year, hot and dry in daylight and almost as hot at night; and now it was raining and the temperature eighty or thereabouts. Where did the rain come from? The rain belonged in the north. The rain mocked him no less than the silk-string hammock and the forgotten dream. He remembered that one of the colors was yellow. He had bought her a scarf yesterday but couldn't remember the color. He thought he had left it at the restaurant. He thought, One less souvenir. The rain made no sense. It was not supposed to rain. Rain was verboten until the rainy season, that was the way things were set up. Living was difficult when nothing was dependable. Probably that was why he received hazardous-duty pay, soon to be increased, according to Ed Coyle. Maybe he would take Ed to a resort hotel in one of the ancient ports. Find two girls and drink gin and tonics all day long, tell lies to the girls. The girls could tell lies back. The lies would cancel each other out. If the dream was so damned colorful it would have red along with yellow and probably some blue. Harry thought about the colors but they refused to arrange themselves. Only paint on a palette, the palette lacking a brush. No canvas, no easel. No atelier. At last he poured a cup of coffee but took too large a swallow and it burned his tongue, causing him to cry out.

Marcia, the secretary, said the ambassador was running a little bit late. She handed Harry the Washington newspaper, just arrived via the daily pouch from the Department. He turned to the sports page but found it difficult to concentrate on the baseball scores. A double in the ninth swept the Chicago series for the Yankees. The reliever lost the game for Boston. He looked over the top of the newspaper to find a photograph of the president of the United States on the wall, a most unusual image. He was wearing heavy spectacles and looked exhausted. The photograph was personally inscribed in an illegible scrawl. Next to it was a candid shot of George Kennan, he of the celebrated Long Telegram, counseling containment of the Soviet Union, a document Kennan insisted was perversely misinterpreted by his successors at the Department, and in Congress and the White House as well. Kennan and the ambassador had been great friends, then fell out over the Long Telegram or some other telegram, but they had apparently made up, making up being a common trait among diplomats. Really, an essential trait given the exigencies of diplomatic work. Kennan was famously difficult and the ambassador famously easygoing, so it was an attraction of opposites. Harry wondered if such friendships always came to grief. A marriage of opposites often worked out, each having an empty space that the other filled. Something like that. His mother was easygoing and his father wasn't. His father wanted today to be very like yesterday and his mother didn't. His mother was excited by tomorrow, the dawn of the new day and so forth, whereas his father saw unspecified difficulties, illness or foul weather or a moronic call on his valuable time. Harry considered himself easygoing, quick to forgive. Well, that depended on what he was asked to forgive, the specific gravity of the request. Some acts were impossible to forgive entirely or even partially. These unforgivable acts were too numerous to name. Carelessness, for example, heedless of consequence. Or all too aware of it.

Harry looked again at granite-jawed George Kennan. He had been out of government for many years but retained influence through his books and lectures. Harry tried to imagine himself at fifty or sixty years old and responsible for relations with a leader as malicious as Joseph Stalin. He could not. Hard enough even to imagine Stalin and the mountains of dead he left behind in his great experiment, corpses beyond count. Diplomacy was a great calling but you had to have the nerves for it and the wind, the confidence to look the American president in the eye and say, This is what must be done. Probably to do this successfully you had to have lived through the most desperate days of World War II, the outcome in doubt, and the Great Depression before that. You had to believe without question in the virtue of the American experiment, the project itself. Not that the nation was blessed by God. God's purposes were enigmatic. At the very most you had to believe that God was not frowning. God did not disapprove. But His thumb wasn't on the scale either.

The times have changed, Harry thought.

The men in charge were insecure, hence the war.

He closed his eyes and drifted off. God and Kennan went away. Harry conjured the German hospital ship under way on the open ocean, steaming through drizzle, everyone excited at the prospect of home, industrious Hamburg and its riotous nightlife. What did the Germans call home? *Heimat*, more than merely a dwelling or a city, a profound state of mind. Meanwhile the passengers had the featureless ocean to gaze upon, hoping that a dolphin or some other sea creature would show itself. At some point the vessel would have to put in for refueling. He had no idea where that would he. Probably somewhere in the vicinity of the African coast, one of the ancient ports like Mombasa or Aden. They would remain a few days, allowing the crew shore leave, though neither Aden nor Mombasa promised much in the way of sightseeing or recreation. Even so, they would be thinking of Hamburg and *Heimat*. Sieglinde would be dreading Hamburg, the place she disliked so. She did not care for Hamburg's past, nor the weather, the north wind and the icy rain that came with it. Neither did she care for the men, Germans of the big blond type. Perhaps that, too, was a tall tale.

Harry?

He peeked from behind the newspaper.

Harry, you're talking to yourself. You said "Aden" and then you said "Mombasa."

I was thinking of ancient port cities.

Mmm, Marcia said. Well. The ambassador's waiting.

Announced by Marcia, Harry stepped through the doorway of the ambassador's office, not as spacious as one expected. But they were short of space at the embassy, so many new arrivals, even the ambassador was asked to make allowances. The old man was seated at his desk, telephone in hand, his feet up, scanning a telegram. He waved Harry to a chair without looking up. Basso Earle said, Give me a minute, Harry.

Harry stepped to the window and stood looking into the street while the ambassador turned his back and spoke quietly into the telephone, not a word audible, but his exasperation was palpable in the rise and fall of his voice, here and there an ambiguous grunt. Harry watched a one-legged man struggle on the sidewalk, leaning heavily on two crutches. He wore a black beret and a shabby wind-breaker against the drizzle. Every step was painful. His right leg, severed at the knee, looked to be a heavy appendage. He was very old and gaunt, stubble on his chin. He looked as if he might collapse at any moment, and then he turned the corner and was lost to view.

Harry, the ambassador said.

Good morning, sir.

Listen to me. Learn something. You will be an ambassador one day. When that happens you must expect to receive telegrams and telephone calls from Washington. Any time of the day or night, usually without warning. Always be polite. Sometimes this will be difficult. More difficult than you can imagine, because what they are saying to you is so god damned stupid. But do it anyway. Be patient.

Yes, sir.

However, there are exceptions to every rule.

Yes, sir.

You will be tempted to scream at them.

I understand, Harry said.

Choose your moment for screaming. This was not one of the moments.

I'll remember, sir.

Well, he said. Let's get to business.

Basso Earle III was a Southerner from one of the parishes near New Orleans, a career foreign service officer of great ability who had declined to enter the family business, which was politics. In Louisiana politics was dangerous business. His grandfather did jail time and his uncle was obliged to expatriate himself to South America to await the appointment of a fresh governor. They were men who played by the rules, but the rules changed frequently and both his grandfather and his uncle had moments of inattention—call it forgetfulness—and a price was paid at once. Louisiana had the agreeable reputation of easy come easy go, a forgiving nature, a jurisdiction that looked the other way as a matter of course, and this reputation was true as far as it went. It did not include the sin of inattention. Basso Earle knew from an early age that he was an inside man, comfortable at a table or a tête-à-tête in a quiet room somewhere, not especially at ease in crowds or at lecterns or speaking into microphones. He much preferred the quiet word in a receptive ear, and while the word might be painful, his tone of voice was silky and in most instances persuasive. He avoided the press. He could make a speech but preferred not to. Ambassador Earle always took his time telling a story, his head thrown back, an easy smile in place, his hands loosely laced upon his belly—and the more important the story, the more time he took to tell it.

He said, We've had some contacts lately with the opposition. There's disagreement among our analysts as to how reliable these contacts are. That is to say, has someone strayed from the reservation or is he following instructions from his superiors? In other words, are we being played? Are we somehow being set up? They're good at games, you know. Good at chess. Very good at cards. They're born gamblers but not known, generally, for the bluff. Bluffing is not usually in their bag of tricks. Bluffing requires wit and they are not a witty people. Then the ambassador detoured into a complicated anecdote concerning his own experiences at roulette, apparently one of life's signature lessons, for at the end of it he said to Harry, Do you see what I mean?

Harry said, I think so.

Sometimes it's wise to rely on instinct.

Not always, Harry said under his breath.

What did you say?

Not always, Harry said.

Yes, of course, not always. Obviously.

Harry knew he had blundered with an obtuse remark. He smiled and said, In affairs of the heart, instinct can lead you astray.

Lust, the ambassador said.

Lust, Harry agreed.

Risk, reward, the ambassador said, returning to the matter at hand. It always comes down to that, depending on the spot you're in. We're in a spot, as I don't have to tell you. If our enemy wants to talk, isn't it worthwhile listening to what he has to say? Depending on the risk. He hasn't wanted to talk before. We've opened channels in every damned way you can imagine and it's never worked out. We've been up on tippy-toe waiting to be kissed and what we've gotten is a fish in the face. That's a Louisiana expression, Harry. It means shit. One disappointment after another. And here this comes from out of the blue.

An offer to talk, Harry said.

The word was passed up the line, one courier to the next.

Until it reached you.

It reached me, yes.

And you believe the offer is genuine.

I have a friend, the ambassador said. She is a very old friend. I met her in Paris years ago when I was head of the political section at the embassy. Adele and my late wife were very close, a pair of mischief makers. I cannot say that I approved of their friendship. Adele was a rogue, headstrong, an adventurer, very smart. But there wasn't much I could do about it, as I was putting in twelve-hour days trying to assess the various governments coming to power and losing it, only to surface months later. It was exhausting. In those years it seemed there was a new government every month or so. Adele is French but has lived all over the world. She lives here now. She grew up in this country—her father was a colonial administrator in the old days—and loves it, strange as that may sound. I think she likes the heat, and I know she likes the turbulence. She is attracted, if I

58

may say so, to instability. She is well connected with many elements of this society, including the worst elements. Adele is a woman of the Left, well educated, sometimes indiscreet. We see each other from time to time and our relations have improved to the point where she smiles when she calls me a tool of the imperialists. That's another way of saying we understand each other. And when I put the facts of this matter to her, she asked me to wait a few days and she would get back to me after she completed what she called her "soundings." The ambassador paused there, frowning at the word he put in quotes. There was pain in his eyes, too, and Harry had the idea he was thinking of his late wife and her friendship with the adventurer Adele. He said, It took her a week. Last night she came by the residence to tell me that, in her view, this démarche is genuine. She will not swear to it. She did not guarantee it. She believes there is some dissension among the enemy leadership and that confuses the issue somewhat. But she did insist that serious people were involved and that, all in all, it's worth a tumble from us. If we were serious also about talks. Are you with me so far, Harry?

Harry said, So far.

Because I think you're the man for this job.

I'll help in any way, Harry said, fully concentrated now.

You're the right rank, not too high, not too low. In a word, you're deniable in case this somehow leaks. *Which it will not do.* And you have as much experience in-country as almost anyone in the embassy. You don't have the language, that's true, but neither does anyone else. And you've nothing to do with the security services. That's an advantage in these circumstances. Our friends on the third floor could use more cloak and less dagger. They are definitely not trusted by the other side. But most important, you have my complete confidence.

How much does Washington know?

What I have chosen to tell them, the ambassador said.

I see, Harry said.

The Secretary and I are very old friends.

I didn't know that.

Sometimes we talk in code.

Yes, sir.

If this goes wrong, I'm responsible. You too, but less so. The ambassador paused and added, This is what I call a moment of consequence.

Yes, sir, it certainly is.

You must have questions, Harry. What are they?

What's my brief?

Listen. Listen damn hard. Listen to every nuance. Take notes, if they agree to note-taking, which I doubt. Don't make an issue of it.

I understand, Harry said.

Go in a skeptic, stay a skeptic. Look on it as a visit to an especially disagreeable lawyer whom you might learn something from. How's your memory?

Good, Harry said. I have more memory than is good for me, to tell you the truth. More than I need sometimes.

The ambassador offered a wisp of a smile. He said, This will probably come to nothing. The track record with these people is pretty dismal.

On the other hand, Harry began.

Maybe not. Maybe they see an advantage. They initiated this after all. It's their play. The iron does seem to be hot. When it's hot, it's time to cook. At any event, clear your desk. You leave tomorrow.

Where exactly?

South to the mangrove swamps, their turf. You begin in one of the southern market towns. My driver will take you there. You will be met, and from then you're on your own. I wish I were younger, I wouldn't mind this assignment. It might actually lead to something important. It might be the first step out of this god damned mess. The ambassador slapped his hand on his desk and stood up. Harry stood also. The meeting was at an end.

This could be dangerous, the ambassador said.

As you say, Ambassador: No risk, no reward.

That's the spirit, Harry. I do wish we knew more about them. I mean their command and control. Personalities and names and backgrounds to go with the personalities. The man you meet could be a country lout or an honors grad from the Sorbonne. Odd, isn't it? We've been here for some time and they're still mysterious. We're an open book. They know our order of battle down to battalion level, names and capabilities. They know my grandfather was a jailbird, for chrissakes. They probably have a dossier on you. By the way, who's Sieglinde?

Harry was startled. Sieglinde?

Yes, Sieglinde.

A friend. She's gone away now on her hospital ship. Back to Hamburg.

Don't look so surprised. We keep track of our people. Part of the job. This is an unstable environment, in case you haven't noticed. The ambassador stepped to the door, and when he spoke his voice was soft. I've saved the most important business for last. This operation is classified top secret. If it leaks, it's scandal time. The idea of treating with an enemy as disorganized as this one is a no-go in Congress and elsewhere. There would be a firestorm that could threaten this effort for good. The Secretary and I are out on a limb. Of course we have the president's backing. We're not rogue elephants, although I'm not entirely confident, if worst came to worst, we wouldn't be left drifting in the wind. I cannot stress enough the need for absolute discretion for this moment of consequence. You are to say nothing to anyone. If anyone asks about you, they'll be told you're on leave. You've wanted some leave and are owed some leave and in a few days you'll be back at your desk, as always. Questions?

None, Harry said.

Good at keeping secrets?

Always have been, Harry said.

Yes, that's your reputation.

Need-to-know, Harry said.

61

Need-to-know, the ambassador replied. And no one does.

The press would go crazy, Harry said.

Yes, they would. They don't like us, you know.

I'm not sure they understand what it is that we do. Actually.

They're addicted to fracas, the ambassador said, opening his office door. He put out his hand and said, Good luck. He added a few more details about the rendezvous in the south, recognition procedures, a timeline. The ambassador suggested that Harry travel light and, obviously, unarmed. This kind of work, a weapon doesn't mean much. Theoretically you are their guest. They promised safe passage; we take them at their word. And for your journey I want you to have this. The ambassador reached into his pocket and took out a flat round case the size of a fifty-cent piece. The case was gold, the ambassador's initials on one side and on the reverse a date. Compass, he said, a gift from my dear wife many years ago. When you return, I expect it back. But for now it's yours. Who knows? You might need it. It's always brought me luck.

Harry took the case and snapped it open. It had the look and feel of a fine timepiece. I'll keep it safe, he said.

And one last thing, Ambassador Earle said. A friend of yours arrives tomorrow. I'll have to tell her the cover story, you on leave. She will be disappointed. She certainly did want to see you and sends her regards.

Harry barely managed to ask the question: Who's that?

Congresswoman Finch, he said, the battle-ax from the Foreign Affairs Committee. She's leading a delegation to assess how things are going, meaning when do we take the gloves off and let the army fight as it was trained to fight. How in God's name do you know her?

Friend of the family, Harry said. And with that, he took his leave. In the outer office Marcia handed him an envelope. Greenbacks, she said. One thousand U.S. In the event of an emergency. You sign for it here, she said, and handed him a pen and a slip of paper. Harry signed, tucked the envelope into his jacket pocket, and hurried down one flight of stairs to the street. He paused a moment, squinting into the morning sun. The street was crowded with cyclos and taxis, here and there an army jeep. The temperature was near ninety and rising. His mind was crowded with questions to which there were no ready answers. He thought of them as gaps, a tumultuous landscape in deep shadow. He did not know where he was going, except it was south. He did not know whom he was to meet, not a name or a rank or an age. He did not know the agenda, if there was one. They had given him one thousand U.S. in the event of an unspecified emergency and Marcia had leaned close, touched his elbow, and murmured, Stay safe, Harry. Take care. He carried the gold compass in his pocket, a good-luck charm. And all this guaranteed by a Frenchwoman named Adele, a woman of the Left barely trusted by Basso Earle. Trusted just enough to—smooth over the gaps. Harry could hear the undertow of excitement in the ambassador's voice. His confidence was contagious, a kind of American fever. Harry lit a cigarette and noticed the tremor in his fingers. Not fear but anticipation of the sort a man might expect on his wedding day, flowers in the church and a mighty organ groaning in the choir, a beautiful girl at his side—and out of sight but palpable, the shadow line dividing past and future, or youth and maturity. He was embarked on a great voyage, alone at the helm. The street filled up and Harry marched away to his villa to stuff a few things in a duffel and wait for the ambassador's driver.

Three

S IX DAYS LATER, Harry awoke in a string hammock in the damp heat of early morning. He had not slept well, bothered all night long by insects and unsettling dreams. He lay still and heard the feral rustle of the jungle, indistinct and undefined except for the sudden meow of the camp cat and, a moment later, the waking cry of a bird. How many days since he had bathed? Five days? No, six, counting the night in the market town before he had set out at dawn on his mission—the ambassador's much-discussed "moment of consequence" that now appeared to be a moment of no consequence. Harry eased himself out of the hammock and stood, listening once again. He had heard heavy breathing during the night, unmistakable sounds of lovemaking and not for the first time. Unmistakable was probably the wrong word. In the deep jungle anything was mistakable, including heavy breathing. The jungle was disorganized, without form. He remembered reading somewhere that the deep jungle's shapes and colors were luxurious. They were not luxurious, they were coarse, mean sights, without harmony, the very soul of chaos. The sounds at night were neither benign nor consoling. They were sinister. They seemed to promise harm, even the meow of the camp cat. Harry stood in the doorway of his hut, jungle darkness all around him. He started when something brushed his ankle, God knows what it was. He was damp with sweat on his chest and back, sweat slick as a mirror. They had not bothered to shackle him. If he escaped, where would he go? This terrain might as well have been a concentration camp, the jungle as forbidding as any barbed wire. The first half hour en route he had been blindfolded, slow progress, one bend after another, and then they removed the blindfold. What was the point? One bend was much like another and the path itself monotonous as a piano's middle C struck again and again, all the grace and variety of a jackhammer. The going was easier without the blindfold. He saw no villages on the trail and no signs of human life except the occasional mark of a sandal's tread. He was sorry now that he had thought of the piano analogy. The piano put him in mind of Chopin, and Chopin was not helpful. It would be good to think of something that was, but nothing came to mind.

Harry saw stars through the trees and guessed the time near dawn. They had taken his wristwatch, for safekeeping they said. *Une garantie*, according to Comrade Fat, the one who seemed to be in charge. There were four of them, Comrades Fat, Thin, and Tall, and Comrade Mao, for her round face and sour disposition. The names were Harry's inventions. None of then offered their actual names. Harry was called Yankee. Now someone murmured in his sleep and shifted position, a rustle of bamboo and what sounded like a fart. Harry had a vague idea of direction, and by starlight he could see the two huts opposite his own, and a little apart from them the third hut, occupied by Comrade Mao, and the pit where the fire had been. Harry moved slowly into the clearing, and when he heard the creak of his rubber flip-flops he removed them from his feet and put them in the pocket of his khaki shorts. His mind was working slowly, the effect of fear. He did not know if this was fear of the known or fear of the unknown but it was surely one of the two. His thoughts were discomposed. They were residue thoughts, slippery and barren as slush. He moved slowly, but not so slowly as to lose his balance. Unbalanced, he would stumble. In a few moments he was at the camp's perimeter—and how long had that taken him, three minutes, four? The earth was damp beneath his feet and he remembered now the water along the way, water sometimes an inch deep, other times a foot or more, and he had blundered along while the others complained. He was in the middle of the file, entirely disconcerted when he was blindfolded, Comrade Mao muttering directions. Go straight. Now we turn left. There had been an argument over the blindfold but Comrade Fat insisted on it and then relented when Harry stumbled and fell twice in the space of five minutes. Evidently they were awaiting instructions from a senior comrade, supposedly arriving from a base camp farther south. Days passed and the senior comrade did not arrive. Harry's escort became restive. Without instructions they were adrift. They were difficult to tell apart, except one was fat, one thin, one tall, and one female. They were Munch-faced, featureless; not the Munch of *The Scream* but the Munch of the dead or the ill. Of course when they spoke they might as well have been speaking Norwegian.

And then the senior comrade arrived without warning, striding into camp at high noon—that was yesterday—wearing a pressed khaki uniform with the shoulder pips that signified captain. He ordered the girl to prepare a pot of tea and he and Harry sat cross-legged in the largest hut and talked. The captain did not offer his name so Harry thought of him as Captain Munch. His English was very good. He knew Harry's rank in the foreign service, knew that he was born in New York, had graduated from Columbia, was unmarried. The captain revealed nothing of himself but Harry suspected by his slurred accent that he was most likely a country boy. They talked through the afternoon and early evening without measurable result. There was something coiled about the captain, a muscle-bound suspicion so complete as to suggest obsession. He was ever watchful, switching to French as the afternoon wore on, a flat monotone, occasionally lapsing into his own language without offering translation. His voice carried great assurance, ex cathedra pronouncements as definitive and unassailable as a recitation from an especially reliable dictionary. Harry listened for any hint of irony or uncertainty and did not find it. Talking to the captain was like talking to a statue—on those few occasions when he was invited to speak. Harry had the idea that the captain regarded him as a particularly obtuse student.

All would be satisfactory in his country when the Americans departed and until that time—nothing. Departure was the precondition for peace. Nothing else mattered. Everything else was by the way. The puppet administration was not serious. They were lackeys of the American empire and would collapse soon enough when left to their own miserable follies, ignorance, and corruption. They were in any case unable to defend themselves. They do not understand that their army belongs to us and would assert itself at the proper time. The war was already lost and the Americans knew it and yet refused to take the necessary step. A simple step, really. Quite logical. This is a strange mission you have undertaken, Monsieur Sanders. On whose authority are you here? Harry replied that he was here on instructions from the American ambassador to listen to what the captain had to say. To hear the views from the other side. He had hoped they might have an exchange of views, find points of agreement, some mutual understanding that might help bring light to the darkness. There were already many dead. There will be many more. Perhaps—and here Harry smiled and stated in well-rehearsed Vietnamese—we could have a moment of self-criticism.

A part of your own dialectic, I believe, Harry said.

Where did you get such an idea?

Your chairman has mentioned it many times.

The captain shrugged, a show of annoyance.

I know a man who thought such a dialectic would be helpful in his marriage.

I do not understand, the captain said.

It wasn't, Harry said. Helpful.

The captain had been chain-smoking all this time and now he lit another Old Gold and looked off to the west. Dusk was coming on, the air lifting and cooling a degree or two. They sat for a moment without speaking. Harry wondered how the captain's mind worked, if there was anything in it besides ideology. He gave the impression of filtering everything through the ideology and then leaving it to age like fine whiskey, growing deeper and richer, more profound, a whiskey without impurities. Certainly that was what he wanted for his country, a regime without impurities. If only to please himself, Harry decided to take the conversation in another direction, sports, films, music. But the captain had no interest in sports and had not seen a film in years. He tried to remember the last one he saw. *The Four Hundred Blows* he said suddenly. A French film, worthless, depicting a state of ennui. A tedious affair, the camera moving in and out of metro stations. *The Four Hundred Blows* was self-absorbed, another example of French personalism. It was not instructive. It was not logical. The captain said he had no time for films. He had no interest in films that were incorrect and there was no place for them in the Party. He looked directly at Harry and said, I want a simple thing. A people's government. A government therefore without corruption.

The ambassador had instructed him to listen, listen damn hard. Harry had done as instructed without recourse to pen and notebook, which in any case had been taken from him. He had listened and listened and decided now to tell a story of his own, his last evening in Paris en route to the war zone. That evening he went to a recital, a pianist playing Liszt at a small *salle* off the Champs-Élysées. A countrywoman of yours, he said to the captain. A disappointment at first. She was tentative at the piano and Liszt does not respond well to tentativeness. However—and here Harry smiled at the memory of her—she was lovely to look at, tiny, small-boned, wearing a flowing amber tunic over white silk trousers. Around her throat was a gold necklace with an emerald pendant the size of a chestnut. Seated alone in a box seat, stage left, was an elderly Frenchman, quite tall with snow-white hair, immaculately dressed

68

in a dark suit with a white silk scarf. His arm rested casually on the railing of the box. He never moved during the recital—a short program, a nocturne, the Sonata in C Minor. If the Frenchman had been sitting for his portrait, the artist would have been Max Beckmann. The Frenchman watched the pianist with a private half-smile, as though he were watching a cherished daughter. And I go into such detail, Captain, because halfway through the program a miracle occurred. Her tentativeness vanished and she threw herself into Liszt, attacking the piece with the passion, one might almost say the fury, of one of the Russian virtuosos or Liszt himself. She seemed to gather confidence as she advanced, bending over the keyboard as her fingers flew left and right. And when she finished the Frenchman rose to join the storm of applause. When she took her bows she looked so delicate that the slightest breeze could carry her away. But appearances were deceptive. She was made of steel, at least as far as her music was concerned. The evening concluded, the Frenchman vacated his box and disappeared into the crowd. Onstage, two workmen were peering into the interior of the Steinway. It seemed that in the final two minutes of the Sonata in C Minor the pianist had broken a string. Do you know how unusual that is, Captain? As for me, I thought I owed myself something more after such an evening, so I strolled down the avenue thinking about this girl, your countrywoman. She wore an emerald at her throat and she played like an angel. A story from Europe, Captain.

I do not care to be adrift in a European world, the captain said.

A thrilling evening, Harry said. She played beautifully. If she had been a young American I would have been very proud.

The captain looked at his fingernails, expressionless. He said, Our diaspora is not large and much of it finds refuge in Paris. Paris is a grail for them, especially the women. True comrades prefer native soil. Our ancestors are here. I have no doubt that your pianist is from our South, probably a landowning family. Their daughter was educated abroad so that she could play your Liszt in a *salle* off the Champs-Élysées. These people, they own land and have import licenses. This one is better off in Paris playing foreign music. Here, she is a parasite.

Harry replied that she was much appreciated by the audience. A standing ovation. Three curtain calls. Many in the audience were in tears.

What was her name? the captain asked. No doubt she has taken a French name.

But Harry had forgotten the pianist's name.

The two sat smoking as dusk came on. The suddenness of it was always a surprise, an invisible hand on the cosmic meridian. There were no sounds elsewhere in the camp and Harry wondered if the others were asleep. He thought that in other circumstances this meeting would be an agreeable interlude, conversation of no particular significance, two friends discussing the day's events and planning for whatever came next. Exploration was poor today, perhaps something will turn up tomorrow. There was so much terrain still to cover. However, things did not always proceed according to plan. Mistakes, errors of judgment, bad luck. Chance always played a role. Chance married to unreasonable expectations, a lethal combination.

It's a disappointment, Harry said. We've come to know each other, not intimately but well enough to speak cordially. Yet we've made no progress.

The captain did not answer, unless his grunt was an answer.

It's a shame, really, Harry said. This dead end.

I am not certain what it is you want, Monsieur Sanders.

Nor I you, Harry said. This meeting was your idea. Your side's.

That is not true.

I believe it is so.

You are in error, the captain said.

Harry summoned a smile. We'll have to begin this dialogue sooner or later. Next month, next year, the year after. It's inevitable. The longer we delay, the more difficult dialogue becomes—

Au contraire, the captain said.

—because positions harden. I suspect you find time on your side but the longer this war continues the more blood will flow, your country awash in blood. Rivers of it. You cannot imagine the force we can bring to bear. Armadas, aircraft beyond count. Six, seven divisions of troops. Surely there is a way this can be avoided.

The captain did not reply, seemingly lost in thought. Then he looked up and smiled, a wide bright smile of undoubted sincerity. Harry was taken aback, then realized that was the point of their war. Throw everything at us. Throw everything you have. Throw the hydrogen bomb, and at the end of the engagement we will remain and you will be gone. The greater the odds, the greater the victory, a victory that will be written about for generations, for a hundred years. A thousand years. Harry had been waiting for an insight and now he had his insight, bleak as it was.

So our conversation is at an end, Harry said.

It would seem so, the captain agreed.

A waste of time, Harry said.

Not entirely, the captain said.

I am already overdue. My ambassador will worry about my whereabouts. If you can lead me to a secure area, I will take my leave.

That will take time, the captain said. Not a long time. Perhaps a few days. Arrangements are being made.

The agreement was: safe passage for me.

Nevertheless, the captain said.

Nevertheless what? Harry said.

You will not be harmed, the captain said. But for your part, it would be wise to exercise patience. Reflect on where you are and who you are and who you are with. This mission of yours is—controversial. Not everyone approved.

He slowly stubbed out his cigarette and put the butt in his pocket. Harry thought there was something petulant about him now, a show of boyish insurrection, his voice rising when he said the word "controversial." The captain said nothing more and strolled away. Harry watched him go, then fell into a worried sleep.

Now he stood at the perimeter of the camp in the early morning wondering what came next. He was not a wilderness man. Connecticut was not wilderness. He remembered sitting around campfires twenty years before, listening to the complaints of boys. He was a Cub Scout. On overnight trips to the hills around Salisbury the pack and its leader sat in a circle and told stories while the campfire blazed, ghost stories and other stories. Harry was recognized as the storyteller of the troop and always went first, weaving fantastic tales of pirates and other outlaws lurking just beyond the ring of fire. There were many villains—ghosts, savage Indians, Nazis, and the pitiless infantry of the Japanese Imperial Army—but everyone preferred pirates. Harry got so wrapped up in his story he half believed it himself, the peg-legged captain and the first mate with a parrot on his shoulder, the captain's wife with Dracula's long teeth. They were supposed to be learning about the woods and how to survive on a tin of water and a shard of flint, little else. A hatchet and native cunning—except there was no native cunning, only a half-dozen ten-year-old boys and the scout leader, Mr. McDonald, overweight in a royal-blue shirt and khaki shorts, high-top tennis shoes, and a yellow neckerchief. Mr. McDonald was a postman by trade, a disciplined walker. Everyone was asleep by nine p.m., except Mr. McDonald, who read mystery novels by flashlight. That was the sum of Harry's experience in the wilderness. He wished now he had been attentive when Mr. McDonald told them about navigation by the stars, the North Star and the Dippers and Orion's belt, but he had not been, unable to imagine the usefulness of such knowledge—yet another failure of his imagination. He remembered lying awake and wondering what lay beyond the circle of light and wishing he were older and able to explore on his own. The wilderness was unpredictable. That was why it was called wilderness. Late one Saturday afternoon the group had gotten lost, blundered, mistaking one trail for another. Mr. McDonald, studying his map, declared that every-

thing was fine, absolutely fine, they'd reach the trail just ahead . . .
Except Harry could hear the fear in his throat, the little cough after
"just ahead" and a surreptitious peek at the flimsy trail map in his
hand. Harry heard it and pretended it wasn't there, that the cough
and the tremor around the edges of Mr. McDonald's voice were the
result of a long day spent with unruly boys, not fear and discompo-
sure. He had heard a similar rustle in the voice of Basso Earle, courtesy and Southernness, its sinuous sentences speculative yet sure-
footed. His voice was not quite confident. It was the summoning
of confidence, as in his account of Adele, the leftist rogue whose
friendship with Basso's wife was — dubious. And toward the end of
their conversation, Basso asked, Who's Sieglinde? As if to signal
knowledge of his private life. At the time he had thought little of it,
beyond his own surprise. But now when Harry thought about it he
wondered if denial was a part of his own inner makeup, his world
view, the way he got on in life day to day. Not believing what was
in front of his eyes. Of course it was. The odds were always stacked
against, and the way around it was to ignore the odds. Diplomacy
itself had illusory aspects. Smoke, and then mirrors.

His mission was straightforward, textbook stuff. Harry would
meet his counterpart and either something would come of it or
nothing would. Probably nothing would, yet there was value in observing the enemy up close, listening to what he had to say and
how he said it. What was important to him. That was the ambassador's point, simply to begin a conversation and see where it led.
Words could lead anywhere. We have to begin somewhere, the ambassador said. There will be negotiations, sometime, somewhere,
and we must look on this as the necessary prelude. The clearing of
throats. If we decline a parley, Harry said, isn't that a show of weak-
ness? Danger was minimal. What would they gain by holding captive or harming a junior foreign service officer? Give me a brief,
I'll follow it to the letter. Mostly I'll listen. As he ruminated, Harry
wondered if he wasn't back around the campfire in the Connecticut
woods, spinning tales about pirates beyond the circle of light. But

he had to admit also his backthought: If he was successful, what a coup! Harry was the first mate with the blue parrot on his shoulder and a double-edged sword at his waist, the one who came from nowhere to settle whatever scores needed settling. During their last conversation the ambassador recounted the Secretary's doubts. Are you certain that Sanders is the man for this mission? He's awfully young. A bit brash, isn't he? Yes to all of the above, the ambassador replied. But he's an awfully bright lad. Not lacking in ambition. More to the point, not lacking in mettle. And he won't go beyond the brief. I'd say it's worth the chance. What do we have to lose?

Harry heard a stirring in the camp, and from somewhere in the jungle the cry of a bird, and next, from far away, the thut-thut of a helicopter's rotor—but the sound may well have been something else, a truck perhaps, or a farm vehicle. As if there were Deere tractors in the far south of the wretched Delta, a swamp, notoriously difficult of access. But if it was a truck, that would mean a road, and Harry had seen no roads en route to the camp. It occurred to him then—such were the uncertainties of the jungle atmosphere—that the thut-thut was a motorbike come to fetch the captain. Harry scurried back to his own hut and smoked a cigarette. He heard chatter among the guards and some laughter. The thut-thut ceased. But soon enough it began again, receding as the motorbike sped away in the direction it had come from. Harry was disappointed that the comrade captain had not thought to say goodbye, nor to explain the "arrangements."

He dozed in the morning, then spent the rest of the day reading Conrad's novella *A Smile of Fortune*, in which a young sea captain is attracted to a strange monosyllabic young woman, with its scenes of high erotic power that put Harry in mind of Sieglinde. But she was never very far from his thoughts. That evening Comrade Thin, a carbine over his shoulder, took up station a few yards from Harry's hut. Madame Mao appeared from the darkness to hand him a plate of rice with a bit of fish on the side, along with a glass of lukewarm water. Harry ate the rice and part of the fish, undercooked and tasteless except for the smell. He drank the water and when he went outside to take a leak the soldier with the carbine was at his elbow. Harry went back to the hut and climbed into the string hammock. Sleep came surprisingly quickly, though it did not last for long. Sometime after midnight he fell from the hammock, retching, drenched in sweat. The smell was foul. He cried out and someone came to the hut's entrance and looked in but did not speak. He went away and Harry heard soft voices and then no voices at all. He retched again and again until he came up dry, and then he slept, still sweating. He began to shiver.

It rained in the morning, a steady clatter on the bamboo roof of the hut. Little rivulets found their way to the interior and soon his shorts were soaked. The water was cold. His head was on fire and he had no medicine to ease it. What he needed was aspirin, a simple over-the-counter bottle available anywhere. He tried to climb back into the string hammock but found he had no strength. For most of the day he lay in vomit and rainwater, and late in the afternoon he slept once more. He had terrible dreams the second night, fantastic shapes and colors he could not identify. He believed he was lying on the steep slope of a mountain of the sort depicted in Japanese scroll paintings, gnarled trees clinging to a high precipice, a straw hut dead center, an old man in a kimono leaning on a crook and looking skyward. Pigeons whirled above the old man and seemed to mock him. Harry tried to bring the picture closer but it receded as he looked at it and finally disappeared altogether. He thought he was losing his mind. He heard some movement in the camp but had no idea who it was. His vision was furred and fractured as if he were looking through cracked glass with someone else's eyes. He lay a long time trying to focus, wondering if all this was a nightmare. With effort Harry raised his head and saw a bristly dragon the size of a calf, and when the beast turned toward him he saw it was an ordinary barnyard pig, black in color, rooting around the other huts, snorting as he went. Harry had the idea the pig was a creature from Asian mythology, the counterpart of a unicorn or a centaur. Rats figured in there somewhere. Snow-white hares. A brown bear. A yellow snake was coiled beside the campfire, its flat head moving from side to side. The smell of it all was ghastly, rotting flesh and something more besides. Harry was certain he was losing his mind and still he wondered why no one was there to shoo away the pig. His mouth was as dry and thick as parchment. His head was still afire as if his brain were frying. Smoke from the dying campfire burned his eyes, the scene before him indistinct and without meaning. He was in a zone of no meaning and was very much afraid. He had no idea where he was or how he had come to be there. When next he looked the pig had gone away. The rats and hares and the brown bear had vanished. The snake crawled into the firepit. He tried to remember the name of the girl in Conrad's story, the monosyllabic girl indifferent to the ship captain's charms. The name was gone. He slept, dreamlessly this time. When he awoke his head was almost free of pain and his eyes mostly focused except for the fur. He gagged again but nothing came up. He was empty inside, the interior of him a kind of wasteland or battlefield, scorched earth. Harry stretched both his arms and crawled to the entrance of the hut and saw that he was utterly alone. He was very weak but pulled himself upright.

He said softly, Hello? But there was no answer to that.

Who's there? But no answer to that either.

He stood with his back resting against the hut but after a moment he sank to his haunches and waited, breathing heavily. He watched an insect alight on his wrist. Harry moved his thumbnail, thinking of it as a miniature guillotine, a way of asserting control. Appreciating the situation. Then he thought better of it, the insect was a pretty creature, feathery blue wings and a black body. Harry moved his wrist and the insect flew off, leaving a tiny spot of blood. He wondered if it was a tsetse fly and then remembered that tsetse flies were native to Africa. He wiped the blood away and squeezed the spot dry. He remained on his haunches looking at the dead campfire and thinking about the comrade captain and the girl guard, Madame Mao, the one with the plate of rice and rotten fish. She never smiled, not once. They were anonymous to him. He did not know their names or where they came from. They were surely local militia, otherwise they would have been supplied with Kalashnikovs. The carbines were no doubt stolen from one of the many American arsenals. The guards were disciplined, though, keeping to themselves, rarely speaking or smiling. Their sexual adventures at night were a diversion. Harry remembered the underdone fish and the rice thick as glue and the cup of warm water. He knew also that he had been abandoned and would have to leave this place alone and at once.

He returned to the hut and put on shorts and a clean shirt from the rucksack. He shook loose a cigarette from the pack and with difficulty—his hands were shaking—lit it and immediately began to retch. But the spasm passed and he sat for a while blowing smoke rings and wondering what came next. Tobacco smoke was a comfort, gathering in the hut as it would in a badly ventilated tavern. All that was missing was a jukebox and a sympathetic bartender in a white apron, someone feeding quarters into the jukebox. He held that thought, remembering the bar near Columbia that he and his roommates went to. There were two shuffleboard machines and a dartboard, Sinatra on the jukebox, also Mabel Mercer and Billie Holiday, the Benny Goodman Orchestra. It was a hell of a good jukebox, best in the neighborhood. Beer on tap. No fights. The bartender's name was Fred and he had a daughter, Fredda, a pretty girl enrolled at Barnard. An aspiring poet, Fredda often helped her father behind the bar. Those were good times, none better. But they didn't teach survival skills at Columbia. Shortsighted of them.

He had only the vaguest idea where he was, and when he stubbed out the cigarette he realized that the smell inside the hut was appalling and so he shuffled out into the dusk, stumbling once, weak as any invalid. Adieu Columbia. Adieu Fredda. The dying sunlight hurt his eyes and he heard once again the cry of a bird and, less

77

distinct, the usual jungle rustle. He saw green everywhere around him and butterflies here and there. The trees were tightly wound with vines and all of it had the aspect of a botanical prison. The other two huts were empty, with nothing left behind except a crumpled cigarette pack, Chesterfields. No food, no water. Dusk came quickly as it always did. He thought of dusk as a shroud pulled by invisible hands and when he looked up he saw a starless sky. He checked his rucksack and saw that his stash of Chesterfields was missing. Furious, digging deeper, he discovered the ambassador's golden compass where he'd left it. His wallet was undisturbed. The envelope containing one thousand U.S. was there, too, everything present and accounted for except the Chesterfields. Enemy cadres were said to be puritanical, a quality essential to their self-image as liberators and egalitarians, hard-wired, as opposed to the selfish ethics and opportunism of the oppressors, worse than the corrupt French. All the same, Harry decided to count the money and found it all there. Probably they had decided that at some fine ideological level Chesterfields wanted to be free, a kind of indemnification for looking after the American. Where he came from, cigarettes were plentiful and cheap. It was not theft. The cigarettes were communal property. This was well known. Then he remembered they also had his wristwatch.

Harry had no idea how long he had been sick, surely two days, maybe longer. For all he knew it might have been a week, a decade, the war over and done with. He was Crusoe with no Friday. His gut was still knotted and he continued to sweat, his back and his chest, his stubbled face. When he put his hand to his forehead he knew he had a fever, not high, a low-grade annoyance. Now time moved in slow motion, an eternity between one second and the next. Then time hastened, almost a swoon. Suddenly he was on the ground once again and retching and moments later in deep sleep. Harry woke up a dozen times during the night, hearing strange noises, blackness all around. The jungle vanished. His thoughts were discontinuous, rapid arrivals and departures in all directions. The voice in Harry's head was not his own, but it was insistent and personal, a warning of the perils ahead. He heard the voice but could not see the face of the speaker. Was it true that vines contained water? The speaker had no idea. He had never seen a jungle. He lived in Connecticut and there were no jungles in Connecticut, only stone walls and fields that rolled off to the west. The speaker shrugged and in a moment was gone, back to wherever he had come from. Harry was alone in an empty house, blood-red walls and bone-white ceilings, no windows. He wondered how he had come to this misfortune and then recollected his reliance on denial. The means by which a young man got on in life day to day, a pretend world of danger and folly that always yielded to illusion, if the illusion was powerful enough. Illusion always defeated fact. He was the piano with the broken string, way up high on the treble clef, the one that promised a melodic lightness of spirit, counterpoint to the ceremony of the bass. Harry fell asleep again, dreaming now of evenings at Fred's bar, the first mate with the blue parrot on his shoulder, a moment that slid easily into a slender girl with an emerald necklace rattling Liszt's cage. The applause went on and on, Sieglinde beside him now clapping furiously. So it was evident that Harry was not done with illusion after all.

He was awake at first light, mostly clearheaded and without rancor. It occurred to him to brush his teeth. He found another pair of shorts and a clean shirt and stepped into the morning sunlight. The jungle's green curtain did not move. Harry thought it wore the tortured face of one of El Greco's saints. A godforsaken face, morose and resigned, and behind it somewhere a Bach fugue, austerity itself. An agitated silence gathered around him.

The place was cursed.

There was one path out and he took it, moving with caution, pausing often to rest. It did seem to him that the jungle had eyes, thousands of them, staring at him with blank indifference. One of the species of palm bore fruit and he decided on no evidence at all that the fruit was sweet, meaning not deadly. He ate it one small mouthful at a time and felt better at once, his parchment mouth softening. Harry was careful where he put his feet and after a while, perhaps fifteen minutes, perhaps an hour, he realized he was barefoot. The sandals were back in camp, and that mistake nearly brought him to tears, but he moved ahead nonetheless, there being no satisfactory alternative. Each step was identical to the step before. The jungle vegetation was unchanging. He knew he was not thinking straight but there seemed no alternative to that, either. When the sun was high he took a long rest, settling under one of the giant palm trees. He looked up to see a beautifully woven spider's web, the spider dead center and waiting one foot above his head. The creature was the size of his thumb, black and yellow markings. He did not have the strength to move and hoped that was also true of the spider. His feet hurt and his vision was blurred. He dozed, and when he opened his eyes the spider was still there, dead center in its web, something imperious about it. He glanced at the trail, a few signs of use, not many. It was not a trail designed for civilians, too narrow, frequent detours for no apparent reason, no litter. Then Harry noticed a tire track about the width of a motorbike's. He had missed that and wondered what else he had missed. Lost and confused, not alert, his only resource was his head, and his head was crippled, as clumsy as a clubfoot. If he was not careful he would find himself stumbling into a base camp, the wrong base camp, and he would be worse off than ever, a captive once again; and a captive without "arrangements," including the false promise of safe passage.

Harry decided some exploration was necessary, so he ventured off the trail and into the bush, thick underfoot and thick at eye level but better above, though difficult to see clearly. The sun was barely visible above the canopy. The terrain was brutal, impassable in bare feet with no machete. The only way forward was the trail, so he retraced his steps to the spider's web, noting that the spider had vanished. He could see no more than fifteen feet ahead where the trail jogged right. He had no choice but to follow it wherever it led. Then he heard voices behind him and quickly crouched, his knees sinking into the damp soil, his body hidden by an umbrella-sized palm frond. He remained there as two girls dressed in black cotton trousers and black sandals passed by. He could see only their lower legs and feet. They appeared to be unarmed but soldiers of the revolution nonetheless. They walked as if out for an afternoon stroll. One of them was humming to herself, keeping time to the slap of her sandals. Harry remained a minute or more until the girls were well beyond him. Then he stepped back onto the trail and trudged on. The girls had shapely ankles and tiny feet. Probably they were couriers. He wondered if they were caught up in the revolutionary spirit, foulmouthed, revering Che. What the hell. They wouldn't know who Che was. Che appealed to American girls. The sun was lowering and Harry knew he must find a bivouac for the night, someplace safe. He wouldn't know what was safe and what wasn't safe. There was no safe place. He craved a cigarette but there were no cigarettes, and if he had one and lit it he might as well send up a flare. Almost without him noticing, his eyes closed and he was asleep.

At dawn Harry woke with a start, uncertain where he was. He had used his arm for a pillow and now the arm was asleep and tingling. He heard the cry of a bird and a rustle somewhere in the bush. His joints creaked as he rose, trying to ignore his thirst and ravaged feet. He moved off staggering and an hour later paused for rest. But no sleep came and he went on, the trail twisting, filled with butterflies, unless they too were an illusion. And then he saw that the trail branched. He had no idea what lay beyond. The trails were without markings of any kind. Harry knelt and saw right away the tire tracks bearing right. So the decision was made for him and he turned left. He had to believe that luck was with him. Scant evidence of that so far except that he was still on his feet. He knew he didn't have much left. He had been walking since daybreak and for all he knew he had been going in circles, but now the trail branched and he actually had a choice to make. He had been lucky so far, although he had made many mistakes. He had made every mistake in the book, beginning with leaving his sandals behind. Oh, Christ, and the rucksack also, with the envelope with one thousand U.S. and the ambassador's gold compass. His wristwatch was gone and he couldn't recollect if they had taken it or he had lost it or simply left it behind. And where was Conrad? No doubt in the comrade captain's pocket and the question now was whether he would find Conrad logical and correct or counterfeit coin, one more Polish aristocrat playing at politics, the usual colonialist propaganda . . . Harry wanted to think he was one up on the comrade captain because otherwise his own incompetence was breathtaking. Again and again he turned a word over in his mind. Idiot. Idiot. Idiot. He looked around him, the jungle bushes closing in on the trail. His surroundings now seemed to him more than feral. They were malicious. But even so he moved on, remembering a story Tolstoy told in one of his novels. A holy man charged with the duty to lay his hand on a woman in order to cure her was instructed to place his other hand in fire and keep it there until his fingers were cinders. That was to ward off temptation. The holy man said, I would rather ruin my fingers than ruin my soul. Harry examined the story this way and that, believing it had some strange relevance to his own situation, a story of blind faith after all. But where was his own temptation, unless it was the mission itself? In the past temptation had been his friend, more or less. Now, instead of cindered fingers he had ruined feet. In any case, the mission was kaput. Idiot.

All this time, since his unanswered Hello? at dawn the day before, he had not spoken aloud, as if this perilous land were an open-air monastery. The silence around him was churchly, just a rustle now and then and the creak of wood. The morning sun filtered through the trees and seemed to break into pieces, falling light through a clerestory window. He had the idea that silent religious were watching him from the shadows, their heads bent in prayer. Harry had once or twice been tempted to go on retreat, some remote place where speech was forbidden except during services, and that speech was in the form of song. The first obligation was to pray. The second was to study. The most devout Trappists forbade even study, preferring mortification. Harry and his college roommates had worried the matter, concluding finally that none of them would be good at self-denial or mortification. They were in the world whether they wanted to be or not. Well, they wanted to be, and for the present Columbia and the city were the world. Temptation was everywhere and easily yielded to, especially when the girl was willing. When she was not willing, which was too often the case—well, you packed up your sorrows and went home. This jungle offered no temptation. It was a temptation-free zone and also a milieu that discouraged prayer. God had nothing to do with this place, ruled as it was by incoherence. A prayer was at some level an insult. But Harry said a few words anyway. Talk was cheap. And no one was listening.

His reverie feathered away, shoved aside by the memory of Sieglinde in the silk-string hammock. Where was she now? How was she doing? He had no firm idea of the ship's route home or its speed. Could be she was in the vicinity of Ceylon. He imagined Sieglinde at the stern rail watching the ship's wake or on the lookout for large fish, fish the size of a Steinway. Certainly she was far away and gaining distance each day. She had the entire world to disappear into. Harry stared at the trail and thought about Sieglinde and how she was doing and whether she regretted leaving him. Maybe she was practicing her scales in order to play Chopin for the crew while the vessel sailed on. She had no more idea where he was than he had where she was. They had each disappeared from the other's sight. He did hope she wasn't standing barefoot and lost in a godforsaken jungle, no help at hand. A lurid jungle nightmare would serve her right. Nothing in Hamburg or the vicinity of Hamburg would have prepared her for this. Unlike the Connecticut woods, he thought, with its vicious squirrels and ominous robins. Where was Mr. McDonald now that he was needed? Come to think of it, where was Siegfried, son of Sieglinde in the Wagnerian scheme of things. Did all Wagnerian heroes come to a bad end, impaled or consumed by fire? Harry pondered that, to no settled conclusion. He touched his stomach. He was ravenously hungry, his stomach as empty as his operatic reverie. Just then he heard the trill of a bird and then an abrupt silence, the song broken even as the trill's echo continued.

Behind him a twig snapped. In the heavy jungle silence the sound seemed as loud as a pistol shot. He froze, and all around him was a fresh scent, sour and alien. He tried to concentrate but his mind did a swoon, a fear-swoon, an icy wave of a swoon, fear of the known and the unknown. His left leg began to twitch and his feet hurt so badly that he believed that if he moved he would lose his balance. He had come so far with such care and now that was finished. His thoughts were disorganized. The sour and alien smell came close enough to touch. Harry told himself that he had to turn and face the intruder but still he did not move. He knew that not moving was a signal of surrender and so he turned slowly, it seemed to him a bone at a time. He found himself staring at a long-haired boy, an unpleasant-looking boy standing five feet away with a carbine in his hands. He wondered if this boy was one of those taken from Village Number Four, a country boy, inexperienced. But the look in his eyes did not signal inexperience. His sneer was the sneer of any street-corner thug accustomed to getting his own way. And so they faced each other, Harry a full head taller but bent so that they were almost at eye level. With an effort, he straightened himself, his arms at his sides. The boy wore a ragged khaki shirt and shorts and rubber sandals. Harry noticed that whereas his own limbs were scratched and bleeding, the boy looked as if he had only now stepped from his own front door. He was clean-shaven, even the sneer. Still, the boy said nothing. The carbine was secure in his hands and now Harry heard the familiar click-click, the irritating on-off of the safety catch. He looked the boy in the eye and knew for a certainty that the next move was his and that he must summon every ounce of what remained. His head was clear and his heart like ice. Harry erased his mind of all doubt—and flung himself at the boy, arms wide, butting him in the head like an animal, the boy falling, his head striking a tree root. He was dazed, his eyes closing, his hands reaching. He said something unintelligible. Harry seized the carbine and shot him dead.

The noise was tremendous, an explosion that sounded and resounded like the clap of a bell in an empty church. Harry stood over the boy, the carbine still in his hands. A second shot was unnecessary. His eyes wide open now, the boy stared at him with a look of—not malevolence but the utmost astonishment, his eyes already blurring over. When he died his eyes did not close. His mouth relaxed and in a moment the astonishment was gone, replaced by the bland and innocent look of any youngster at rest. The color of his eyes went from black to gray. Harry watched all this with horror and disgust. He sat down heavily and put the carbine aside.

My God, he said aloud.

He looked away but that didn't help. Harry noticed a spot of blood between his toes and wiped it off with his thumb. Then he wiped the thumb on his shirt. He had no idea whose blood it was, his own or the boy's. He sat very still, listening for any alien sounds. But all he heard was the usual jungle rustle behind the buzz in his ears.

The boy's shirt was bunched up around his chest, a result of the fall. Harry looked closely and saw a small hole, bruising around it. There was no blood. The wound had cauterized. Harry stood with difficulty, still looking at the bloodless wound. He heard the trill of a bird and covered his eyes with his hands, in his own way trying to turn the clock back. But the clock did not turn and when he looked once again the boy was still there, his eyes open. Harry noticed now that his fingernails were neatly trimmed, his slender hands smooth, as if he were a boy from the city. Probably he was. He had a biography like anyone else but Harry would never know its details. He had a name but Harry would never know that either. He remembered the girls who had passed by many minutes before. He was trying to find a justification for what he had done but none came to mind in any coherent way. The boy and his carbine had come along at the wrong time and Harry did what anyone would do in a war, kill the enemy before he killed you. That had coherence but it did not help.

My God, he said again, in a growl that surprised him.

He picked up the carbine and flung it into the jungle and knew at once that he had made another mistake. Who knows when another murderous teenager might appear on the trail and require execution? He found it difficult to move. When he walked he felt as if he were walking on razor blades. But there was more to do. Averting his eyes, Harry took the boy's feet and moved him into the bush. His sandals fell away and Harry picked one up, looking at it this way and that, measuring it against his own foot; but they were much too small for his own use. Christ, he had killed a child and now he wanted the child's sandals. Next move would be to rifle his pockets for any cash on hand. He had a wristwatch too. Well, that was stupid. He had had no choice in the matter, none at all. The matter had been his life or the boy's life, and if things had worked out differently it would be him on the ground. The boy carried a weapon and from the look of him—his sullen face, his stance, his purchase on the carbine, his stealth—knew how to use it. That much was certain. It was Harry who had been in the wrong place at the wrong time, and the boy had paid the price.

He looked around him, collecting the scene, storing it for reflection later, including the unsettling detail that the boy had not bled. No blood on him, no blood on the trail except the blood from Harry's feet. Everything about this day had been excessive and he wondered if the country had some special capacity for suffering, a magnet that drew unwelcome visitors. The visitors were charmed by the capital's French colonial architecture, and the sandy beaches to the east and north, the raw mountains of the center where people went to escape the heat and hoped to come upon an elephant or a tiger. The Chinese, the French, and now the Americans. The people themselves were not much noticed. They were said to be belligerent, holding within them a fierce pride and stamina. In a certain sense they were unlucky, not that they would ever admit it. They kept to themselves. Their culture was incomplete, no literature to speak of, no painting or sculpture, no music of their own. Of course that was the visitor's opinion, often with a caveat. Conceivably much was hidden, and in any case there was little interest in the thoughts of the visitors. Harry remembered the boy's look of astonishment at the moment he was hit. He dropped the carbine at once, as if it were on fire or simply too heavy to hold. And Harry himself thinking, as the boy died before his eyes, What in God's name am I doing here? Something about his situation—and he could not think what that something was until he came upon a simple word. The word was immodesty.

Harry turned and started down the trail, widening now, room for two men abreast. He picked his way along, limping badly, his footprints stained with blood. The ground softened and before long he was ankle-deep in water, black water filled with dirt and twigs, small leaves, boiling with insects. The place was a greenhouse for the nurture of tropical diseases, yet people lived there, got along from day to day, the war something like an afterthought. His thirst was homicidal and he scooped up a handful of tepid water and swished it around his mouth, then spit it out. The water was tasteless and he supposed that was a good sign. Also, his fingers had not turned to ashes or dust. He was pleased with himself, showing discipline when he spit out the water. Then he decided discipline was a luxury and scooped up another handful of black water and drank it down. He felt his stomach turn but the water tasted sweet. He was taking a chance, though. He wished he knew the boy's name and where he came from, which village. Otherwise his death was anonymous, an event lost to history. Well, it had happened all right. There was a dead boy in the bush. Of course at some point he would be found. The carbine, too. It wouldn't take much guesswork to identify the killer. The killer was the Joe from the American embassy, the ambitious one who thought that a negotiated settlement would end the war, a modern Congress of Vienna or Treaty of Westphalia. The negotiators would wear swallowtail coats, champagne all around after the signing. Harry was the one who did understand, at last and about time, that the war would not end until the Americans got out of the way. And there was a death to be reckoned with, one among so many. All right, Harry said to himself, that was enough. What was done was done. Yes, but it was terrible. Necessary, yes, but that didn't make it any less terrible. Disgusting, really. But old news. There was a task at hand.

He stumbled on. The light continued to fail. In a few moments he came to a dry clearing, and beyond the clearing deeper water, black water covering the roots of the trees and bushes. Spanning it was a makeshift bridge, two thick logs lashed together, no railing. Branches with strings of vines hung over the bridge and he could not see the end of it. After a few yards the bridge disappeared into jungle darkness. Harry stood at the bridge and did not know if he could manage it even if it could bear his weight. He thought not. Balance was required to make a successful crossing and he did not believe he had balance. Balance was out of the question. His thoughts were scattered every which way. He did not trust his judgment. He was bent over with fatigue and sorrow and his feet hurt terribly. He refused to look at them now, turning his face away. He explored the soles of his feet with his fingers, deep ridges, cuts, blood, loose flesh. A toenail was missing on each foot. Well, he was alive at least. Retreat was unthinkable. He had come so far and now there was this last thing. He bent his head and said a little prayer, the Lord's Prayer and Newman's prayer. *Lead Thou me on!* He asked for safekeeping and a pleasant afterlife for the boy. Harry stood at the bridge knowing he had this one chance. There was no other. The bridge was a kind of gift, perhaps an omen. It had arrived from nowhere. He decided to count himself lucky and so he took the first step.

Left foot on the left log, right foot on the right log. He said to himself that he was good with balance, superb really. Balance was his long suit, it always had been. He had always thought of himself as a balanced personality and others agreed. Reliable Harry. His fatigue was temporary. Danger was temporary. He need only summon this one last effort, having come so far, needing only a little more balance. The log was slippery and he found it easier to walk sideways, both feet on the right-hand log, the one that looked sturdier. He moved ahead by inches, looking into the jungle wall, wondering at the wildlife concealed there. When his right foot touched a knot he teetered and managed to lower himself to a sitting position. He rested, gathering strength. Harry eased himself over the knot and continued on in that way, a few inches at a time. Before long he lost sight of his starting place. He supposed he had traveled twenty feet or so and had no idea how many more feet there were or if the bridge simply petered out, decayed from disuse. Here and there the wood was rotten. He wondered who used it other than the comrade captain and his command. Perhaps there were aborigines in the swamp, Stone Age people with highly developed survival skills. A thick vine touched his forehead and he brushed it roughly aside and watched it fall, turning in the air, mouth agape, striking the water and slithering away, leaving a miniature wake. His heart stopped cold. He thought he would faint from fright. He sat without moving, his hands trembling, his vision blurred. He believed he had witnessed a miracle. When Harry looked at the black water he saw a congregation of tiny flies of many colors landing on the water and rising from it as the dusky light continued to fail. In a moment the flies disappeared.

And then his hand touched dry land. Harry rolled off the log and lay there, breathing hard. When he got his breath under control he listened for a minute or more, hearing nothing but the usual jungle rustle. He rose awkwardly to his feet and continued along the path, stumbling over roots and branches and the heavy palms that obscured the ground. He reckoned he had ten minutes of light. He must quickly find a bivouac, some safe place to rest for the night. He thought of climbing a tree but gave up the idea. Trees were not safe. There was no safe place here. Nothing was peaceable. The jungle ruled with surly indifference. Even the animals were not safe from one another. Harry looked up and not ten feet away he saw a Burmese parrot perched on a vine, its blue helmet and tail, its lime-green wings and yellow breast, its eye markings that suggested a dowager's pince-nez. The creature was identical to the parrot kept by the ambassador's valet, brought out for special occasions and urged to speak, which it refused to do. The Burmese parrot was said to be long-lived, friendly when it felt like it. When friendly the parrot would perch on the valet's shoulder while he served canapés. At the moment the parrot was watching a butterfly, Harry thought, with evil intent. He clapped his hands but neither the butterfly nor the parrot paid any attention.

A good omen, Harry thought, two harmless creatures keeping their distance. They were colorful, too. Defiance was vainglorious, and in that spirit he fished around in his pockets and discovered under a Kleenex a single Chesterfield. He lit it with a flourish, blowing one smoke ring and another and watching them collapse in air that seemed heavy with its own sweat. The odor of tobacco was suddenly all around him as if he were in a cocktail lounge or the bleachers at the ballpark. Harry thought it was a good idea to make his own rules for a change, so he sent up the flare. It would make no difference because he had definitely used up his own luck and the jungle was now in charge, despite the parrot. Probably the jungle had been in charge all along. At such a time there was no reason not to subvert the natural order, collect a reward for perseverance, let them know he was still alive and on his feet. Harry whistled an old tune as he continued to stagger along the path, widening now. He dropped the cigarette and raised his foot to stamp on it and remembered that he was barefoot. He left the cigarette butt to smolder, a souvenir for anyone who happened by, and that would be the end of his willfulness—call it hubris. Nothing here was familiar to him, but that was the normal way of things, utter unfamiliarity. He did believe he had come athwart an actual road, one lane, deeply rutted. He felt pinpoint drizzle and sat, the better to await what came next. In the middle distance he could see twin moons. Their light was brilliant, blinding almost, as if the moons were close enough to touch. He could clearly see his bare feet and his legs, welts on his knees and shins. He was filthy. Rain was in his face and he made a visor of his hands and the lights before him seemed to dip. He realized he was twenty feet from a truck. He heard the rattle of the truck's engine and then it, too, fell silent. Harry was alone in the drizzle and exposed in a bath of electric light.

I am unarmed, he said, his voice a kind of frog's croak. He heard a door open and close and then a hand was at his elbow. The driver was a full head shorter than he was, wearing the blue trousers and homespun shirt of a workingman. He said something unintelligible. His eyes were wide with—not fright, perhaps confusion. He looked Harry up and down, offering his hand, guiding him in the direction of the truck, a strange contraption, more caravan than truck. Harry wondered if he was dreaming once again. The parrot had been a kind of dream; he thought at first it was a hallucination; the butterfly, too. Now he was looking at an ancient Datsun pickup. In the rear where the truck's bed should have been was a windowless wooden cabin entered by a door displaying a brightly colored drawing of a dragon, a blue and red dragon with slit eyes and a coiled tail, a raptor's curved talons. The driver tapped on the door and opened it. He said something in a warm voice, most polite. Harry placed his hand on the driver's shoulder, steadying himself, and climbed inside. The interior was sparsely furnished, lit by candles. A Chinese was seated on a miniature throne. A boy stood beside him. The throne was crafted from ebony and gleamed in the candlelight. The Chinese—elderly, clean-shaven, hands invisible in the sleeves of his ceremonial robe—nodded warmly in an apparently sincere gesture of welcome. Harry responded with a *Merci beaucoup* but the Chinese did not respond. There were many Chinese in the country, mostly merchants and bankers, along with other, less savory entrepreneurs trafficking in opium, gambling, girls. Desultory efforts by the Americans to involve them in the struggle with the revolution were unsuccessful. The Chinese played little part in the war; business and banking and opium and girls would continue no matter who won. Harry could not imagine where this Chinese had come from, with his grandfatherly appearance and air of civility and hospitality, sitting regally on his tiny throne. Now he indicated a pallet of plump cushions beside the door, inviting Harry to sit. Harry smiled and moved his hands in thanks. It was only then that he noticed the pungent incense in the air and his own foul odor. He felt a tug, the engine coughed, and the truck began to move.

The Chinese said something Harry did not understand. Then he repeated the word.

Harry said, Yes, American.

The Chinese did not respond to that, but if he was alarmed he gave no sign. Then he said something to the boy, who reached behind him and offered Harry a flask of water. He drank all of it in greedy drafts and thanked the boy. The water was deliciously cool. A single draft of water had never meant so much, and then he asked for another.

The Chinese again indicated the cushions beside the door and Harry sat, easing himself onto the fat cushions, making a pillow of the smallest. Every joint ached and he bled from a dozen cuts on his arms and legs. He was sick with fatigue and felt nausea coming on. He wondered what the Chinese made of him, or if he made anything, an American blundering out of the swamp in the darkness announcing that he was not armed—not the normal thing in that part of the world. The language barrier was complete, with the additional barriers of nationality and age. Neither man would ever know anything of the other, except for appearances. The Chinese was surely a mandarin venerable of some kind, a merchant or banker or trader of exotic materials. He had beautiful manners. They might as well have been ghosts, each to the other, except that the Chinese had saved Harry's life.

The boy refilled the flask from a jug and handed it to Harry, who drank half. The boy was wide-eyed and careful not to approach too closely. No good could come of familiarity with a stranger. The Chinese said something more to the boy, who dipped a cloth into the jug and handed it, dripping, to Harry. He slowly washed his hands and face and when he was finished sat dumbly while the Chinese stared into the middle distance, expressionless. The boy curled up and went to sleep at the old man's feet. Rain continued to fall in a steady tattoo against the roof. The truck moved cautiously, no more than ten or fifteen miles an hour, pausing often to slide in and out of ruts, the engine laboring. Harry thought the heading was north but it was impossible for him to know for sure. He was beyond caring. The swamp was forever behind him. The slow-motion roll of the truck made him drowsy and he lay back against the cushions and despite his best efforts fell asleep, the sort of heavy dreamless sleep that, when he awoke hours later, seemed itself a dream, something not real, a dream of no-dream. It took him a moment to reconcile where he was and who he was and how he had got there, wherever he was, with the Chinese and the boy. He shuddered, remembering his passage across the log bridge, the vine snake, the spider in its web.

The truck came abruptly to a halt and he heard conversation outside, inches from his head, an argument of some kind. The driver was arguing with someone and then Harry heard taps at the door. He looked with alarm at the Chinese, whose features were impassive. But then the Chinese shook his head and put a finger to his lips. The argument went on for some time, and eventually, with a sigh, the Chinese rose and stepped to the door and rapped sharply, twice, a signal of impatience. The argument, if that was what it was, ended and in a moment the truck's engine came to life and they drove off. The Chinese returned to his throne and sat, his hands again concealed in the sleeves of his ceremonial robe. The boy continued to sleep. Outside, the rain ceased.

Soon they were driving on pavement, at most twenty miles an hour. Now and then the driver honked and Harry imagined bicyclists making way. He could hear other cars, trucks, and motorbikes going in the opposite direction. He had no idea if the time was morning or evening or somewhere in between. He had no idea how much time had lapsed since he stumbled from the jungle swamp and saw headlights. When the truck stopped Harry heard voices all around them, shouting and some laughter. The voices were rough and he feared he had arrived at the base camp after all, delivered to the headquarters of the comrade captain. But that was unlikely. Impossible, really. Perverse. All but inconceivable.

The Chinese muttered something.

I beg your pardon? I don't understand.

The Chinese nodded.

Harry shrugged and gave what he hoped was a smile.

Bonne chance, the Chinese said pleasantly as the rear door opened, admitting a blade of sharp morning sunlight into the cabin. The driver stood at attention beside the door. Beyond him was a street filled with carts and automobiles, cyclos, people going about their everyday business, uniformed schoolgirls walking in single file. Dogs in the street, a portable kitchen selling soup, a sidewalk café awaiting the lunch trade. Harry hesitated before easing himself to the pavement. He felt lightheaded, so much noise and movement, frightening in its ordinariness. He was disoriented. Bare yellow sunlight hurt his eyes and dust rose in little clouds all around him. Across the street was a cream-colored villa with an American flag hanging limply from a second-floor window. This was USAID House, two guards dozing in wicker chairs at the entrance gate. They looked scarcely older than boys except for the carbines they carried. Harry looked back inside the truck. To the Chinese he made the Buddhist gesture, his hands together, bowing deeply.

He said, I thank you.

The Chinese spoke a few words of acknowledgment.

I wish you good health. *Bonne chance*, Harry said.

The Chinese nodded. He was impatient to go.

And good fortune, Harry added. He realized he did not want to leave the protection of the Chinese, the safety of his cabin. It was a miracle they encountered one another; a few minutes either way and they would have passed in the night. Harry had found a safe harbor, a providential event, and he had never believed in providence. His days in the jungle were still more real than the turmoil of the street in front of his eyes. The jungle was a green wall of silence except for the rustle. He had adapted to it as prisoners were said to adapt to their captors. Starlight at night was a reminder of the past, and the brutal heat of the day promised a perilous future. The jungle, like the high seas, did not seem to be a place where people belonged. Human beings were outsiders. Youth was essential. Old men would never survive such surroundings. The heat was killing, then as now. This little town where boys carried carbines was even more perilous. The clamor of the street was painful to hear.

The driver nudged Harry aside in order to shut and lock the door. And then he was gone and a moment later the Datsun pulled away and was lost in the midday traffic. Harry stood in the sunlight, already beginning to sweat. Traffic was forced to detour around him, people staring as if he were an apparition. Americans naturally carried authority, and Harry had no authority, with his stubbled face and wounded legs, his derelict's clothing. His eyes were haunted. When he approached USAID House the guards leapt to their feet at once, carbines unslung. They told him to leave, and leave quickly. He was not wanted at USAID House, property of the American government. Probably he was drunk or befuddled by some hallucinogen, so popular among the American neocolonials. In that way they resembled the colonials of decades past. That was how they got on from day to day, hallucinogens and whiskey.

Harry took a step back, uncertain how to proceed. His vision was weak. When the guards began to shout, a middle-aged American appeared at the front door of the compound. He was brutish, heavy-bellied, swarthy, his eyes invisible behind thick-lensed sunglasses. He wore a sidearm. He stood, arms folded, his tight smile almost a snarl. The American came down the steps slowly, his irri-

95

tation obvious now. He stood at the gate and said something Harry could not hear. The American moved his hands in a peremptory way. Then Harry was on the pavement, his feet suddenly turned to sand. A bicycle stopped inches from his head. A crowd began to gather, laughing and jostling one another. Harry looked at the white sky, remembering the last few feet of the long bridge when he thought he would surely sink into the swamp. He had no idea how he had survived it. Harry felt himself falling into a tangle of bicycle tires. His elbow hurt as he tried to rise, having no idea now where he was. He had been with a Chinese and now the Chinese was gone. Then the brutish American was bending over him, his face giving a look of pure amazement.

My God, Sergeant Orono said. It's you.

Four

HARRY WAS IN a half-light of consciousness. His long sleep in the truck had not refreshed him. He felt as if he were drugged, in limbo, neither here nor there. The brutish American had taken charge, waving his pistol at the crowd that had gathered. His voice was loud, a threatening voice. This gave Harry no comfort. He had the idea he was now in a jungle of another kind, without protection. His head was on the pavement and he was looking at a bicycle tire and a sandaled foot and he wondered if the comrade captain had returned and he was somehow in the enemy's base camp, more useless conversation ahead. His mission, whatever it was, had failed and he himself was breaking down, running on empty, blood on his hands.

It took the director of USAID House an hour to find a local doctor. She did what she could, patching and stitching, but she had neither the skill nor the equipment to assess internal damage. Harry was unconscious and unresponsive. Meanwhile, Sergeant Orono made an urgent call to the embassy to let the ambassador know that Harry Sanders had turned up dazed and bleeding but more or less intact, very weak and not entirely lucid but not life-threatened either. That was the opinion of the local doctor. Harry himself was in no condition to offer explanations for his sudden appearance on the street in front of USAID House. What's this all about anyway?

Sergeant Orono asked the ambassador's secretary. What's he doing here and where has he been? But the ambassador's secretary would not be drawn except to say that she would inform the ambassador at once. When she returned to the telephone she instructed Sergeant Orono to prepare Harry for the trip to the capital and to accompany him. A helicopter would be sent. He was to tell no one of this journey. He was not to mention Harry's name. Was that clear? Yes, ma'am, the sergeant said, but he thought it all most peculiar and below the line. Something not quite straight about it and the secretary spoke to him as if he were the hired help. He was not the secretary's property, he was the property of the U.S. Army. But Sergeant Orono was trained to follow orders, so he did as he was told, even if the order came from a civilian. He was fond of Harry Sanders. The young man had sand.

When the helicopter arrived in the capital the ambassador himself was on the tarmac. An ambulance was idling nearby, two nurses and a doctor on hand. The ambassador shook Sergeant Orono's hand and thanked him for his efforts. The military attaché was present also, standing a little apart from the others. The ambassador called him over to say he would write a report for the file, copy to the commander of U.S. forces; Sergeant Orono deserved a commendation. He said to the sergeant, Did Sanders say anything at all? No, the sergeant said, he was in pretty bad shape. The ambassador nodded and went away to supervise the offloading of Harry from the helicopter to the ambulance. In a few minutes they were all gone except for the military attaché, an aging lieutenant colonel who shook the sergeant's hand and said, Well done. Was it true that Sanders had said nothing? Yes, the sergeant said, can you tell me what this is all about? The attaché did not reply but raised his eyebrows in a gesture that said, unmistakably, Civilian fuck-up. The attaché seemed almost pleased at the turn of events. He left in a staff car and Sergeant Orono climbed back into the helicopter for the return flight south.

Harry woke up the next afternoon, still dazed. A tube led from his right arm to a bottle hanging from an aluminum stand. He grunted something and a nurse was at his side, asking how he was feeling. She gave him a cup of water and told him not to gulp it. He asked where he was and she said the name of the hospital. Harry recognized it, a private hospital near the port. He said, Is the German hospital ship gone? She said, My goodness yes, left two weeks ago at least. Harry went back to sleep, and when he woke two hours later the ambassador was in the room, sitting quietly in the chair next to the bed, reading a file. When he looked up and saw that Harry's eyes were open, he smiled warmly and patted him on the shoulder. Can you talk? Harry nodded weakly and reached for the water cup and drank some. The ambassador produced a Chesterfield, lit it, and held it to Harry's mouth. Harry nodded gratefully and took a long drag and coughed roughly once, and again. The ambassador snuffed the cigarette and waited until the coughing stopped.

He said, Thank God you're back. We've been terribly worried.

Harry mustered a smile and said, Me too.

Things went badly, the ambassador said, half question, half statement.

Harry nodded.

Did they mistreat you?

He did not reply right away. He said finally, Not really.

Any progress?

No progress.

You learned nothing from them?

Nothing, he said.

Nothing to report?

Nothing of value.

The ambassador sat thoughtfully a moment, making a note on the file. He said, Go back to sleep. When you're fit we can talk at length. I want to know the full story. You should be up and about in a week or so. They think you have a parasite. Not a serious parasite, they assure me. I decided not to inform your kin and now there's no reason to, at least not right away. We can discuss that later. The hospital staff has been told to admit no visitors. But I'll be by from time to time to see how you're getting on. Your feet are a mess. Did they tell you that?

No one had to tell me, Harry said. They both looked at his feet, swathed in bandages so that they looked twice their normal size. The ambassador said, You did a fine job. I'm proud of you. We all are.

Harry grimaced and turned his face. He said to the wall, Did it leak?

We contained the leak. The leak wasn't your fault. Get well. We'll talk when you get well.

Harry sat up suddenly and groaned. It's gone, sir.

Gone? What's gone?

Your compass. I'm sorry. I left it behind in my rucksack. It's in that damned hut. And the thousand U.S. That's gone too. How can I explain that to the auditors?

The ambassador laughed. Forget it. There's so much American money floating around this embassy that it might as well be a bank. The thousand U.S. is a drop in the bucket. Less than a drop.

My carelessness, Harry said.

Don't worry about it. After a pause, he said, What else?

I killed a man, Harry said.

Ambassador Earle did not reply, waiting for an explanation. When none came, he said mildly, How did that happen?

A boy came up behind me on the trail. He was militia. He had a carbine. I knocked him down, took the carbine, and shot him in the heart. He died at once.

Harry, the ambassador began.

He was only a kid.

In uniform?

Not a uniform that you or I would recognize. Khaki tunic, khaki trousers, no badge of rank. The carbine was probably one of ours, stolen.

Tell me all of it, the ambassador said.

100

Harry was sick of it, sick of the details and sick of the outcome, sick of thinking about him, his look of—he supposed the word was awe. He stared at the ceiling for long minutes, hoping the ambassador would give it up and wait for another day. But Basso Earle was a patient man, known for his endurance. Endurance became him. Harry stared at the ceiling and recited, in a thick voice, the facts of the matter, the long trek and pausing on the trail, the snapped twig that sounded like a pistol shot, turning to find the boy with the sullen face. Harry described the pain in his feet, rushing the boy and knocking him down, picking up the carbine and firing. His voice broke once but he gathered himself and continued. The carbine in the jungle, the boy dragged off the trail. Later he pushed a heavy vine to find not a vine but a snake coiling in the air, the snake's mouth wide open, its snow-white fangs—

Yes, I see, the ambassador said.

Harry was silent once again.

You killed him in self-defense.

Yes, Harry said.

Well, there's no doubt of that.

Do you want it in my report?

Ambassador Earle thought for a moment, the focus of his eyes somewhere in the middle distance. Yes, he said finally. Bare bones. Don't call him a boy. You don't know his age. Asians, it's difficult to know for certain.

Harry nodded listlessly.

Don't fret about this, Harry. You did what you had to do and thank God you did it, the ambassador said. He gave Harry's hand a squeeze and left the room. Later, the ambassador admitted that the interview had been exhausting. Punishing, really. When he left the hospital room he brushed by the nurse with a tray of food. He turned to say that she should pay special attention to Harry Sanders, who had been—heroic. Back at the embassy, he told his secretary that Harry looked like death twice warmed over but seemed to have his wits about him. He looks older. He's aged ten years and

I'm afraid that his usefulness to this embassy is at an end. I'll find him a new posting, a good one. Harry was out of his depth. Maybe we all were. He lost my gold compass, the one I gave him for good luck. Can you imagine?

The poor boy, the secretary said.

Yes, the poor boy, the ambassador said.

The private hospital was known as the Singapore Sling, owing to a generous endowment by a Singapore businessman whose daughter, years before on a visit, had emergency surgery and against all odds survived. Harry laughed when he heard the story, thinking of the Connecticut Window at Église St.-Sylvestre. Supervision was lax, even negligent, at the Sling, and in the evenings all but nonexistent. One duty nurse looked after the twenty-five patients in the twenty-five rooms, fully occupied at all times. Everyone seemed to come and go as they pleased so long as they were ambulatory. Ambassador Basso Earle visited one more time and did not appear again, sending his secretary instead with an armful of books and American newspapers and magazines, a box of chocolates, a carton of Chesterfields, and a postcard from Harry's mother. His parents had flown to Barbados, spur of the moment. The secretary said the ambassador had been called back to the Department for consultations but would return soon. When Harry asked if anything was wrong, Marcia replied, Oh, no, it's the normal thing when there's a flap. But Harry was not reassured.

On the fourth night, bored to distraction, he decided to take a walk to the harbor. They had outfitted him with oversized slippers to accommodate the bandages on his feet. Harry used a cane because his feet hurt but gave it up after a block and sat on a sidewalk bench to wait for a taxi. He was breathing hard. Walking was a mistake, his balance was shot. In due course a taxi arrived and he asked to be taken to the port, quay number one. The quay was deserted, so quiet, not even a prostitute in sight. He sat on a piling at the water's edge reflecting on this nocturnal city that had become his home. Once he left it, he believed he would never return. He knew it better than any city in the world, knew its boulevards and alleys, its cafés and restaurants and churches, knew the Chinese quarter, knew the hotels and embassies and even the zoo and the golf course near the zoo. When he was older he would tell stories about the capital, its nightlife and working life, its mood flying from giddy to sinister and back again. There was romance, too, as in any wartime capital where the rules were flexible. The war zone conferred license, not on the epic merry-go-round of London during the blitz, perhaps because there was no blitz here. Danger was elsewhere, in the countryside, where if you made a false step you could be shot at close range and die without so much as a spot of blood. The capital would be well remembered by anyone who had been here—the heat, the sudden storms.

Harry watched a riverboat glide by, above it a brilliant parachute flare illuminating the river's far shore. Certainly he would tell stories about Village Number Five and the other places he had been, a long bridge to the back of beyond, the Singapore Sling, his villa with its silk-string hammock. The stories would not involve high diplomacy, George Kennan in Moscow or Belgrade, because there was no high diplomacy here. Perhaps low diplomacy, an unsuccessful mission into the swampy southern jungle, for example. Surely that mission would be forever classified, sealed away in a filing cabinet in a government warehouse, to be released in fifty years or not at all. Cities and their rivers cast shadows, and he knew that these would cast shadows as long as he lived, moments of truth so to speak. If Harry were an artist, the shadow would be Matisse falling on his hand at the upstroke. Harry watched a junk motor up the river, no running lights. The cargo would be contraband. In a short time, maybe as short as a year, the Americans would arrive in force and the city would change its spots once again, welcoming on the surface but something infernal beneath. The lights along the quay went out and the river was silent.

The junk disappeared around the bend of the river, barely visible in the darkness. Harry thought again of the zoo and its crippled elephant and toothless tiger. At least they were safe in the zoo. In the bush they wouldn't last the night. A prostitute stuck her head out a window and when Harry didn't wave she disappeared into the interior darkness. The sky was filled with stars, spoiled only a little by the winking lights of a jet aircraft high overhead. The café on the corner was empty, its doors closed. The taxi waited at the curb. He watched the river's current, sluggish as it worked its way to the sea, little eddies visible here and there, turbulence from mysterious underwater currents. He thought he would remember this moment for a very long time. He hailed the taxi.

Harry decided to look in at Café Celine, see if anyone was around, have a drink. His feet hurt and he wanted to sit. He was happy to find Ed Coyle at a table, deep in conversation with Yves. The room was not half full, no one else he knew. When Ed saw him he gave a wide grin and began to clap. Yves stared at him in disbelief. Others in the room looked up, then returned to their drinks. Harry slowly lowered himself into a chair, overwhelmed at once by Ed's questions. Where had he been? And what was with the cane? The slippers? There were rumors everywhere. You look like hell, Ed said. Yves disappeared behind the bar and returned with a bottle of wine, then crooked his head and said they should continue in his office, a comfortable office with all the amenities, where they could talk privately.

You should not be here, Yves said when they were settled.

Harry took a swallow of wine and smiled.

I've heard you're at the Sling. That true?

I'm supposed to be released in two days.

Where have you been? Ed asked.

On leave, Harry said.

Did you pick up the cane on leave?

My feet hurt, Harry said.

So you've been on leave and now you're at the Sling.

Ed, Harry said, lay off the questions.

Some reporters nosing around, Ed said.

Reporters don't know anything.

They see a mystery. They want a solution to the mystery. And Basso's gone away to Washington for consultations. And there's a rumor he's not coming back.

Yves smiled. Was it successful? Your leave.

Harry lit a cigarette and said it was.

Except for the feet, Yves said.

They're on the mend, Harry said.

And what the hell's that? Ed said, pointing at Harry's wrist, the livid lump the size of a golf ball.

Insect, Harry said.

What kind of insect? That's the damnedest thing I ever saw. Does it hurt?

Burmese wasp, Harry said. Vicious critters.

I never heard of any Burmese wasp, Ed said.

Well, now you have, Harry said. Doesn't hurt. Smarts a little.

My car is here, Yves said.

Go with him, Ed said. You're all in, Harry.

I'll take you back to the Sling, Yves said.

All right, Harry agreed. He was exhausted. His feet had turned to sand once again with no feeling except pain. When he stood, he teetered dangerously, and if Yves had not taken his arm he would have fallen. Even so, he stood upright at last, finished his wine, and stumbled out the door with Yves's help.

Harry spent not two days more at the Singapore Sling but four, released on a Thursday afternoon with enough drugs to stock a pharmacy. The doctor offered a final prognosis. The parasite was stubborn but would in time go away. Watch your diet, Monsieur Sanders. Avoid alcohol. Harry's feet were another matter, permanently damaged. The doctor said, I have stitched what I could stitch. I have cleaned out the debris. The right foot is worse than the left. You will learn to live with your feet. I have given you painkillers but try to use them sparingly. They are addictive. Surely there are disability benefits in your foreign service. If there are not, well then, you are out of luck.

Harry said, What happened to the German hospital ship?

They went away. Good riddance to them.

Why good riddance?

The doctor looked at him strangely. They are Germans, he said.

They did good work here, Harry said.

They were dilettantes, the doctor said. Making restitution, I suppose. My family died in their war. All of them. I am the only survivor.

Ed Coyle had fetched clothes from Harry's villa, chino trousers and a polo shirt. There was also a sealed note from Basso Earle. *Welcome back. Stay at home. Don't come to the embassy until I send for you. Stay off your feet.* No one was at the nurses' station so Harry walked on, emerging into full sunlight. The afternoon was very warm. He took the first taxi he saw and arrived at his villa at five p.m. The houseman was waiting, eager to hear where Harry had been and why he was using a cane. Harry did not reply to either of these questions. He asked Chau to bring him a gin and tonic, no lime. He would be on the terrace. If there was any cheese in the fridge he could bring that also, and a plate of crackers. Thus fortified, Harry sat in his bamboo chair and thought about his feet, swollen, lightly bandaged, still hurting. He had rashes on both legs and his left wrist was sprained, probably the result of his tussle with the boy soldier. The bump on his right wrist had diminished, though not by much. He placed a wedge of cheese on a cracker and ate it, following up with a gulp of gin. He took the vial of painkillers and shook two into the palm of his hand, then decided to leave them for later. Allow the gin to do its work without interference. The cat eased up to the chair and sniffed his feet. Harry told her to go away but she paid no attention. Instead, she yawned and settled next to his left foot. For a while he stared at the hammock and the ficus tree and thought about Sieglinde, remembering when she suddenly cried out, mistaking the cat's tail for a snake.

He heard Chau's voice from the kitchen. Mr. Harry, a telephone call.

Who is it?

Mr. Coyle, Chau said.

Tell him I'm not here.

He knows you're here.

Tell him I'm asleep.

Yes, Mr. Harry.

Tell him I'll call him tomorrow.

At that moment Harry preferred solitude. He took another swallow of gin and ate a cracker. From somewhere nearby he heard music and thought it was Chopin. He sat up. The melody was faint. It could be anything, Chopin or Mama Cass or Sinatra. For the hundredth time he reflected on Sieglinde's mysterious departure, no warning, no note. He thought that was unlike her, but he didn't know her well enough to know whether it was unlike her or not. Maybe abrupt departures were the normal thing for her. So long, see you tomorrow, but tomorrow never came and that was the last of her. Probably she was an unstable personality, abrupt departures being part of her makeup when things got difficult. Complicated. God, he missed her. It was a physical ache, somewhere in the pit of his stomach. All in all, the strangest period of his life—first her, then the journey to the jungle, the boy, the Chinese venerable, the Sling, events enough for a lifetime. Maybe not quite a lifetime. But the voice he heard in his dreams was Sieglinde's. Daydreams, night dreams. It all seemed too fantastic to credit. She was out of reach now, though, perhaps somewhere in the Indian Ocean. What sort of speed would a hospital ship make? Of course the ship would be at full throttle, everyone eager to see Hamburg, except for Sieglinde, who hated Hamburg. If she hated it so much, why did she board the ship?

The hell with it, he said hopefully. Harry called for another gin and tonic, no lime, and thought about his future. Basso Earle would want him out of the way for a time. He had leave coming. He could go anywhere he wanted. Then, on an intuition that came from deep within him, he closed his eyes and began to count. Sunday was the fifth of the month. Today was Wednesday, the eighth. He shook his head and began to laugh, more chortle than laugh and undeniably rueful. He was sitting alone in a bamboo chair with a glass of gin and a slice of cantal on a cracker. Chau was in the kitchen preparing a light dinner, or so he promised. The lowering sun filtered beautifully through the trees and the air was soft. Somewhere nearby was music he could not identify. He was meeting the ambassador in the morning but he did not want to think about that now. Today was his birthday. He was thirty years old.

Five

THE OFFICE OF Ambassador Basso Earle III looked more like a private study than a government bureau. There were no in boxes or out boxes. With one exception the pictures on the wall were personal, his late wife at table in Galatoire's, his two grown sons as teenagers in baseball uniforms, his father and mother at railside of a tourist boat bound for Cuba, a group of friends in climbing gear on a hilltop somewhere in Provence, passing around a wineskin. The exception was a candid photo of a young Basso bent at the waist listening to a jaunty FDR, a cigarette holder in his fingers, a rare glimpse of the president in his wheelchair. A long spear and a set of sculling oars rested in a corner. Also, there were bibelots on the various tables, a sculpture from India, a scale from China, a gold cup from Iran, and a brass cornet that the ambassador insisted once belonged to Louis Armstrong. The room was inviting. There seemed in it an absence of crisis.

The ambassador said, How are you feeling?

I'm fine, Harry said.

Your feet?

Some pain, not enough to worry about.

I see you use a cane.

For the time being, Harry said.

All right, the ambassador said. Tell me your story.

He wanted a written report for the file but first he wanted to hear the full account in Harry's own words, from the moment of contact in the café around the corner from USAID House to his return a week later. Harry went through it all, day by day, the conversations with the comrade captain, the captain's sudden departure, his own illness, and finding himself alone in the camp. He had the feeling that once they had him they didn't know what to do with him. They were wary, quite brusque. He described the guards and the young woman, peasant cannon fodder. The comrade captain was educated, good English, good French, with a single message: The Americans had to leave or there would be no peace, not now, not later. That was his point, not exactly a news bulletin. He was not interested in discussion. He was irritated with argument. Harry went on to give a general description of the camp, the food, the weapons, the makeshift huts, the fire. One thing about the comrade captain: He was humorless. He rode a motorbike, smoked cigarettes, rarely spoke to his compatriots. He was the lord and they were the vassals. Of his trek from the camp Harry was circumspect. It was a long way. Once he was obliged to move off the trail to avoid two teenage girls. Later on he killed a soldier. Harry told the story in twenty minutes, realizing as he went through it that fundamentally his trek was a long walk under a hot sun and not much more, except that someone died. He had forgotten to mention the snake. The rest of it was a blur. The ambassador had few questions, and when Harry was finished the older man sat lost in thought for a moment, and when he did speak his voice was little more than a whisper.

Tell me again about the dead man. How did that happen?

He came up behind me. We fought. I shot him.

But you were not armed.

It was his gun, a carbine. I took it from him.

Jesus, Harry, the ambassador said.

He looked to me not much older than a teenager.

What happened to the body?

I dragged it off the trail. Not very far. They'll find him soon if they haven't already.

And the gun?

I threw it away.

Was that wise?

Not wise, Harry said. But I didn't want any more to do with it. My luck was used up.

Could've gone the other way.

Almost did, Harry said.

You showed great presence of mind.

Harry remembered his fear and the turbulence in his head, his irresolution and the terrible noise when the gun went off. He fished inside his jacket for a cigarette and said nothing more.

OK, the ambassador said. I'll tell you what went on at my end. The ambassador paused, gathering his thoughts. Our dear ally the host government got wind of it. Not the killing, the meeting between you and the comrade captain. An awful flap, thanks to their paranoia that sooner or later we'll sell them down the river and retreat to San Francisco. Not an unreasonable fear. They thought we were making a separate peace and this was the first step. They believed that the meeting was at our instigation. What does that suggest to you?

Disinformation from the other side. The Reds leaked it.

Looks like it, the ambassador said.

The thing was a setup, Harry said.

Pretty much, the ambassador agreed.

The whole damn thing was a waste.

The ambassador did not reply to that.

We had to do it, Harry said. Negligent not to. It could have been real, the genuine article. And if it had been—

But it wasn't, the ambassador said, an edge to his voice. None of this was your fault. You handled yourself very well, start to finish. Neither of us knew the rules of the game because it wasn't our game, a thought you might tuck away for future use in case you continue in our business, which I sincerely hope you will. He raised his eyebrows and smiled. And you got out in one piece, a pretty good bit of navigation.

Harry had one more question. He said, Your friend. What was her name? Adele. Did Adele shed light?

The ambassador shrugged.

I'm sorry, Harry said.

Don't be.

They sat in silence a moment, and with a heavy sigh the ambassador said he wanted Harry to take his leave immediately. Go now, he said. Go anywhere you want, the farther away the better. Believe me, you do not want to be caught up in this. And you won't be, at least I don't think you will be, if you make yourself scarce. Strange thing is, your name has not been mentioned. I mean, the Reds haven't mentioned it in their sly commentaries. I suppose you could give them a pat on the head for that. They adhered to that part of the code. Everyone else, including the newsies, are busy turning over every rock in the garden. Who's the mystery envoy? They're assuming he's one of the third-floor chappies, hence the mystery. Very odd because the Reds adhere to their own code of conduct, not our code of conduct, but in this one instance they've played along.

Do you think you won their trust?

No, Harry said.

I don't think so either.

As for me, the ambassador said, I'm another story. Washington may need a head and I'm the head on offer. Funny thing is, I've liked it here. I like the country. I even like the people, and they're not a likable people. But I intend to retire anyway, next year or the year after. I have a place on Nantucket and I think I'll go there, maybe write my memoirs, everything except this last episode. It's too early for a drink or I'd offer you one. Let me know where you'll be, telephone numbers and so on. This thing may still blow up.

Have a good leave. When you return I may be here or I may not be here. I do expect to be called back to Washington. More consultations, but this time they'll end with my retirement.

Dumb of them. The enemy claims a scalp.

Just so, young Harry. Just so. Complicates matters for them, doesn't it?

Harry stood and offered his hand. The ambassador took it and they shook.

It's been a pleasure, Harry said, as if he had come by for a drink at the end of the day instead of meeting with a boss about to be heading into early retirement.

Me too, the ambassador said. I do hope this business hasn't put paid to your career. I don't want that to happen and I'll do what I can to prevent it. The old man's face grew cold, a twitch to his jaw and a hardness around the mouth that Harry had not seen before. An ambassador had a variety of faces, one for every occasion. Basso Earle also liked to hide behind his accent, the crushed syllables and slow diminuendos, slippery as glass. He gave the impression of being slightly hard of hearing. In other words, an easy man to underestimate. He did not sound the way an ambassador was supposed to sound, vaguely British like Dean Acheson or High Church like Foster Dulles. Basso Earle had a sly wit, and in telling a story, its ins and outs and twists and turns and frequent digressions, he sounded almost French. He'd been successful from the beginning, his first posting as second secretary at embassy Rome working for a political appointee, Boston born. They got on famously. The Bostonian was a student of Italian culture, its uses of illusion, brio on the surface and melancholy beneath. An attractive people, he thought, ill served by their wretched church. They had no talent for governance, but that, too, was more subtle than it seemed. Fundamentally, Italians did not wish to be governed. They wished the appearance of government, meaning a mighty bureaucracy, quite another thing. Alas, in Boston the Irish and the Italians did not get on. A pity. Each had much to learn from the other.

Basso was popular in the Department, taking care not to insult those he stepped over on the way up because they were eternal, like Nosferatu, and knew how to insult back. Everyone had friends, and friends looked after one another as friends were supposed to do. Basso Earle had friends on every continent. Typical of him that he should choose Nantucket as a place for his retirement. A whaling island of the previous century, independent of spirit. The people were hard as iron and the accent was a fortress.

Ambassador Earle retreated now to the safety of his desk, looking down and reading something, a sarcastic frown. Harry was at the door and knew that it was time for him to go. He knew also that this was probably the last time they would meet, at least in this office. He said, Goodbye, Ambassador. I'd work for you anytime.

Remember, the ambassador said without looking up, our business is not a straight-line affair. We deal with curves and switchbacks, the yes that means no and the no that means maybe. We are obliged to be comfortable with ambiguity. I have always thought that in diplomacy you are the master of your own fate so long as you keep your eyes wide open, understanding always that things can turn on a dime. It's wise to take the long view, Harry. Be patient. The black cat is there somewhere and now and again it'll come for you.

Harry stopped by his office to collect whatever he would need for his trip. There was a raincoat and he took that, along with his checkbook and his passport and some stationery for letter writing. He put these in a canvas bag, along with a manila envelope from Marcia. On the way out he looked in at Ed Coyle's office but Ed was not there. Outside the building, he stood in the raw heat, already beginning to sweat. A cyclo driver stopped at the curb but Harry shook his head, preferring to walk. Across the street the one-legged veteran with the black beret was on his usual rounds. Harry watched him a moment, listening to the erratic click of his crutch.

He said to himself what he always said, Poor old bastard. Harry waved at him with his cane but the old man did not wave back.

He walked slowly, the canvas bag over his shoulder, not heavy but bulky. In twenty minutes he was in his own neighborhood and five minutes after that was walking up the driveway of the villa and into the kitchen. Chau was not there. Harry poured a large glass of lemonade and thought about his leave, where to go and how to get there. He was dubious about a vacation taken alone at a resort hotel in an unfamiliar country. He stood on the porch with the glass of lemonade in his hand and looked at the silk-string hammock, a kind of mockery. He had never been to Australia, but Australia was a far distance. Hawaii was even farther. He had no idea what you did in the Philippines except visit Bataan. Climbing in the Himalayas was a possibility, a view of the summits of Everest and K2. He assumed the road to the mountains began in Nepal but wasn't sure. He remembered his feet and decided the Himalayas were a bad idea. Someone had told him that the west coast of Malaya was pretty, good beaches, a good climate, decent food. The accommodations were adequate and not expensive. There were guesthouses all along the shore. The fishing was superb. He would need a library, half a dozen books at least. A couple of bottles of gin. But he could buy the gin at the airport; three bottles would be about right for a two-week stay. Harry lit a Chesterfield and blew a smoke ring, still staring at the lawn, shaggy at the edges. The hedges needed trimming. He sat in the bamboo chair and fished around in the canvas bag for the manila envelope. In it he found six letters, three from his family, two bills, and one with unfamiliar handwriting, though he knew at once whose it was. The postmark was Tananarive and that was a puzzle, unless the hospital ship was equipped with jet engines.

Sieglinde wrote that she was sorry not to have been in touch before but she had been on the move. She had quit the ship at Columbo and taken a plane to Tananarive. She had always wanted to see Madagascar, for the flowers and the wildlife. It was very beautiful and she thought she would stay for a week or so. And then resume her odyssey. By the time he got this letter she would be gone, most likely.

I did not say goodbye, she wrote, because goodbyes are always painful to me. I never know what to say. Whoever I'm saying goodbye to doesn't know what to say either, and so it's painful, especially if the likelihood is that we won't see each other again. The ship's departure was abrupt and there was nothing I could do about that. I stood at the rail and watched our city recede. The captain remarked that we had done some good, being there. Saved lives. Helped scores of children. But our time was up. We had overstayed as it was. When he asked me if I had enjoyed myself I said yes, but I did not wish to go further than that, even though we had come to know each other quite well and were in the way of being friends. I had no wish to tell him about us. And if I had chosen to, what would I have said?

Harry looked up from the letter, her words recalling her voice, its rise and fall, and her accent. She had never hidden behind her accent. Just then it was as if she were sitting beside him and talking, her hands expressive, the rise and fall of her voice very nearly a song sung parlando.

I am looking at the sea while I am talking to you, she wrote, huge thunderheads to the east. I am assured they will not bother us today, perhaps tomorrow. I am on the verandah of my little cabin. Dusk is in the air but still an hour or so away. I wonder about you, where you are and what you are doing. I imagine you upcountry somewhere. Is there a Village Number Six? I bet there is. And if there is, that's where you are. I meant to tell you our last night together that you needed a haircut. I'm a good haircutter and I would have given you one, no charge. But I forgot to mention the haircut. I think there were many things I forgot to mention and one of them was—to tell you how much I care for you. How much I worry

116

about you in the war. Please stay safe. I think you can sometimes be reckless, my Harry. Do not let them push you into doing something reckless. I feel you are all too ready for reckless adventures. But I should talk. That's my way, too.

When Harry turned the page he found her writing now in green ink. Evidently she had stopped and continued the letter later. But there was no mention of that. However, she did change course. A fresh thought.

I know nothing of my family, Sieglinde wrote. I was so young when my father was killed and my mother was lost to me not long after. My memory of my father is contained in a snapshot. My mother began to disappear almost at once. My aunt in Lübeck is dead. If there are other family members I have no idea who or where they are. I worry about this. I worry about what sort of people they were. Where did they live and what did they do? Were they human-ists—or the other kind? Did any of them resemble me? If I saw one on the street would I recognize her? I know there are places you can go to find out such things but I have never found the will to do so. I believe it would take years, searching records, searching birth certificates, old telephone books—assuming my family had tele-phones. Where to begin? I could spend a lifetime and I refuse to do that. And perhaps I was afraid of what I might find. These were terrible years, terrible years. I did not choose to be German but it is my burden, is it not? I was put at odds with the world. And the odds grew longer from day to day. I am in every sense orphaned and I feel great loathing for Hitler's war. The war took my family from me and showed not one iota of remorse. It is a great fault line and not only for me. I listen to you talk about fine country houses in Connecticut and the good living that supposedly went with it, and I do not know what to make of this. Of course I am envious. How could I not be envious? And I also know that you and I have some-thing between us that is quite apart from my Hamburg and your Connecticut and your ancestors and my own. But I do find myself alone in the world and I fear that will go on and on. That is why I am in Tananarive to look at the animals and the flowers. To watch the thunderheads to the east. Rain tomorrow. I know no one here. And no one knows me.

I do not know how I can live a normal life. My love, my heart is broken. I am lost.

With you, I am afraid of what I might find.

When Harry arrived in Tananarive two days later, he drove from village to village on the east coast looking for Sieglinde. He spoke to restaurant owners and cyclo drivers and proprietors of guest-houses, describing her, a German woman, five feet five inches tall, ash-blond hair, a shuffle-walk, a sad face. He found no trace. If someone truly wants to disappear there are always ways and means to do so. On the fifth day, with no success at all, he gave it up and rented a one-room villa on a pleasant cove with a good restaurant nearby. He stayed a week, beachcombing and reading one novel after another, getting a bronze tan. Late each afternoon he returned to the porch of his villa with a drink and a bowl of peanuts, waiting for Sieglinde to appear. He made another drink, and a third, before walking to the restaurant for dinner. Harry had the idea that Sieglinde might simply appear, out of nowhere as it were, and they would fall into each other's arms and be together forever, leading a normal life. He was devoted to proving the ambassador correct. Surely it was possible that, from time to time, a man was master of his own fate.

A group of Americans had rented a large villa at the cove and were always in the restaurant when Harry appeared to take his corner table. On the second night they asked him to join them for a drink in the bar. When they asked him what he did for a living he said he was traveling, no fixed destination. He did not go beyond that and the Americans did not press the point. They were pleasant enough Americans, two lawyers and their wives, a businessman with his girlfriend, a doctor and her husband. The doctor warned

Harry about the sun; there were alarming studies about skin cancer and the like. They had all been to school together and traveled as a group each year. Harry was interested in hearing what constituted a normal life in America and they obliged with stories of their country club in the Chicago suburbs, the annual Darby and Joan golf tournament, summer dances with a jazz band from the South Side of Chicago. Their children were doing well at New Trier. All in all the region was prospering, except for the Negro element. But in time the Negroes would catch up. Education was the answer. Harry nodded. Nothing new so far. They were all mildly tipsy, Harry too. He asked them what was doing politically in Chicago but got no clear answer beyond the comment that the Democratic machine ruled with an iron hand. They were not political. Politics was a distraction. They did not recall whether the governor was a Democrat or a Republican. Harry was careful not to mention the war and they didn't either. The evening wound down. Harry took his leave with a glass of cognac and wandered back down the beach to his villa. He had only two days remaining. He sat on his porch sipping cognac and thinking about a normal life. He knew it required money, the more money the better. Good health, certainly. Children who did well. Nothing wrong with a jazz band on a summer evening. Sieglinde must have a particular definition of normal life. She never mentioned money.

Harry sat awhile on his porch, watching the stars disappear as the front moved west. He took small sips of cognac, wanting it to last. He was very tired but did not want to go to bed. He wished he had asked them about the war, its place in their lives. War conversation did not occur to them. Harry wondered about the government of Madagascar, if there were communist elements. Probably there were. The Russians were active in Africa. He had no idea about the government of Madagascar. The war had been his life, crowding out events elsewhere. He was not up to speed. Harry fell asleep on the porch with the glass in his hand, waking near morning, bright shafts of sunlight and a light breeze from the west. The weather front had not moved one inch and the air smelled of peaches. The front looked to be a permanent fixture in the eastern sky.

Two days later in the airport, Harry picked up one of the British newspapers. A three-inch-high headline announced that his embassy had been bombed, one dead, six injured, and the injured included two marine guards. Ambassador Basso Earle III was not present; he was believed to be in Washington for consultations. The dead man was a political officer, Edwin Cayle, thirty-one. The idiot reporter had misspelled Ed's name. Ed had been standing at his office window when the bomb exploded and had been killed by flying glass. The bombing occurred at ten a.m., when the embassy was at full staff. Among the injured were three women, including the ambassador's secretary. A cordon had been established around the building, which was closed until further notice. The bomber—and here Harry lifted his eyes to the ceiling, thinking about Ed Coyle, always among the first to arrive at work. Harry gave himself a minute, then finished the paragraph. The bomber was a one-legged army veteran. Eyewitnesses said he removed his beret and set himself alight, and moments later the bomb exploded. American officials said the bomber was a familiar figure in the district but no one knew his name.

Inside the paper, together with photographs of the damaged embassy, was a sidebar datelined Washington. The story cited unnamed American officials denying reports of a recent meeting with high-level communist military officers. The meeting was said to be the first known contact between the adversaries. Absolute falsehood, the American officials stated, disinformation designed to sow distrust between the allies, a well-known communist tactic born of desperation. There was no such meeting and would not be one until the communists laid down their arms, ceased terrorizing native villages, and promised to pursue their objectives in a nonviolent manner. The United States and its allies were always open to constructive discussions.

The newspaper article noted that rumors had circulated for weeks that an American embassy official had met with communist representatives at an undisclosed location in the south of the country. It was unknown if the alleged conversations had produced results. But an American official said that the embassy bombing was answer enough as to whether any contact with the enemy would have official endorsement.

Six

SIEGLINDE DEPARTED MADAGASCAR by ship the day Harry arrived by air, neither aware of the proximity of the other. Sieglinde watched the coastline disappear with the certainty that she would never again see Madagascar, an island that seemed to her forlorn despite the exotic animals and flowering plants, a profusion of color. The people were friendly but reserved. They were very poor, often malnourished. Sieglinde was restless and felt herself in the wrong place. Whatever in the world inspired her to go to Madagascar? Surely not the dozens of species of bats. She devoted her days to beachcombing and her nights to stargazing, lost in thought. The first few nights she stopped in at the hotel bar for a glass of Löwenbräu, but after some unpleasantness with a French bush pilot she stayed away from the bar and finally bought passage on a steamer bound for the Mediterranean. Each day brought her closer to Germany, though she did not consider Germany her destination. Sieglinde stopped for a day in Aden, then continued on through the Suez Canal to Cairo, where she visited the pyramids and rode a camel. She thought that in their massive gray brutality the pyramids could well have been designed by Hitler's architect, what was his name? Herr Speer. Sieglinde was often the object of scrutiny and conjecture, such a pretty young woman traveling alone. From her distant manner she was assumed to have suffered misfortune, no doubt of a sentimental nature, an affair of the heart. She discouraged conversation yet was adventurous. She rode the camel as if born to it, arms spread wide as she held the reins and cried, Hut! Hut! That night she attached herself to a tour group from California and spent the night in the desert.

When anyone asked, she said she was traveling to Hamburg.

Do you have family in Hamburg?

Yes, my sister.

And your parents—

Yes, my parents also.

It's a pleasant city, Hamburg.

My family is in the shipping trade.

How interesting!

I hope to be home for Christmas, Sieglinde said. It is always a great celebration in my family. Roast goose. Gingerbread.

Oh, it sounds like a feast.

It is! Sieglinde said.

Leaving Cairo, Sieglinde had begun to worry about money. Of course she had her savings with her. She had been careful to put aside what she could during her time on the hospital ship and had been frugal in Madagascar. She had been paid in deutsche marks and the exchange rate was favorable, but now she put herself on a regime, coffee for breakfast, a salad for lunch, a simple dinner in a café. She had always paid her own way and hated worrying about money now, like some disappointed shopgirl. Sieglinde stopped at Tripoli and went overland by bus to Tunis. She had no fixed destination. She told herself she would know it when she saw it. Harry was much on her mind during this journey. When she thought about the silk-string hammock, the details of that night came vividly to mind and she smiled and giggled and smiled again. Harry so athletic, and gentle, too. Had she ever been happier? At last she was living in the present moment. She remembered also Harry's rapt expression as he stood on the stairs of his villa watching her play Chopin. Less happily she recalled telling him of the war, her father's death and her mother's disappearance, Hamburg in flames, the nation on its knees. What could he know of that in Connecticut! He lacked imagination. He could not comprehend the situation in Europe. He had never in his life been hungry. Never breathed ashes in the air. He had made a joke involving the Third Reich and she had felt a chill deep in her bones. He had no understanding of the way things were, owing to his lack of imagination.

Still, he applauded her piano music. He was moved by it. Sieglinde had not touched a piano in months and was surprised at how quickly it all came back to her, phrasing and tempi. Of course Chopin reminded her of Europe, and Europe of the war, and she did not wish to think of either one.

Her thoughts were scattered. She had taken to calling herself a wanderer. The hospital ship had been her home and now it, too, had gone away. She wondered if she should have stayed on board until Hamburg and then shipped out again when it received orders. There were rumors that the next ports of call would be in the Baltic, if the Russians would consent. She remembered her years in Rügen as a child. The beaches were mostly unclean and the water frigid. Why on earth would she want to visit the Baltic?

In Tunis she took a bus to one of the nascent resort towns on Tunisia's east coast and stopped there, finding work as an x-ray technician in a local hospital that dated from colonial times. The x-ray machine was primitive. All business was conducted in French. The three doctors, two French and a Tunisian, were brusque. All three were exploring ways and means to emigrate to Marseilles. Watching them work, she thought them no more than competent. Sieglinde settled into a routine, putting in her eight hours and returning to her hotel on the edge of the resort, close to the beach. Each evening she went for a long walk and drank a cold Löwenbräu on the porch of her hotel as dusk settled. One night she looked up and searched, unsuccessfully, for the Southern Cross, remembering it as one of Harry's failed quests. It had something to do with the Polish writer Conrad, she'd forgotten what. And now she would never know. At times she thought she had made a terrible mistake leaving Harry, at other times not at all. Theirs was a doomed love affair. The precise reason she could not name, except to reflect again and again on how different their childhoods were, how different their upbringings, how different the societies from which they had sprung. Their personal histories at no point connected and Harry seemed so confident of the life he had chosen. Was there room in it for someone else? They were parallel lines that would never touch. Still, her thoughts turned to him each day, where he was, how he was doing. What had become of Village Number Five? She hated thinking of him in the jungle yet again. Sieglinde read a newspaper when she could find one, always turning first to news of the war, when there was news of the war. A brigade of American troops had landed, the first organized fighting unit in the country. Surely the brigade would bring the insurgency under control. She had no idea where Harry fit in. When one of the articles referred to the embassy bombing weeks before, her breath caught in her throat. The article mentioned one fatality, the fatality unnamed. She was appalled. She had no idea how to learn the identity of the fatality. The obvious solution was to write Harry at the embassy, but then she would have to give a return address and she did not want to do that. She decided finally to call the embassy. She had the number and the next day she went to the post office to book the call, and when the embassy operator answered, Sieglinde's voice was so soft and shaken that she was asked to repeat the name. Harry Sanders, she said, and the operator said that Mr. Sanders was no longer at the embassy. Sieglinde said, He was not hurt in the bombing? No, the operator said. He was not hurt. Mr. Sanders was reassigned. When Sieglinde asked what posting, the operator said she could not answer that, but if the caller wished to write Mr. Sanders a letter, the letter would be forwarded. Sieglinde hung up, her eyes filled with tears. At least he was safe. But she wondered where he was.

At the hotel in the Tunisian resort town—it was a resort in name only, and the hotel was more rest house than hotel, though it did have a pleasant dining room that looked over the sea—Sieglinde fell in with a team of archaeologists conducting a dig to the west of town. They were confident they had found a colosseum that dated to the fourth century. The team was composed of four men, British and American, and a woman, a Canadian. One night, seeing she was alone, they asked Sieglinde to join them for dinner. They were in the midst of a friendly dispute concerning the dimensions of the colosseum, presuming it was a colosseum and not an agora. They were at the beginning of their dig, the British arguing for large and the American for small. The Canadian woman, Suzanne, called the dispute bootless since they would know the answer soon enough, meaning sometime that year. Suzanne looked at Sieglinde and rolled her eyes—they were listening to a typical male dispute in which patience was ignored. Of all the disciplines in all the world, archaeology called for patience. Only from patience would intuition arise. Suzanne asked Sieglinde what she was doing in Sfax, of all places. Sieglinde said she was traveling with no fixed destination. She liked places near the sea and had fetched up at Sfax faute de mieux. And was she alone? Yes, alone. Sieglinde told Suzanne that she had found work as an x-ray technician at the hospital and that would keep her going until she moved on, perhaps Italy, perhaps somewhere else. Suzanne did not inquire further except to ask if Sieglinde had medical training beyond x-ray machines. Yes, of course, Sieglinde said. She had had a year of medical training, one of the requirements in Germany.

You could tend to a broken bone, for example.

Yes, Sieglinde said. Later, certainly, hospital care would be necessary.

And you could diagnose tropical diseases?

Some of them, I suppose. Yes.

Stomach disorders?

If there were medicines available . . .

Suzanne pulled her chair closer and poured them both a glass of wine. She said, We have need of a medical person. The desert is very tough. Snakes, scorpions, strange maladies. Other than our team we have twenty locals for the heavy digging. Someone is always being injured or falling ill and then one of us has to take him to the hospital here. We waste time. If we could put together a pharmacy and a medical tent, could you do—what has to be done? Ailments and broken bones and the like. This would save us time. Save us money. I think I have seen you at the hospital, Sieglinde.

It's possible, Sieglinde said. Truthfully, it's not a very good hospital.

In this part of the world, Suzanne began.

It's what we have, Sieglinde said.

It's interesting work, ours. We live in the desert and once every few weeks we come here for a few days off, a sort of rest-and-recreation thing. We get on very well. We've known each other for years. We are compatible and I think you would be compatible, too. Our work is slow work. We'd teach you how to go about it and when one of the natives got sick or stung by a scorpion you could look after him until we could get him to a hospital. Probably you could do what the hospital does and do it better.

Also, Suzanne said, I would like some female company. What do you say?

Would I be paid?

Of course, Suzanne said, and named a figure.

It's more than I'm making now, Sieglinde said.

We have funds, Suzanne said.

How long—

You would have to give us a two-month commitment. After that, if you want to go away no one would stop you. We're not running a prison.

Two months, and then if I didn't like the desert, I could go.

Exactly, Suzanne said.

Maybe it's time I settled for a while, Sieglinde said. I was about ready to give it up here and go somewhere else.

You have been traveling a long time?

Long enough, Sieglinde said.

I would like to do what you're doing, Suzanne said. Moving from place to place, no fixed itinerary . . . Her voice trailed away.

They were sitting on the porch of the hotel, the one facing the sea. At distant points over the water were ships' lights. The air had a pungent smell, not unpleasant. It was different from tropical air. Probably it was the desert that made the difference, dry air mixed with sea air. The effect was somnolent and Sieglinde yawned, thinking of the prospect of two months in the desert excavating a fifteen-hundred-year-old colosseum (if it was a colosseum). She looked at the men across the table. The argument had ended and they were throwing dice for the check. Their faces and necks were deeply tanned, their arms bruised and scratched. Suzanne had joined in the dice-throw, and when she was eliminated she turned back to Sieglinde. She said she had been married once but the marriage had not taken—that was her phrase, "not taken"—and she had returned to her archaeological work, suspended when she followed her husband to Los Angeles. He was an actor waiting for a break, and she waited with him until it seemed obvious to her that the break would never come, or come in an incompatible way. Los Angeles was said to be hospitable to those waiting for a break but Suzanne had not found it so. People were hospitable if they thought you could help in some way with the break, if you had connections, a school friend or an uncle in the industry. After a while her days were consumed with quarrels and so she left and found work with her college friend Ted. She nodded affectionately at the man with the dice in his fist, a heavily muscled redhead with hair so tightly woven to his scalp that it looked like an animal's pelt, now muttering some incantation over the dice. Ted was a miracle worker with

128

angel money and now they were a unit, she and the four men. They had enough money for a year's work and had to show progress before another grant was approved. Suzanne laughed. She said, A year is nothing in this business. A year is a snap of the fingers. But we're making progress.

You like the work, Sieglinde said.

I have a passion for it, Suzanne replied.

Digging things up.

Very old things.

What kinds of things?

A shard of pottery, Suzanne said. Something that may or may not have been a statue's kneecap. There's definitely something here. We just don't know what it is. What's interesting is the finding out. I'm not so sure about the colosseum. That's Ted's hunch. He likes to think big, Ted. That's an advantage because most everything we find is so small. It's good to have a goal if only as something to disprove. There was a sudden roar of laughter from the men, dice game over, Ted the loser.

Sieglinde looked up to find a plate of clementines, peeled and quartered, before her. The tall American, the one called Joseph, had said little during dinner, and now he looked at her and said, For you.

Sieglinde thought that the nicest gesture.

Thank you, she said.

My pleasure, Joseph said.

Sieglinde heard something in his voice, an irregularity, and asked, Where do you come from in America?

Joseph said he came from all over. He had started out in a small town in Wisconsin and went on to the university at Madison and after that the University of Chicago, trying to discover what it was he wanted to do with his life. At Chicago he became interested in archaeology and the work of Schliemann, his life and times, what some would call his banditry. Joseph wanted to learn how it was done, the identification of the place, and the digging itself. His first dig had been in Central America, not a very challenging dig. He went on about the dig in Central America, a Mayan dig that didn't disclose much, and fell silent. Sieglinde waited for him to continue but evidently he had said all he wished to say. She thought Joseph had an interesting face, skin pulled tight over his cheekbones, large ears, wavy brown hair, a forehead that seemed to rise to the heavens. He was slight of build. He had an open smile and a soft voice, so soft that it was easy to miss the irregularity, but to Sieglinde it was like a fist to the face.

The evening came to an end. Nightcaps were ordered and after a short discussion of the morning drill, all gear in the lobby by five-thirty a.m., coffee on the verandah, wheels up at six, the party broke up.

Suzanne walked Sieglinde to her room, Sieglinde silent.

Suzanne said, Is anything wrong?

Sieglinde said, That Joseph. He is not American.

Of course he's American. He's from Wisconsin.

I do not believe he is from Wisconsin.

I've known him for ages—

What is his age?

Joseph is—thirty? About thirty. He's a gifted scientist.

Sieglinde said nothing.

If he's not American, what is he?

He is German, Sieglinde said.

Why do you think so?

I can hear it in his voice. It's easy to miss, but it's unmistakable. The German language. When you listen carefully as I was doing.

That's the Wisconsin accent.

Wisconsin via Düsseldorf, Sieglinde said.

I can't hear it, Suzanne said.

It's German, definitely.

And does that make a difference?

Sieglinde was silent a moment.

Maybe it does, she said finally.

We have immigrants in North America, Suzanne said. We are a continent of immigrants. My grandfather came from Ireland. My great-grandfather, the other side, came from Holland. Some came over on the *Mayflower*, others arrived yesterday. So what?

You are right, Sieglinde said. It makes no difference.

But you are upset.

I was surprised, Sieglinde said.

He's very gifted, Suzanne said.

Yes, you said that.

You'll see, the way he goes about things.

Good night, Sieglinde said, and went to her room.

The dig was conducted not in the desert but on hardpan at the approaches to the desert. There was little vegetation and no trees above shoulder height. The terrain was flat, the line of sight extending for miles, the horizon a long thin line. Here and there were declivities but they were hardly noticeable. Sieglinde had never seen a country so bleak. The sun was already high when they arrived in the Land Rover, soon followed by a truck carrying the workmen. For a while no one moved. The heat was ferocious, boiling in the clear air, blue sky above. From time to time in the distance they would see a caravan, always, it seemed, moving east. Occasionally they would see a single camel and the camel's driver, a nomad going who knew where. Sieglinde was told they were likely Tuareg, inhabitants of the southern desert, an austere people who lived by their own mysterious rules and regulations. They seldom ventured north. The Tunisian workmen had constructed a lean-to with a canvas roof against the sun. Sieglinde stayed under it for most of the first day, getting used to the heat and blinding light. Soon enough a workman appeared with a wounded foot and twisted ankle. She had never seen skin so tough. It resembled old leather. She dressed the wound and wrapped the ankle, all the while looked at with high suspicion by the workman. Suzanne had told her to expect that. They do not trust women. They especially do not trust women doctors. Pay no attention, though it's difficult not to. They are from another century, these people. And, do you know what, we're the intruders.

They had stopped at a pharmacy on the way from Sfax and bought supplies, splints and surgical tape, iodine and other antiseptics, and a range of medicines that would treat snake and scorpion bites, though they had yet to see a snake. There were remedies also for gastric disturbances and headaches, which did seem to be epidemic.

Sieglinde thought of the archaeological patch as a place where time stopped. In the shimmer of midday nothing moved, not a leaf, not a twig. There was no wind. The earth did not stir. The sun made its indifferent transit and precisely at noon all work ceased with a clatter of tools and presently the plaintive cries of the faithful praising God. The workmen made their way to their tent and the archaeologists to theirs. They ate sparingly and went down for a nap and no matter how lethargic they were, sweat continued to rise and ooze down foreheads and chests. Often in the afternoon a fugitive breeze came up, not enough to stop the sweat but enough to moderate the heat a fraction. From the moment the breeze arrived—it was impossible to know its origin unless it was the hand of God Himself, so fervently prayed to by the faithful—time appeared to revive also, advancing at a pace so slow as to be barely noticeable, and in a moment forgotten. After the first few days Sieglinde found she liked the patch, the barrenness of the terrain, the heat, the absence of time passing. The outside world was over the horizon, unaccounted for. A good place to collect yourself, she decided, unlike Madagascar and its many demands. During the heat of the day no one spoke unless they had something to say of the work itself, the discovery of a pottery shard or a block of stone that may or may not have been part of a building's foundation. At dusk, the workmen returned to their village, the foreigners gathered under the tent, normal conversation begun once more. Sieglinde said little, preferring to listen to her new colleagues. She learned that

Ted, along with being a genius at writing grant proposals, had private money of his own, so that if temporarily they came up short, he helped out. They had constant problems with bank drafts and the blizzard of numbers and cosignatures that accompanied them. Ted was the de facto leader of the entourage but did not insist on leading unless no one else wanted to. The Englishman Paul was much the best educated in their group, always hauling out a quote from Coleridge or Gibbon to brighten the cocktail hour. They called it, French-fashion, *un cocktail.* Paul's schoolmate Christopher was a pixie, vastly erudite but fond of dirty jokes and cockney rhyming slang. He also slept badly, often waking the group with groans and shouts that signaled a nightmare. Christopher was embarrassed and contrite but there was nothing he could do about the nightmares except to sleep away from the others, and that was deemed dangerous, one person alone in just a sleeping bag. So everyone put up with the nightmares and after a time became accustomed to them. Every few nights Christopher brought out his tape recorder, the latest model from New York, and played an opera. *La Bohème* and *Tosca* were his favorites but he also had tapes of *Norma* and *La Traviata* and Wagner's Ring cycle. Sieglinde thought it enchanting: drinking a gin and tonic in the dark and listening to opera, the quality surprisingly good. The evenings usually ended with an accounting of the events of the day, what was uncovered and the prospects for tomorrow. The pace was glacial but no one seemed to mind. Harry Sanders slipped further into the closet of her memory, threatening to disappear altogether — and then someone would make a remark that reminded her of him, and the door would open a crack, and close soon after. She wondered where he was and if he had found a new girl.

One night after the music, Joseph arrived at her side with two glasses of wine and asked her where she was from in Germany. She said, without enthusiasm, Hamburg, and Joseph nodded in a complicit manner and said, Berlin for me. Born in 1935, he said, the last good year. Good being a relative term, don't you agree? She said nothing to that, having no wish to discuss Germany. Joseph said his family actually lived in Potsdam, but he always thought of Potsdam as part of Berlin, only forty-five minutes on the S-Bahn. His father worked as an accountant at Babelsberg studios. He loved motion pictures and every once in a while would bring an actor or actress home for supper, one of the young ones living hand to mouth. My mother would roll her eyes and set places for them at the table, resigned to an evening of stories concerning the tribulations of the cinematic life. As if the tribulations were unique. I was so young, Joseph said, I remember them only vaguely. But even a child can apprehend glamour, and perhaps a child most of all. Don't you agree? My father was encouraged to join the Party so that his job would be secure. Of course by then Babelsberg was an arm of the Ministry of Propaganda. Some arm, Joseph said, sipping his wine, raising his eyebrows. They were sitting in camp chairs, Joseph leaning close to her, a little closer than she would have liked. He had a musty smell; she thought of it as the granular smell of the desert. His face was tanned to mahogany, his teeth white as milk. When he smiled, what she saw were teeth and deep creases either side of his mouth. She thought him handsome in an actorly way. His gestures seemed timed. He was certainly aware of himself and the effect he had on people. Women. He looked like a man who could take care of himself and whoever was with him. Still, he had come a little too close so she pulled her chair back a fraction and as she did so he smiled, perhaps a smile of apology, perhaps of something else. His easy assurance disarmed her. She heard the German language in everything he said; his *s*'s were the giveaway. She liked his soft American voice and wondered if he missed his language. She had not spoken German since she had left the hospital ship and did not speak it now, but she heard it in his every word.

She said, And what then?

My father became a Nazi, Joseph said. He didn't wear the armband but I'd call that a detail. He loved Babelsberg, loved the craft, loved the people. I would say he loved the dreams that film people had. Film dreams were more real than their own dreams. Still are, I suppose. And everything went to hell soon after, including Babelsberg. The Soviets arrived, Ivans everywhere in Potsdam and Wannsee. What they did to women was unspeakable. The excuse was that the horrors of the eastern front had made them into brutes, scarcely human. What do you think? There's always an excuse. I saw a French documentary not long ago, the heroism of the Resistants. By this account, the Resistance made D-day possible. The Americans and the British lent valuable support to the Resistants in their successful liberation of Paris. Do you believe that? We live in a turnstile of lies.

Joseph lit a cigarette and blew a smoke ring.

So the Ivans came, he went on. By then I was living with my grandfather in a little village in the Black Forest, one narrow road in and the same road out. The war was far away. We were so remote, I don't remember seeing a single soldier, German, American, or Russian. And suddenly the war was over, and that was strange because in our village it had never truly arrived. People did not know what to think. Hitler was dead. Who would look after them now? I have no idea what happened to my parents. We Germans are unnaturally meticulous when it comes to recordkeeping. It's a kind of religion with us, don't you agree? Statistics of all sorts, no statistic too small to be noted, especially where human beings are concerned. Who died. Where they died. How they died. Our house in Potsdam was destroyed utterly and I assume my parents along with it. That was my grandfather's belief when he told me they were missing. But I have no idea, really. That is a blank space in the time of my life. We had relatives in Milwaukee and in 1947 I went to Milwaukee to live with them, an interminable voyage aboard a tramp steamer, and then a train to Chicago. They were kind people, older people in their sixties, not in the best of health, and I believe the last thing they wanted was a twelve-year-old boy with little English and very bad memories. But they were forgiving, and hospitable, and determined that I forget my German past and become a good American boy. I was told not to discuss the war, nor my father's work at Babelsberg. I was never under any circumstances to mention the Führer. Milwaukee was filled with Germans who had rapidly Americanized themselves, beginning before the Great War. Often they changed their names, the first step in assimilation. My aunt and uncle in Milwaukee went easily from Braun to Brown. They wanted to separate themselves from the old country, and who could blame them? But it was difficult for them, and for me, too. The accent was hard to lose. And if you liked pilsener and schnitzel, well, you liked pilsener and schnitzel instead of Coca-Cola and a hot dog. My aunt and uncle are dead now. They had no children of their own, only me. And I got out of Milwaukee as soon as I could. And I did not go back. So that's my story. And you?

How did you get to the university?

I was always a good student. And I had a colorful past.

A refugee, Sieglinde said.

Yes, a refugee. Now, your turn.

I spent the war near Hamburg, Sieglinde said, and that was all she said.

I won't ask you about it, Joseph said.

Sieglinde shrugged and looked away.

I like talking to you, Joseph said. Shall we speak German?

Sieglinde shook her head.

I'm out of practice, Joseph said.

I can hear it in your voice.

I know that. I knew it when I first spoke to you. And you recoiled a little. Why did you recoil?

I suppose I did, Sieglinde said. What of it? I was surprised. I assumed you were English or American like the others. I was surprised when you weren't. She fell silent again, and then she said, I think it's fair to say I am escaping Germany. Trying to. I am trying to find a normal life for myself. She paused there, knowing she had said too much without saying enough. She said, I do not think I can find a normal life in Germany because Germany is not a nor-

136

mal country, divided in two. And they say that's a good thing, the division, not so many of us within one boundary. They say we have an economic miracle and perhaps that's true. You should see Hamburg, where forty thousand souls were lost in a single night's bombing. Now almost no trace of it, the bombing. We keep our heads down and produce goods, machine tools. Automobiles. We have elections. But there are everywhere ghosts, and the machine tools and the automobiles and the elections cannot dispel the ghosts. I have no relatives there that I know of. My family has vanished, disappeared from the map.

We are both orphans, Joseph said.

I suppose we are, Sieglinde replied. I do not like to think of myself as an orphan.

Nor I, Joseph said.

He handed Sieglinde her glass of wine, untouched. She took the glass and sipped a little. The others had gone to their tents. She could see light in Suzanne's tent. The other tents were dark. She wondered if she had made a mistake, listening all this time to Joseph's story, so like her own except the American part. There were so many Americans in the world. Everywhere she went she found Americans. Americans went everywhere and seemed untroubled. She wondered if she had made a mistake leaving Madagascar. In Madagascar she knew no one and no one knew her. She had given it up too quickly, not the first time she had given up something or someone too quickly. Apparently she did not possess the German thoroughness gene. Instead, she was strenuous and too eager to call it a day, not much difference at all between arrival and departure. Looked at in a certain way, they were the same thing. She was ill at ease. And now here she was talking about her disorderly past with a stranger from Milwaukee. He too had a story. Well, everyone had a story. Because they had one didn't mean she had to listen to it. Sieglinde finished off her wine and stood. Joseph stood also and took her hand.

He said, We are displaced persons.

I suppose so, Sieglinde said. I would say stateless.

Perhaps, he said. Will you stay on here, then?

For a while, Sieglinde said.

Joseph's tent was identical to the other tents, twenty feet long by twelve wide, the canvas of a color similar to the hardpan underfoot. Mosquito netting covered the tent flap. He pushed both aside and preceded her into the tent, where he lit a kerosene lamp. The wick flickered and then caught, casting a yellow light into the interior, hard dark shadows. Sieglinde paused inside the tent flap, startled by what she saw. A figured carpet covered the hardpan. A canvas chair and a table piled high with books were next to the lamp. Two steamer trunks sat opposite, more books atop the trunks. The books gave the room an academic air, as if there were a classroom nearby and students. Hooks in the canvas held sketches, evidently Joseph's. They were drawings of the terrain, various aspects of it, though the line of sight was monotonous. Sieglinde could not see how he found variety. On the hook over the steamer trunk was a print of Caspar David Friedrich's lonely traveler atop a German mountain looking west into the dying sun, smaller mountains in fog between the traveler and the sun. Friedrich called the piece *Wanderer Above the Sea of Fog*. He painted the traveler from the rear so that his face could not be seen, only a slender figure in a black cloth coat and black gaiters, one hand holding a walking stick, no hat. He stood in the submissive posture of the aesthete. Joseph's sketches seemed to take their inspiration from Friedrich, yet there was something subtracted. Sieglinde could not define what, unless it was the absence of human forms, leaving only the bleak landscape of eastern Tunisia. The sketches and Joseph's books suggested a life apart from the ardor of the archaeological dig. Men needed a distraction from their workaday lives. Thinking of that, she thought also of Harry Sanders's piano, so badly out of tune in the tropical heat.

Joseph's tent had a nest-like quality and was spotless and orderly in the way a bachelor's life was said to be orderly, spoiled only slightly by the industrial odor of kerosene. His clothes hung on wire hangers from a hat rack. The ashtrays were clean. On the table beside the books was a carafe of water and one cup. When she looked up, Sieglinde noticed a mobile suspended from the ceiling, turning slowly as she imagined the earth turning. There was no breeze inside the tent, and then she saw above the table a little grilled window fitted with mosquito netting. She had not seen a mosquito since arriving the week before, so that could be bachelor's caution. Joseph sat on the bed, a double cot with a blue duvet and two pillows with white linen covers. He motioned for Sieglinde to take the chair.

Heimat, he said, and she laughed, unaccountably at ease in Joseph's tent. Her own tent was without ornament of any kind, unless you counted a wind-up clock and a bottle of eau de cologne as ornaments. She especially admired Joseph's carpet, solid underfoot and yet soft to the touch. Her single cot had one threadbare blanket, olive drab in color. She suspected it was army issue but she had no idea which army. Her pillow was without cover of any kind, and it, too, had seen years of use.

She said, I expect to find a valet in the closet.

No valet, he said. No closet.

You live nicely, she said. Do you often invite people in?

I never invite people in, Joseph said.

She noticed a photograph in a silver frame on the bedside table, a low-slung building of Bauhaus influence, people milling about. She said, What's that?

Babelsberg, Joseph said.

Sieglinde nodded, admiring the frame. She sneaked a look at her wristwatch, near midnight. She removed her sandals and rubbed her feet on the carpet. She knew that if she did not leave now she would not leave until morning.

A souvenir of my father, Joseph said.

I have no souvenirs except one photograph, my father in his uniform, off to the war. A big smile on his face. He might have been going off to the *bierstube* with friends, a glass of pilsener before dinner. A game of darts. Something like that, except he was in uniform and holding a rifle. My mother took the picture.

What rank? Joseph asked.

Rank?

Military rank. Was he an officer?

Corporal, Sieglinde said. He was good with cars. Probably he was a mechanic in his unit. But he was also a marksman. He loved to hunt and there was plenty of woodland near our village. I wonder if they needed mechanics more than they needed marksmen.

Mechanics, I imagine, Joseph said.

I have so few memories of him, she said.

It's the same with me, Joseph said.

He was killed a week after the photograph was taken.

I'm sorry, Joseph said.

We never knew the circumstances.

Was he returned to you?

No, Sieglinde said. He has no marker. All I have is the photograph.

I'm sorry, Joseph said again.

He, too, was a Nazi.

Joseph did not reply to that.

I have no idea why. My mother told me once that he was not political. He had no interest in politics or government. He enjoyed being with his friends. He liked to hunt and he loved cars. I don't understand.

Joseph said, Probably his friends joined and he joined, too. Solidarity. All for one, one for all. My father joined to save his job. He loved the films. So he joined the Nazi Party to stay in films.

At least he had a reason, Sieglinde said. My mother said nothing beyond his being nonpolitical. Of course much was left unsaid in those days. And what was said was so often not the truth.

Does it matter to you?

Sieglinde was silent a moment, weighing the question. She said, Yes, it does.

To me also, Joseph said.

So there we are.

You must try to put it away—

How do I do that?

It was so long ago, he made whatever choices he made. My father, too. From this distance it's impossible to know why they did what they did. Your father, my father. Cogs in the machine. In any case, they are gone now.

Does it matter to you?

Of course it matters. And what have I taken from it? I've refused to be a cog in a machine. That's my answer. Your father loved cars, mine loved the movie business. Joseph opened his mouth to say something more but evidently had a second thought, because he lit a cigarette and blew a smoke ring and said nothing further. They sat in unsettled silence. A breeze had developed and the tent billowed slightly, creaking. Here and there were spots of dust in the air. Joseph reached under the bed and came up with a bottle of schnapps and a cup. He filled the cup and walked the few feet to Sieglinde and handed it to her.

A nightcap, he said. It's good schnapps.

She took a swallow and handed it back.

He said, Did your mother survive the war?

I don't know that either. She went away and did not return.

A missing person, Joseph said.

I do not believe she survived. I made an effort to find out, not a very big effort I think. I didn't know where to look and I was perhaps frightened of what I might learn. She abandoned me. What sort of mother does that? She was not right in her head. I don't know where she went after she left me. She could be anywhere. But surely now, so many years later, she is dead. If I saw her I would not recognize her.

Joseph nodded sympathetically at the phrase "so many years later . . ."

I don't want to talk about her, Sieglinde said.

141

All right, Joseph agreed.

Sieglinde look around the tent and said, Your sketches remind me of Friedrich.

He said, Yes. The Nazis claimed him, you know. Heroic melancholy and all that. His reputation suffered terribly, but then, after the war, he was rehabilitated. An artist is not responsible for his admirers. That was the idea. For God's sake, Friedrich was born in the eighteenth century. Died a recluse, I think. But his work is in all the museums now, a part of our artistic heritage. They say you have to be German to appreciate him, in the way that you must know our language to appreciate Goethe. He does not translate easily. I'm not so sure about Friedrich. It seems to me he could appeal to anyone with a romantic streak. It is not only Germans who are romantic.

Do you think the French are romantic?

Oh, no, Joseph said. The French are worldly. That's a different thing.

Americans are romantic, she said.

I would not say romantic. I would say optimistic. Yet it is true that optimism is a precondition of the romantic temperament. So I cannot disagree with you entirely.

Americans can be anything, Sieglinde said. They take pride in their makeovers, a nation of actors, or should I say playwrights, each examining her own story. That's the myth, anyhow. A nation in an eternal state of rewrite. She thought then of Harry Sanders, wondering if she was right in thinking of him as a romantic. Well, of course he was. But she could not imagine Harry on a mountaintop staring into fog, a wanderer. She did not think he was in any way a wanderer, but she conceded also that she did not know him well. She did not know his heart. She certainly had never had a conversation with him that resembled this one. Such a conversation with Harry was unthinkable owing to his nationality. She had never before considered nationality as an ingredient of loving someone or thinking about loving someone. Could it be true that nationality was destiny? Americans would surely think so, accustomed as they were to living among so many tribes, all of them with a claim to freedom—of movement, of worship, of anything that came to mind. Why, they believe their nation is under God's protection! Or was it destiny, in a way that a recessive gene determined hair color or mental illness. Germans were bound together by their language, not an easy language to learn and, once learned, impossible to forget altogether. Nationality was surely destiny if you were a German of the twentieth century. So many ghosts.

He said, What are you thinking about? You have a strange look.

Do you think nationality is destiny?

If you are German it is.

That's what I think too.

No one lets us forget. Not that it is possible to do so. Our history is our companion, not always but sometimes.

But we, you and I, were but children—

That's true, German children who endured terrible times.

We are not the only ones. Polish children, Russian children, children of the Balkans. Jewish children. Even British children.

We were defeated.

Yes. So were they. So many dead. The cities in ruins. Everyone except the Americans.

I was involved with an American.

Tell me about him, Joseph said.

No, Sieglinde said. It's over now.

Did his Americanness bother you?

It did, in a way I can hardly describe. I was very—fond of him. But I feared that we would never understand each other. The important things. I thought, Sieglinde said, giving a little abashed laugh, that he would never be able to read my mind, whereas I was able to read his with no trouble. He wore his heart on his sleeve, that one. He was a lovely man.

So you did understand him. He didn't understand you.

He was not as interested in his history as I was in mine.

What did he do? Your American.

143

He is a diplomat.

Did you love him?

I think I did.

And where is he now?

I don't know, she said. He is somewhere in the world, attending to the diplomacy of the American empire. I imagine he's good at it. I expect he will go on to a brilliant career, and in a couple of decades I will pick up a newspaper and find that he's secretary of state. Wouldn't that be something? I'll write him a note: Remember me? Sieglinde, your German girl.

That would be something all right, Joseph said.

Sieglinde was looking at Joseph's sketches. She said, You do not draw people. You draw landscapes.

Sometimes I put a person in my landscapes. Not often. Not if I can help it. I can put an American in the next one if you like.

I like your landscapes, she said.

I'm glad you do.

And don't make snide remarks about my American.

Not a snide remark, he said. I meant it.

I'm worried about the absence of people in your work.

I like nature, he said. And naturalness. German naturalness.

Maybe here and there a woman, she said.

All right, he said. I'll put you in the next one.

As an example of German naturalness?

Why not?

Don't be foolish. Not me.

Who then?

An old woman.

An old woman, he said. All right. He plucked a sketch pad from the hook behind him, and a pencil from the bedside table, made a few quick strokes, and handed the result to Sieglinde. She looked at it and nodded in admiration. He had drawn a portly woman from the rear. She leaned on a walking stick and gazed off in the distance to a ruined colosseum. Her hair was gathered tightly into a bun, her shoulders bowed under the weight of sticks tied with a rope. In her posture was the very essence of endurance. Sieglinde stared at the sketch a long moment, marveling at what could be made of a few short strokes — a bun, roped sticks, heavy shoes, a broad back.

Joseph was sitting in half-light, sharp shadows cast from the kerosene lamp dividing his face. The shadows were all around him. His skin had an artificial glow and now he appeared lost in thought, a kind of midnight reverie. Joseph looked up when the tent billowed, the canvas snapping in the wind. More dust was in the air and Sieglinde wondered if they were on the leading edge of a sandstorm. If they were, Joseph did not seem alarmed. He was lost in thought, his expression unreadable as if carved in mahogany. The canvas rippled in the wind and Sieglinde rose to leave. They had said what they had to say. The conversation was at an end, for the moment anyway. Sieglinde peeked out the tent flap. All the tents were dark.

He said, Don't leave.

She said, I must go. We work tomorrow.

This is not work. It's a fantasy. Ted's fantasy.

You mean there's no colosseum.

No colosseum, Joseph said. Oh, there's something. Dig long enough in Europe or North Africa or the Middle East and you'll find something. But I doubt that it's a colosseum or anything else of significance. Ted is a genius at raising money. He raises their hopes and they give him money.

Sieglinde said, I must go. Really. She opened the flap and stepped outside. The wind died. The sky was full of stars. She located the Dippers and Orion's belt. The night air was cool. Joseph stood behind her, his fingertips touching her elbows.

He said, Can I ask you one thing?

Yes, she said.

He said, Did you ever spend time in Berlin?

No, she said. I have never been to Berlin.

Oh, you've missed something. On the first day of spring, if it isn't snowing or otherwise disagreeable, the beer gardens arrange their tables and chairs outside in the light. Prussian light is as clear and delicate as fine crystal, a pale light but warm all the same. The light has hibernated during the winter, gone to wherever the sun goes to. The terrible Berlin winters when weeks go by without the sun, and when it deigns to shine it is thin, a thin light, more a suggestion than a conclusion. You can feel it on your face, a grueling wind and a sun that delivers no warmth. All that changes in a day, a page turned. Springtime is something else, something almost—epic. The girls pull their skirts to their knees and the men open their coats and loosen their ties. I will take you to Berlin some March and you'll see. No place in the world is like it. You cannot mistake it for another city in another region of Germany or anyplace else. That, too, is what it means to be German. A spring day, a glass of pilsener, perhaps a little cake. Berlin on that day is—prodigious.

Sieglinde smiled. She had always thought of Berlin as coarse. Also promiscuous, but even the promiscuity had its coarse aspect.

Someday it will be our capital once again. Not in our lifetime. But sometime.

When that happens I will join you there.

Have you really never been to Berlin?

No, she said, never.

His fingers pressed harder on her elbows. She was undecided whether to return to Joseph's tent or move along to her own tent with its threadbare blanket and hard cot. His fingers fell away but she could feel his closeness. Sieglinde looked at the dark outlines of the tents and the barren land reaching to west and south. First Madagascar, now this. She had no idea what she was doing in Tunisia except getting on from day to day. This was not a normal life. Her plight, if that was what it was, suddenly amused her and she laughed out loud. There was nothing to fear here. Joseph's fingers returned to her elbows and they turned together and retreated into his tent.

PART II

Seven

T HIS WAS HER first visit to Washington and the first time she had seen Harry since his home leave from Asunción the year before, two strenuous weeks in the West—Yosemite, the Grand Canyon, one expensive weekend in Las Vegas, a peripatetic holiday. Now they were in Washington for briefings before taking up their new post in central Africa, the journey via Paris, where they would be married. They put up at the Mayflower and late in the afternoon on their second night Harry explained about the reception for the British chancellor of the exchequer at one of the downtown clubs, the invitation thanks to Ambassador Basso Earle III, now retired, Harry's boss during the war. Harry went on and on about Basso, a boss who had become a good friend. There would be grandees aplenty at the reception, the French ambassador, the American secretary of state. Her eyes grew wide—my God, she had nothing to wear! So at the last minute they took a cab to Georgetown, to the little dress shop on Wisconsin Avenue, where she found a black shift off the rack that fit perfectly. Of course she was nervous, who wouldn't be, entering this recondite world of Harry's, a world that seemed to have its own language and customs, its specific rituals and manners. She stuck close to Harry, who was careful to introduce her around, always supplying a title and a posting—the Washington bureau chief of *The Times* of London, the

Japanese ambassador to Washington, the deputy assistant secretary of state for East Asian affairs. How do you know these people? she asked. Oh, Harry replied, you see them around. You meet all kinds in this business. She thought, All kinds?

Soon enough Basso Earle took them in hand and suddenly they were at the top of the food chain — the French ambassador, the director of policy planning at the Department, and then she found herself shaking hands with the vice president of the United States, a beefy figure with huge hands and a crooked smile. She was standing with the Saudi ambassador and the chairman of the Senate Foreign Relations Committee. The conversation appeared to flag, and when she looked around Harry was nowhere in sight. She was standing in a cone of silence without a word to say for herself. And then she was alone, the vice president and his suite disappearing down the marble staircase. She looked about her in a panic and realized then that there was no need to panic. She was twenty-five years old. She was a young woman in a room filled with old men and their capable wives, and so, with a spring to her step, she took a glass of champagne from a passing waiter's tray and looked for someone interesting to talk to. She decided to avoid the circle of women standing a little apart. She had the idea they were talking about their children.

May had a wonderful time at her first diplomatic reception. Later in her life, when these events became as familiar as old shoes, she would confess that she liked listening to the grandees, the ones who had known Stalin, met Hitler, sipped wine with Mussolini and champagne with Churchill, advised Roosevelt, took instructions from Marshall, played bridge with Eisenhower, and sat at the feet of Mao, waiting for a gnomic pronouncement. They were very old now of course. But they had phenomenal memories, conjuring the texts of cables sent decades before. They were attractive men, well turned out in bespoke suits cut in a prewar style, suits of heavy serge or pinstriped flannel, wide lapels often displaying a mysterious button or tiny band of cloth. They wore white hankies situated just so in the breast pocket, a vest and often a watch chain, more often than not a bow tie. Also, they were forever quoting or citing other men she had never heard of, like Walter Lippmann or the poet Miłosz or Arthur Koestler. That was the way it had gone at that long-ago reception at which she had made but one gaffe, mistaking Dean Acheson for the chancellor of the exchequer; laughter all around except for Mr. Acheson, whose mustache bristled. She had been introduced to an especially attractive older man, an ambassador somewhere, George Kennel or Kenner. She did not catch the name but the title alone always did the job. They never got her name straight either, May Huerwood. She was forever being called Mary or Margie with a hard *g*. Mostly they called her "young lady."

She was standing in a group with Harry, Basso Earle, the Polish ambassador, and Ambassador Kennel, who was apparently a statesman of some renown. Harry stood a little taller when he spoke to him. The Polish ambassador, in high good humor, was explaining that he and his wife had a parlor game, identifying the causes of World War I. They had a dozen or more causes, the development of the battle tank, the murderous example of Antietam, the general boredom in the chancelleries of Europe among them. And now they had a fresh candidate, utterly unexpected, most interesting.

Ambassador Kennel raised his eyebrows.

Walt Whitman, the Polish ambassador said.

This was the thrilling insight of his compatriot the great poet Miłosz. Miłosz proposed that in the years before the Great War, Walt Whitman was widely known and revered throughout Europe but had a truly fanatical following in just one country: Yugoslavia. The revolutionary anarchists of Sarajevo were inspired by Whitman's songs of democracy, his faith in the virtue of multitudes, his evident disdain of the ruling classes, his unorthodox sexual arrangements, altogether a new American man. They believed Whitman a much greater soul than the hypocrite slave-owning capitalist Jefferson, whose deeds did not match his words. One of the Whitman-drunk anarchists who had taken to the streets of Sarajevo on June 28, 1914, was Gavrilo Princip, and when Archduke Franz Ferdinand *mit frau* arrived in a horse-drawn coach, Princip produced a revolver and shot him dead. This, the spark that set all Europe ablaze. What was the statistic? Fourteen million perished. All of it the responsibility of Walt Whitman.

May watched Kennel's mouth approach a frown, which after a moment seemed to dissolve into something resembling a smile. Kennel did not look like a man who appreciated whimsy. Whimsy would not be in his repertoire. Yet there it was, a small tight smile—and then he turned to Harry.

Basso tells me you've been posted to Africa.

Yes, sir, I have, Harry said.

Looking forward to it?

We are, yes, Harry said, nodding at May. Very much.

It's a good place to begin.

Do you think so? Is there room for diplomacy?

Yes, I do. But very difficult. Not much room.

Harry nodded.

So few structures.

Yes, Harry said.

The logic of the African situation must be allowed to work itself out, the ambassador said.

Harry looked at him blankly. Sir, could you develop that thought?

But the eminent diplomat did not elaborate. A brooding look came over him, a look almost of grief. He seemed wrapped in a tremendous stillness, as if time itself had come to a halt. He ambled away to say hello to the Soviet ambassador, a frosty handshake and a few mumbled words, and then he was gone.

In the years to come May thought often of that evening at the downtown club in Washington, her introduction to Harry's neighborhood. She had never before been in company whose milieu seemed to be the world itself, its enmities and alliances, its instability and bother, its evident danger. The world's troubles seemed to float in the room, a part of things no less than the high ceilings and chandeliers, the curtained windows and daffodils in cut-glass vases, and the waiters with their trays of champagne. She supposed that the object of it all was to seize the future, make it predictable, bring it to heel—or otherwise leave the logic of the situation to work itself out. A parlor game that turned on the causes of World War I! Did that keep them busy in the evening? The reception was breaking up, a line forming near the marble staircase where the chancellor of the exchequer was shaking hands, offering a particularly warm smile to May, holding her fingers a little longer than was strictly necessary. So good of you to come. I hope my little party wasn't a bore. His silver hair was combed in little wings over his ears and his blue eyes sparkled. He was quite tall and lean. He bent close to her to say something but May did not catch what it was. She thanked him and moved off, looking for Harry, but Harry was nowhere to be seen. May did notice the Polish ambassador's barely concealed look of contempt as he watched Kennel and the Soviet diplomat in a tête-à-tête before the Soviet abruptly turned and disappeared into the crowd waiting to shake the chancellor's hand. May knew so little of this world and its contents and discontents, waters she had never navigated or thought to navigate. This was her first reception after all. She knew there were shoals but did not know where they were or what they looked like, and then she had an inkling. The chancellor of the exchequer continued to shake hands with departing guests but now and again he looked across the room at May with a private smile. She noticed that his hair wings had lost altitude. Lecher, she thought, and turned her back. My God, he wasn't a day under seventy years old. Whatever was he thinking? Well, what he was thinking was plain enough and that caused a private smile of her own. Receptions of this sort would be her milieu from now on and May knew she was equal to it. More than equal. At the same time, wouldn't it be wise of her to keep her distance? As she watched the company move en masse down the staircase she made a resolution to keep her wits about her as she and her newly minted ambassador husband-to-be moved from one posting to another. They would grow old together but she was determined never to lose her essential self, her particular way of seeing the world, the fundamental Mayness of May. It would be so easy to become entangled in this seductive atmosphere, so worldly, populated with outsize personalities—"figures." It was not celebrity. It was something beyond celebrity, this inside world, a kind of private club, the members' faces recognized in Washington and nowhere else. The Undersecretary of State. The Chief of Naval Operations. The Chairman of the Federal Communications Commission.

Then Harry was at her elbow, and as she looked at him, his tousled hair and proud smile, she imagined them years hence at an important embassy somewhere in Europe, Harry the American ambassador, first among equals. She would have her own life during the day, and in the evenings preside at glittering events. Glittering, but down-to-earth too. American menus. American music. And in due course they would find a pretty retirement villa in the American West, somewhere near their grandchildren. Harry would take a teaching job while he wrote his memoirs. She would ride horses every day and in the evenings do what normal people did, whatever that was. Play Scrabble. Go to a movie.

Harry's arm was around her waist.

Oh, he said, you were great tonight. Just great. Everyone said so. Did you have a good time?

Better than you can imagine, May said.

PART III

Eight

CONSIDERING HIS AGE, the ambassador was in good health, aside from some arthritis, allergies in the spring, bouts of insomnia. His feet had troubled him for forty years and so he used his whalebone cane for any distance longer than a city block. His hours were regular, as predictable as the consoling chime of an old clock. He lived alone. Visitors were rare. He owned a car but seldom drove it. During the day he listened to music and read, biographies mostly (so confidently composed, so unreliable), often took a walk at dusk, half a mile up the road to the village for dominoes and an apéritif in the café, occasionally two apéritifs, before walking home in the darkness, carrying a flashlight for safety. He was known in the village as a reliable man, good-humored, good at dominoes, often called upon to settle disputes of a factual nature. Did Austerlitz precede Jena or follow it? Was America's greatest test of horseracing the Preakness or the Belmont?

In the evenings the ambassador watched movies from Hollywood's golden age, Bogart and Boyer, Dietrich, and at midnight the late news, a street demonstration in Paris, early returns from the Asian capital markets, more dead in Iraq and Afghanistan. Three times he had spotted someone he knew from former days, young men grown old, weary-faced, incongruous in bush jackets and floppy hats, cargo pants, thick around the middle, often (and more incongruously) bearded. They were the ones in horn-rim eyeglasses standing in the background at the impromptu press conference at Kandahar or Mosul, replying to impertinent questions concerning the aid mission or the drug trade, government corruption, secret negotiations with the Taliban, civilian casualties, indices—"metrics"—of progress, the always elusive estimate of the situation. Listening to them he could only recall his own war, the same excuses, the same lame optimism. Rome wasn't built in a day. Americans are an impatient people. So few Westerners could speak Pashto. The ambassador had heard that the State Department was shorthanded, so a number of recent retirees were encouraged to sign on with one of the many private consulting firms to come back on board as a contract hire. Some of them were from as far back as Indochina, familiar with the routine, the paperwork, and the rest of it. Pass the physical, secure the relevant clearances, you're in. Serious wages, all benefits, a six-month stint, back in the game, a last hurrah for Uncle Sugar. So they kissed the wife goodbye, called the grandchildren, and left the eight-room Greek Revival in Camden, up in Maine, or the condo in Clearwater, down in Florida, and signed on, bringing with them the army-issue backpack that had last seen duty at that hill station in the central highlands—what was its name? But he had forgotten the name. The ambassador had romantic thoughts about offering himself, but his age and his feet argued against it and perhaps his experience was not precisely the experience the government required. Harry was not a field man except that one time. Nevertheless, he always offered a smart salute to the disheveled figure on the small screen. God bless. Come home safely.

When the screen went black Harry Sanders did not move but sat quietly, deep in his memory, dozing. He knew he often got things out of sequence. One posting often ran into another. His memory was not reliable that way. When he looked up an hour later he saw to his surprise a naked woman and a middle-aged man in a tuxedo enjoying a glass of champagne on a beach somewhere. A pornographic movie, the normal post-midnight fare in washed-out color.

The beach reminded him of a resort in Asia during the war, and he couldn't think why until he noticed the hut in the distance, its thatched roof shaped like a topi. Harry watched for a while, the girl was beautifully built, and then he was back in his memory again, and she was there too, this time in disguise.

This is part of what he remembered from his fourth posting, perhaps his fifth.

He was waiting in the anteroom of the presidential palace tapping his cane on the toe of his shoe. The windows were thrown open to the afternoon heat, a damp salty heat that carried with it the aroma of garlic. It always amused them to keep the American ambassador waiting, if only to show that they were mortal and you were, too. Then he heard his name and stood to be ushered into the president's office, a narrow rectangle in shape. It had the aspect of a railway car except for the fifteenth-century oil of Aphrodite rising from the sea, an artwork said to be from the atelier of Botticelli. The president rose to greet him.

Excellency, Harry said.

Ambassador, the president replied, in a voice so deep it resembled an animal's growl. Please sit. You would like coffee?

I would, Harry said. Medium sweet.

The president murmured into his telephone and shortly a servant arrived with a tray holding two small cups. The president took a sip of coffee and waited.

Three nights ago, Excellency, goons struck a village. Two dead, three wounded.

I heard something about it, the president said.

Then last night, another goon attack. By all accounts unprovoked. The village was asleep. This time, three dead.

Two, I think. The third is recovering in hospital.

The third man died this afternoon, Harry said.

I am not up-to-date, then, the president said.

Evidently not, Harry said. He took a sheet of paper from his briefcase and put on his eyeglasses to read it. This was a little bit of theater to get the official business out of the way so that he could speak plainly. What he was obliged to read was a four-sentence paragraph that expressed the grave concern of the American government at an attack that was wholly unwarranted and that could only damage relations between the two countries because, as the president well knew, there were implications concerning the eastern rim of NATO, et cetera et cetera, the president of the United States himself greatly troubled at the loss of innocent life, et cetera et cetera, with the government either unable or unwilling to put a stop to it. Harry read the text slowly and left the sheet of paper on the president's desk so that he could read it himself at his leisure.

One always regrets loss of life, the president said.

Your goons, Harry said.

The president frowned. His eyes appeared to moisten. Such a harsh word, he said. They are not goons, Ambassador. They are young men who feel themselves insulted. Humiliated by a minority population. He paused and sighed. I understand a young woman was involved.

The attack was unprovoked, Excellency.

We have different information. As is so often the case.

These attacks must cease, Harry said.

My country has a cruel history, the president said. We have been overrun countless times in two millennia. The Greeks, the Trojans, the English, Carthage, Rome. The Turks. The president paused again, apparently overcome with emotion. He continued with the litany of aggressors: Saracens, French, Persians. It has to be said that the Jews have done us no harm. Nor the Americans, and that is why I speak so frankly to you. You must give us latitude, given our history. These people among us are beasts. Brutes.

The three dead included a woman, aged sixty-five. Shot in her bed.

My information is that she had a weapon.

Her knitting needles?

That is unworthy of you, Ambassador.

Nevertheless, Harry said.

Boys can be rough sometimes.

They were not boys, Harry said.

All inquiries are being made, the president said.

It would be very good if your inquiries resulted in arrests.

We live in violent times, the president replied.

When was it not violent here?

I do not remember such a time, the president said with a smile. I would say that we have not been fortunate.

And there, for the moment, the matter rested. Harry stifled a yawn and sipped his coffee. He had been awakened at five a.m. by his station chief, informing him of the attack. Shall we go look? the station chief said, and they were soon in a car bound for a settlement in the hill country north of the capital. A half hour later, dawn breaking, they arrived at the village. A small gathering of women and a few men met them at the well. Next to the well was an elderly man lying on his back under an olive tree. Rigor mortis had begun to set in. His fingers were rigid a few inches above the earth. He looked as if he were about to ascend into the sky. His beige-colored face was heavily stubbled and his eyes were open. He wore pantaloons and a blue shirt and except for his wristwatch he could have lived in the previous century. His look was one of surprise. No wound was visible and then someone said that he had been shot in the back. The village women were weeping and the men were sullen. The men began to speak, all of them at once. The assassins were cowardly, typical of their race. They had arrived at ten p.m., everyone in the village asleep. They fired indiscriminately. They did not care who they killed. Two more bodies were at the rear of the house. They fired in a cowardly manner. The victims had no means of defending themselves. Harry noticed children peeking around the legs of the men. Harry and his station chief stayed an hour or more listening to the various accounts of the killings. Finally one of the men said, When will you Americans do something?

Harry nodded but did not reply.

Justice is better, Harry murmured, realizing as he said it that to this community justice was vengeance. There was no difference between them.

What did you say? the man demanded.

Rest assured, Harry said, I will do what I can.

Animals, the man said. They're animals. You must do something before they kill us all. He stepped forward and handed Harry a looseleaf binder, insisting that he inspect the contents. Harry knew what was inside but opened it and began to turn the pages, photographs of previous atrocities committed against his people. Women, men, children, some dead by gunshot, others by knife or bludgeon. One photograph after another, some close-up, others taken from a distance. Some of them were obviously years old, the edges furred from fingering. The man's face began to soften as Harry turned the pages. Every village in the country had similar dossiers, dating from years back, scrapbooks meant to show the depravity of the enemy, his vicious recklessness, his bloodlust. Keep vengeance alive. Harry looked aside to see an old woman gather a shawl around her shoulders and bend down to touch the stubbled face of the dead man, as if that touch would bring him to life.

You must control your people, Excellency.

We have many grievances, Ambassador.

You are in control here. You have the authority.

And them, the president said. They must control their people, too.

Still, you have the upper hand.

There are provocations —

On both sides, Harry replied. And last night, an old woman dead in her bed.

Their women are as vicious as the men, the president said. He stood up then. The meeting was concluded.

I wish you good day, Ambassador.

And you, Excellency. My government will be watching your investigation. An arrest would be helpful.

In due course, the president said. And may I offer my condolences.

Harry nodded, uncertain of the reference.

The events in San Francisco, the president said. How many dead?

Six, Harry said. Five wounded.

In a schoolhouse! the president said, his eyes wide.

We have the killer in custody.

Yes, of course. Have your authorities discovered a motive?

The man was deranged, Harry said.

A tragedy, the president said.

Justice will be done, Harry said.

Of course it will, the president said. In due course.

In a moment Harry was outside in the bright sunlight. He stood on the steps of the palace feeling the heat gather. His irritation increased as he took off his suit jacket and motioned for his driver to follow at a discreet distance. He walked through the gate, nodding at the guards standing at attention. In his irritation he noticed that their shoes were not shined nor their trousers creased. He walked across the square and down the street until he found an inviting café, nearly empty of customers, tables arranged under one large awning. The time was six p.m. Harry loosened his tie, ordered a beer, and watched the street, hazy in the late afternoon. The few pedestrians moved slowly. His irritation diminished as his attention began to drift, other villages in other countries, promises to do something when there was no intention of doing anything. The president was an old fox, his smile sly as he mentioned "the events in San Francisco," Harry caught off-guard, which the president sensed at once. He had not read the morning paper nor seen the cable traffic. The president's message: Don't preach to us. He had a point, too. What they both knew and left unsaid was that the foreign aid bill was making its way through the American Senate. That was the meaning of Harry's remark "My government will be watching your investigation." The president needed American money, but he wasn't going to grovel for it.

Harry ordered another beer as his memory drifted to Africa, and before Africa, Paraguay. Then he was in the war again, hostilities mercifully ended now. No more of that, probably for some time to come. He smiled, remembering his villa and the houseman who came with it, the vegetation, quiet streets all around. He had lived very well in the war capital, much better even than here, where he was ambassador. Now he watched four young men in leather jackets and blue jeans saunter down the street and pause in front of the disco, Aphrodite's Disco it was called. Harry sipped his beer and watched them open the door to the disco, and as they filed inside one of them turned around, looked Harry in the eye, and smiled sourly. The other three waited while he lit a cigarette and threw the match into the gutter. The driver was suddenly behind Harry, suggesting that the time had come to move along.

Sit down, Harry said. Have a beer.

I will have coffee, Nikos said.

Do you know those four?

By reputation, Nikos said.

They are bad news, Harry said. You can tell by looking at them.

Juvenile delinquents, Nikos said.

Harry and Nikos sat awhile, not speaking. They watched a line form in front of the disco. Harry focused on a girl, her shuffle-walk, lithe. He could tell she was not of the country. By her dress and her looks and the way she carried herself, he knew she was European. She was unaccompanied, not the normal thing. From a distance she looked so much like Sieglinde that he rose from his chair and very nearly called out. When she turned around he saw that she was not Sieglinde. She looked nothing like Sieglinde. This was not the first time he had been fooled. Stung.

*   *

These many years later, in retirement, the ambassador was said to be in hiding, but that was surely malicious rumor. Anyone who wanted to find him could do so with scant effort, elementary detective work; and there was no evidence that anyone was interested. He had been retired for a decade and his moment of consequence had occurred many years before that. Moment of consequence — Basso Earle's ornate phrase, spoken dryly, his annoyance barely concealed. Basso said, We've broken dishes, Harry. We took a chance and the chance didn't work out. His accent thickened, curdling a little. Now comes the cleanup, always more hazardous than the event itself, more fraught. Not the steak, you see. The sizzle. Not the offense but the shadow of the offense. Not the facts of the matter but the perception of the facts of the matter. We live in dark times. Scoundrels abound. But you know the drill. The cleanup will take some little while — so many loose ends, so much drama — and for obvious reasons you can't be part of that except to be cooperative in the interview. Our cleanup will be tightly held in-house, a board of inquiry, the objective to tidy the record. Make certain that we're all on the same page and so forth and so on, and when our work is done the result will be highly classified because the material can be easily misunderstood. Your mission was not in search of a separate peace, as all those sunshine patriots in Congress would claim if they knew about it. So few people understand what we do and how we do it. Dead ends are part of our business. Dead ends are what we live with. That leaves you, and as it happens a solution is at hand. The Secretary has agreed to send you to a small embassy, head of the political section. How does Paraguay sound? Harry said, I speak no Spanish. Basso Earle said, Learn, adding, after a moment's pause, We'll not forget about you. I admire your work. I admire your discretion, your way of going about things. The Secretary agrees with me. Paraguay's nice. It's out of harm's way. Basso's Louisiana drawl thickened as he went along, the beat in two-four time.

He said, One last thing about the inquiry. Obviously you are an important witness. Remember to answer the question they ask, not the question they neglect to ask. Tell them the truth. Don't go beyond your brief. Understood? And in case you're wondering, I'm the first casualty of this affair. I'll be retiring sooner rather than later, reasons of health. You ever get to Nantucket, give me a call. Tell you something else, Harry. You're an adventurer just like me. It's OK, adventuring. Just don't go all the way every time.

The Department looked after Harry. After Paraguay he was posted to a central African nation. After an uneventful tour as a deputy assistant secretary, Harry was named ambassador to a noisy Mediterranean nation, and in the years to come three more embassies, and it had to be said that these embassies, though quietly important, were on the margins of crisis. They were not, in Department parlance, areas of critical concern. Harry's final posting abroad was a brief tour as ambassador to a bloodthirsty Balkan nation, a tour cut short by misfortune. Harry returned to Washington and the Department Secretariat, a position well behind the lines, as it were, the clock ticking toward early retirement. He knew at once that he was a stranger in the capital, too many years abroad, perhaps too many years as the senior man in the building, practicing his trade in his own way without serious interference. If a note was to be drafted for the Secretary's signature, Harry drafted it, occasionally without consulting the Secretary or anyone else. As ambassador he liked to travel far afield, taking as much time with the local opposition as with the regime, whatever regime it was; and now a trip outside the building meant an hour in a congressman's office or lunch with an important lobbyist. Washington was a greenhouse with the usual suffocating gases. He soon realized that he was a foreigner in his own country. Of course he was not alone. The Department was filled with former ambassadors assigned to this or that bureau. One often saw them taking a constitutional in the Department's wide corridors. They were clean-desk men. Nothing much to do except push paper from one box to another, waiting for lunch, and later in the day, a reception at one of the embassies near Kalorama where he hoped to find old friends, an evening of reminiscence and too much champagne. One year in, Harry took retirement at age sixty-three, happy enough to do so. He had never fit in at the Secretariat, any more than years before he had not fit in at Policy Planning. He saw himself as a man for today and perhaps tomorrow. He was not a prophet.

They gave him a farewell party on the seventh floor with drinks and a fine buffet, clever speeches, and a medal for distinguished service. The current Secretary stopped by for a cocktail. No one was surprised that Harry was retiring and moving to France, where he owned a villa in the south near the sea. France was a museum and everyone joked that Harry would fit in nicely. He had never truly fit in at the Department, where political skills were paramount. A colleague once remarked that Harry Sanders liked the point of the sword, not its hilt. Washington was hilt-work. What was an ambassador anyway but a dapper messenger passing along the Line of the Day. A bit of a hotspur, Harry, at least in his younger days. A capable diplomat, better abroad than at home, better behind the scenes than in the footlights. He did enjoy overseas work, though his wife May was considered a liability—fragile was often the salient word, subject to multiple interpretations. Her health was dubious and she had not known what to expect as the wife of an American ambassador. Africa had been a trial and their subsequent postings—difficult for her. Harry was good with his counterparts and good with the press, arguably too good, too fond of droll stories when he had a glass in his hand. One could imagine Harry being surprised by his own reputation—lone wolf, say, or adventurer, when he considered himself steady and subtle, collegial when the situation called for it. He was very popular with embassy staff.

Of course his colleagues knew he had been, if not sidelined, put out of harm's way, the cause some obscure incident long past, part of the war's troubled legacy, a Rosetta stone no one cared to decipher. A diplomat's life was never an open book, except at the very top of the Department. Harry had killed a man and that set him apart. The exact circumstances were known only by a few. Had he acted rashly? That was the source of the remark that Harry liked the point of the sword. A serious diplomat avoided sword points. A serious diplomat sought common ground, understandings that might defuse a dangerous situation. But still, along with the tut-tut came some admiration. Whatever situation Harry Sanders had found himself in, well, that situation was surely perilous and he had lived to tell the tale — or not tell the tale, for he was known for his scrupulous discretion. Harry's war had broken the rules. There were pockets of silence all over the Department in those days, as if, Harry remarked, most everyone in it had something to be ashamed of.

It was too much to say that his colleagues were afraid of him; Harry was not a man to inspire fear. Instead, his colleagues kept their distance, wary of being identified as his good friend. His was not the sort of star a younger man hitched his wagon to, though he was popular among the women now beginning diplomatic careers. They were the ones interested in point-work and sought Harry's advice, and May's, too. So what good was point-work in South America? Or in frigid Scandinavia some years later? Harry was said to covet an embassy in the Middle East, Syria or Lebanon or Iraq. But those missions seemed out of the question, requiring as they did a steely temperament and exquisite political footwork — no glass in hand when speaking to the wretched press — and the patience of an ox. And then suddenly he was too old and contemplating retirement. As for a mission in the Middle East, some in the Department wished that for him but Harry never wished it for himself.

In any case, the moment of consequence was a dead letter, filed and mostly forgotten. It happened so long ago. The Secretary was dead, his senior staff all dead or in nursing homes. Basso Earle was dead, a long struggle with cancer, his memoir unfinished. Truth to tell, never really begun. A few months before Basso died Harry flew to Nantucket for a last conversation. He had heard that Basso was ill and wanted to pay his respects. They sat in Basso's gazebo at the end of the day, drinking martinis and watching sailboats maneuver on the Sound, a heavy chop owing to the north wind and an incoming tide. The old man's Louisiana accent had thickened over the years, a melodious gumbo that slid and sloshed in its cup. Harry had to lean close to catch the drift. They spoke of places where they had served. Harry's current posting was Oslo, and Basso had some fun at his expense. How're things in wintry Oslo? he said. One scandal after another, I'll bet. Much of a Red threat there? I heard they called Kissinger to straighten things out for them.

But the conversation always drifted back to their war and its discontents, its muddled legacy. Still, Basso said, we tried. We did what we could. It wasn't enough. Or, more to the point, it was too much. Our war turned into an ironist's feast, a smorgasbord of contradictions and false hopes. I always thought irony was small beer, an academic's substitute for action, force always balanced by counterforce. Something lame and exhausted about it, Basso went on, a lack of nerve. Don't you think, Harry? Irony doesn't god damn it lead you anywhere. You're stuck in an eternal rotary, what you gained on the turns you lost on the roundabouts. That's what we have, Harry. That's our inheritance. I'm sorry I got you into it but I'd do the same thing today. You play the hand you're dealt with the chips you're given, and irony doesn't come into it unless you're running some god damned seminar up at Harvard.

Fuck 'em, Basso added.

Twice over, Harry agreed, and then an old name flew into his head. He hadn't thought of her in years. He said, You never explained to me Adele's role in all this, if she had one. Adele, your wife's friend. The mischief maker. The Red.

Adele, Basso said, and grunted.

Adele, Harry said.

I'm glad you reminded me, Basso said. I'd've forgotten otherwise. Wait here, he said, and left the gazebo to walk across the lawn to his house. Harry refilled his glass and sat looking at the boats on the open water, the breeze freshening. All the boats had their spinnakers out, and not for the first time Harry wished he knew how to sail, had an appreciation of tides and wind, knew the difference between a yawl and a sloop.

Then Basso was back, easing himself into his chair with a theatrical sigh.

I'm not sure what happened to her, Basso said. I know she left the country, more or less disappeared. I haven't seen her from that day to this. She wasn't constructive, that's for sure. I don't know what else is for sure. One more unresolved memory. There are so many of them. Isn't it tempting to make a spy story out of it? Adele a kind of Mata Hari. People love spy stories involving women. But I think Adele was only a meddler, one of those who demand to be in the mix. For people like Adele, life outside the mix is no life at all, and if there isn't a mix she'll create one. Probably there's a little more to it than that, though. A few months ago I got this in the mail.

Basso handed Harry the gold compass, the one he thought would bring luck. The compass that was lost on Harry's trek in the jungle.

Harry turned it over and read the initials on the case: *B. E. III.*

It's the genuine article, Basso said.

Yes, I think it is.

A short note from Adele came with it, Basso said. Postmarked London, no return address. One of her friends bought it at a jewelry store, the one around the corner from the Singapore Sling that specialized in secondhand items in gold and silver. Adele wrote that her friend knew at once whose it was. And sent the compass to her so she could send it to me. End of note. Best regards, Adele.

Harry pushed the button that opened the case and found true north. He handed the compass back to Basso.

No no, Basso said. It's yours. My gift.

Basso, it belongs to you.

Not anymore, Basso said.

It's from your wife —

I know, Basso said.

What am I going to do with it?

Basso had fallen silent. His eyes closed and for a quarter of an hour he snoozed. Harry sat with him, watching the boats toss about on the Sound. He drank the dregs of the martini pitcher, the gin watered. These days Harry limited himself to two drinks at a sitting. He moved his chair into the shade and looked again at the compass, its gold facing scratched from use. He didn't want it. The compass had not brought good luck. But he supposed he was stuck with it. Harry stared out to sea at the boats, spinnakers flying, water washing over the bows, the sun brilliant. Nantucket was a harsh environment, windswept, rocky, barren, the antithesis of humid overgrown Asia where tigers prowled, where the nights were nearly as warm as the days. Whenever he thought of the Asian war, which was often, he thought of Sieglinde. He did not dwell on where she was and what she was doing, whether or not she was married or continued her x-ray business. He remembered their brief time together and their misunderstandings. He remembered the silk-string hammock and wondered what had become of it. Probably it was a commissar's hammock now, spoils of war along with the American kitchen, the ficus tree, and the neighbor's cat. He did hope Sieglinde had found whatever it was she was looking for. Surely a man had entered her life, and Harry wondered who the man was and what he did and his nationality. He was not American. Of that Harry was entirely certain.

When Basso awakened, Harry said it was time for him to leave for the airport.

Too bad, Basso said. I was going to take you around to see the houses.

What houses? Harry said.

The tycoons' houses. There are tycoons on the island now. Big houses. Biggest damned houses you've ever seen. Swimming pools. Can you imagine swimming pools on an island? I know some of them but they're hard to talk to. I don't care what they know, and they don't care what I know.

The tycoons lose, Harry said.

171

Basso brightened. I think they do, he said.

I'm glad I came to see you, Harry said.

I'm glad, too.

I wish you'd take back the compass.

No can do, Basso said.

Well, OK. One last thing.

What's that?

Did you ever see the report of the board of inquiry?

Never did, Basso said.

Do you want to?

Basso shook his head. Nah.

Sure?

Damn sure, Basso said. They shook hands and Harry walked away to his rental car. There wasn't much to tell, really. The board of inquiry—three former ambassadors and the Department counsel—deliberated for six months, interviewing the relevant parties and examining the paper trail, what there was of it. Harry was cooperative and when the salient question was asked, Whose idea was this?, Harry replied that he understood it to be a joint venture of the secretary of state and Ambassador Basso Earle. But others may have been involved. The White House, for example. But if they were, he had no knowledge of it. I was too far down the food chain, Harry said. For what it was worth, Harry had agreed with the idea, and agreed also that the probability of success was not high.

And there was no loss of life, the Department counsel said, turning the page, literally and figuratively.

Yes, there was loss of life, Harry replied. I killed a man. Shot him dead. So for the moment the page remained unturned as Harry was asked to explain himself, the circumstances, his own frame of mind. He thought, Frame of mind? *Frame of mind?* So he sketched out the frame of mind, the counsel declining to make any sort of eye contact. It was like talking to the statue of a stargazer. Though he was not asked to do so, Harry described the boy and the carbine in detail, including the moment when he flung himself forward, the boy falling and striking his head, the carbine in Harry's fingers, and the shot—unbelievably loud in the stillness of the jungle. Appalling, really. It was evident to him as he went along that he was giving more detail than was wanted, but he decided to tell it all so that there would be no additional questions, a misapprehension as it turned out. The counsel said, Are you skilled with firearms? Harry said, Not particularly. The counsel said, Would you describe your action as self-defense? Yes, Harry said. But there might have been something short of lethal force . . . He let the sentence hang and went on, But I'll never know. No one will. The counsel ordered the technician to turn off the tape recorder.

The counsel said, Were you of sound mind when you encountered the enemy soldier?

Sound enough to have pulled the trigger.

What I mean is—

I was not myself, Harry conceded.

You were injured. You were under stress.

It had not been a happy day, Harry said.

And there were no witnesses, the counsel said.

No witnesses, Harry replied.

Do you have any idea of the dead man's identity? His name? Did he have a rank?

No idea. I do know that I didn't like him. I didn't like his face, a cruel face, pockmarked in places. A low forehead, high cheekbones, pig's eyes. A nasty customer.

Is that why you shot him?

I had no choice, Harry said.

The counsel turned to the technician and told him to restart the tape recorder.

And what happened next? Take it from the moment you arrived at USAID House.

Harry smiled broadly. Don't you want to hear about the snake?

The board of inquiry took another two months to sift its findings. By that time the war was in full flood, five divisions of American troops in-country and another three still to come. Events were in the saddle. The board was said to have produced a document with the highest possible classification. The results were never made public, and there was some question of whether it had been properly filed. The burn bag was the most likely alternative. There were so many untoward incidents in the war—and so many missions that had no clear provenance. No obvious point of departure and no obvious objective. What exactly did you expect to happen? These missions resembled the art market, the Old Master that had been through two dozen galleries in nine countries, so many dealers, so many buyers, and hard to sort them out because dealer and buyer were often the same person or anyway related by blood or by bed. Somewhere along the line the bills of sale had disappeared. The connoisseur had to rely on his own eye and instinct, qualities honed over many years. While no one could prove him right, no one could prove him wrong either. And so the Steen or the Van Dyck slipped from hand to hand and finally from sight altogether.

The one episode he never explained, because no one asked the direct question, was the Chinese venerable and his boy in the throne room of the Datsun truck. Truth was, the episode defied explanation. Even now, decades later, his hours in the Datsun seemed to him a kind of stop-time, the sudden glare of headlights, the exquisite manners of the venerable, his young son—if that was who the boy was—pouring water. No intelligible word passed between them, unless you counted his fractured question, Amel'can? That, Harry kept to himself. The episode seemed to him to embody something of the supernatural. Of this he was certain: The old man had saved his life. In any case, the relevant parties had all passed on. Harry thought of himself as the sole survivor of a far-flung family, the last repository of an intimate history. And those many facts of which he was unaware or suspicious—well, they were dead, too, and buried. He believed he dwelled in a city of the dead, and they were too numerous to be counted accurately. That afternoon in the gazebo, Basso Earle had asked Harry this question: All things considered, looking back on it now, are you happy you chose diplomacy as your life's work? Harry laughed and said, Of course. What other business is there for someone like me? He laughed again and said, A connoisseur of the counterfeit and the inexplicable.

Each afternoon, round about three, weather permitting, the ambassador took tea on the verandah of his cottage. He sipped tea and watched the afternoon slip away. Harry looked across flat fields to the defile that led to the narrow estuary, a fingernail of the Mediterranean. Along its quays and clinging to the stone cliffs that loomed above it were houses mostly occupied by fishermen and their families. Here and there adventurous outsiders had built villas for summer and fall holidays. The spring, as a rule, was wet, and the winter windy. The fishing village below was approached by a treacherous switchback road. Only the fishermen and the few summer people were allowed in. Parking space was at a premium. On a bright summer day the view of the harbor was superb, fishing smacks next to small sloops and now and again an enormous yacht anchored at the mouth of the estuary, the skipper always careful to leave ample room for passage. Beyond all this was the sea, brilliant in all seasons. The villagers, both breeds, were intolerant of outsiders. There were no amenities in the village beyond a simple bar-restaurant and a fishmonger, open in the afternoons. The fishmonger also sold gasoline at outrageous prices. There were no showers, public toilets, souvenir shops, or gendarmes. The foreign yachtsmen were tolerated so long as they paid in cash and did not linger. The village was notorious all along the coast east of Marseilles for its inhospitality. It was such a pretty location, so welcoming from a distance, so peaceable in the summer light, that from time to time a professional photographer unaware of its reputation would happen by to take pictures only to find himself surrounded by burly men and told to go back where he came from, and it took only minutes for him to pack up his camera gear and commence the long climb up the near-vertical road.

Harry had never been there. His damaged feet could not take

him down and certainly could not take him back up. He watched the comings and goings through powerful binoculars, not that the comings and goings enlightened him. He admired the village's situation, a child's conception of a pirate's cove. Its aspect was medieval, the houses constructed of stone, many of them with wooden porches. The steps leading to them were stone, and at dusk, the sun westering, the houses appeared to be hanging on the cliff without visible means of support. In the early morning, when the small fleet embarked for the fishing grounds, they ghosted through the mouth of the inlet like great whales. In the rain the village was as forlorn as any on earth, the air, the water, and the walls of the cliff an identical shade of gray. With the rain came mist, then fog. When the air cleared, Harry found the boats back in harbor. Harry saw the village as a means of escape. In that way it resembled a crease in a mountain chain, the crease that allowed a climber to descend safely. He knew people who would take him there for a look-around but never bothered to ask them. He liked the idea of its inaccessibility, its oddity and hostility to outsiders. He liked to think of the village as in some sense a version of himself. Harry finished his tea and picked up the binoculars and looked east and west. The sea was empty.

He sighed heavily and stepped off the verandah and onto the path that led to the rear of his house. He moved slowly, using his cane, because the path was narrow and uneven. Under the enormous plane tree was his wife's grave, simple granite with her name, May Huerwood Sanders, and the dates. Whatever the weather, Harry visited her each afternoon, speaking a few words, clearing the night's debris from beneath the plane tree. Beyond the grave was rising terrain with farmhouses and a few vacation villas. The morning silence was disturbed only a little by the movement of the tree's long branches and in the distance the faint hum of an automobile. Harry could hear the sigh of his own breathing. Auspicious, he thought, evidence of life, however slow. He sat on the bench under the tree, resting his chin on the crown of his whalebone cane, a birthday present from May. They were in Oslo then. He was at the end of his tour and awaiting a fresh assignment.

They had taken an afternoon stroll in the neighborhood, and the moment she saw the cane in the window of a men's shop she walked in and bought it, not without difficulty. The owner tried to explain that the cane was not for sale but for decoration, a bibelot. But when pressed he came up with a price, a ludicrous price, but May was not to be denied. For your birthday, she said, though Harry's birthday was weeks off. She immediately threw his old cane into a trash barrel. She said, An ambassador should have a serious cane, an ambassadorial cane, don't you agree? And it will remind us of Oslo wherever we go. White nights. Salmon. Herring. They strolled on, discussing Harry's new assignment. May wanted someplace warm, perhaps a capital near the seashore. The Mediterranean was an agreeable sea. Wouldn't Tunis be a good posting? Horseback riding was her favorite outdoor activity, and she knew for a fact that horses were present in Tunisia. Why don't you suggest Tunis, Harry? He remembered saying that Tunis wasn't a bad idea, knowing that the chances for a posting there were slim to none. He had no special knowledge of the Arab world. He did not speak Arabic. He had read the Koran but concluded that its dreaminess translated well enough into English, always allowing for obscure syntax: "Surely God wrongs not men, but themselves men wrong." He said, What about Greece? All those islands requiring his personal attention, Hydra, Santorini. Santorini was said to be especially fine for bird watching. Bird watching on horseback, he added. May did not reply right away, preoccupied as she was by Tunisia. They walked on. Harry couldn't remember the remainder of the day. Probably they went to dinner at Charlys, grilled salmon with a savory dill sauce. In those days the American ambassador could walk around unencumbered by drivers and bodyguards, especially in Scandinavia; then came Olof Palme's assassination and the rules were rewritten, though not drastically. Then he remembered they did not go to Charlys but dined in with the mayors of Bismarck and Duluth and their wives, in Norway visiting relatives. They had written asking if they could meet for a meal and May suggested dinner at the residence; she had always had an interest in the Dakotas and Minnesota. That was news to Harry. But the mayors were interesting on economic conditions in the upper Midwest. At that time both cities were losing population. A way of life was disappearing. Norway, meanwhile, was prospering.

That was the extent of his recollection of dinner with the mayors and their wives. He tapped May's headstone with the tip of his whalebone cane and lamented his stuttering memory. There were tests available to assess the severity of memory loss and the causes and the prognosis. But what idiot would take such a test? So what? The news was either good or bad, and if bad, nothing to be done but continue to beaver away at crossword puzzles. A sentence of life, as it were, without parole. Now he watched a grasshopper light on the tip of his cane. Harry was not a connoisseur of insect species but, by God, this one was ungainly, all legs. He wondered if grasshoppers were identical the world over or if there were subtle variations like alligators and crocodiles or Germans and Austrians. This one was self-possessed, immobile on the tip of the whalebone cane. Wait him out, be patient, Harry thought. And then in an instant it was gone. Next time someone asked him about retirement he'd tell them about watching a grasshopper and waiting it out, offering his misshapen wrist as a landing zone and having the offer refused.

He rose, tapping the cane on granite.

It's a beautiful day, he said aloud.

A beautiful day for riding horses.

So long, sweetheart, see you tomorrow.

May Huerwood grew up in a hamlet in Vermont's Northeast Kingdom. The aptly named Slother contained a drugstore, a hardware store, a tavern, an IGA, and a Congregational church. The lawyer and the surveyor shared an office above the IGA. Slother was a quiet village except on Saturday nights when the tavern was full. The high school was one of those called consolidated, a low-slung, fawn-colored building that accommodated grades eight through twelve. Students came from miles around. Few of its graduates went on to college, and those who did enrolled at Johnson State College and at once fell behind, most of them, owing to inadequate preparation at the consolidated school. The home life of many of the children was less than ideal. The economy of the region was depressed—marginal farming, some logging, a little tourism, and of course the school and the regional hospital. Slother still felt the effects of the Great Depression. Many of the inhabitants remembered it well and told stories to prove it. People loaded up their flivvers and lit out for California. And many came back. There was a CCC camp and a soup kitchen. Truth was, the town was sore. It was indisposed. Slother had never sent a child to an out-of-state college until May was offered a scholarship, a prize not valued by her family. The school May chose was a small college near Denver. The college had never had a student from Vermont and the admissions director thought that May would add New England sobriety to the classroom, Mrs. Wharton taming Jack London. He was charmed by the idea of a Northeast Kingdom. And May was a fine student, high marks all the way around. Also, she was eager to be quits with Slother. She wanted to see something of the world and Denver was as good a place as any to begin. The admissions director at the Denver school laughed and laughed when May recycled the old adage:

The Northeast Kingdom. So far from God, so close to Canada.

May did have a shadow on her spirit, an inheritance, Harry thought, from her Vermont family, hotheaded and mutinous, vengeful. The far north of the Northeast Kingdom was closed in, a wild terrain of worn-out hills and trackless forests, unforgiving and monotonous. They called it God's country and dared you to disagree. May's parents were suspicious, hard-muscled, expert with firearms, prideful, wary of outsiders. And no wonder. Entrepreneurs from Boston and Providence and beyond showed up from time to time with promises of a resort village or a ski lift, needing only a tax break and some seed money, and always went away with the proceeds. The resort village or ski lift never materialized, God's country vandalized once again. When May arrived with Harry one October afternoon, the Huerwoods' worst expectations were met. The family had the idea he was a socialist sympathizer because he lived abroad and worked for the government, a toxic combination, no different from any sly commissar from the Ukraine or worse. May had abandoned God's country for the devil's, and whatever the consequences for her and her parasite boyfriend, it served them right. Harry had never met anyone like them, not in the most remote regions of Paraguay or the war zone or anyplace else. They were utterly incurious, though fascinated by his cane, which they identified as a fashion accessory like an ascot or pearl-gray gloves, the sort of doodad an Englishman might wear. Bum leg was all Harry said when they asked him about his injury, the word "injury" accompanied by a doubtful smile. Their first day together was exhausting, then infuriating, and yet when they talked about surviving the dreadful winters and the mud-strangled streams, the proper way to fell a tree or quarter a calf, they were informative. They were tolerant of the various communes established in the region, perhaps because everyone had to endure the same weather. No one was exempt. Sam and Esther Huerwood knew what they were talking about and Harry listened attentively. He guessed that their cockeyed political talk was a way of marking a boundary, the way wolves pissed in a circle to mark theirs.

Sam was a large man, well over six feet tall and rugged. His size seemed to mean a great deal to him. When he sat in his big leather armchair by the wood stove, his hands clasped tightly behind his head, he appeared as immovable as granite. Harry sensed that this was an advantage in daily life, a strenuous outdoor life, the forest always encroaching, the weather all too predictable. Three cords of wood were stacked neatly between two ancient oak trees. At night coyotes howled.

May had suffered at their hands but she tried to be understanding, at least when she was talking to Harry. Her voice was soft and filled with regret and forbearance. He knew that her inner thoughts were laden with anger. Regret and forbearance were her public voices. They're hard to know, she said of her parents.

They don't get out much.

They are not worldly people.

They think I abandoned them. Betrayed them. Don't value them. They have a point, I think.

But my life could never be their life. I chose you.

Harry said, I think they're not wild about your choice.

I didn't expect them to be, May said. They never have been before. May smiled and looked away into the forest. The time was near nine, after a second fractious dinner in Vermont. May's sister, Belle, had joined them for dessert, Belle shaking Harry's hand with an iron grip, hugging her father, kissing her mother, finally settling into a chair and lighting a cigarillo, tapping it impatiently on the edge of an ashtray. Belle posed a number of questions about Harry's "prospects," to which he had no satisfactory answer except he was done with the war. In his line of work you went where they sent you. Belle pointed out that in the government you had a job forever; wasn't that the great thing about it? Absolutely, Harry said, cradle to grave. That's what I mean, Belle said. The pay's good, too, Harry replied. I'll bet it is, Belle said. Esther looked disappointed. She had not liked his answer concerning the war. Evidently he planned to retreat in the face of the communist enemy.

Now he and May were alone in the chill of the evening. May said, I think you frighten them.

Frighten them? A rattlesnake wouldn't frighten them.

I don't mean physically, May said.

Harry let his mind drift while May told a rattlesnake story, something about sitting up all night with a snakebitten calf. His thoughts wandered here and there, to evenings in Connecticut and in Asunción, while he looked at the sky for familiar constellations.

A soft breeze moved around them, stealthy as a ghost. May put her head on his shoulder; the scent of jasmine. He said, Your parents. What did they think when you took up Chopin?

May said, I beg your pardon?

Harry returned at once to the present moment. Oh, sorry, he said. I was thinking of something else.

Someone else, May said. Who was she?

Someone I knew in the war, he said.

Where is she now?

Damned if I know. I haven't seen her since.

Was it serious?

For a weekend, he said.

What was her name?

Sieglinde, Harry said.

What sort of name is that?

She was German.

What did Chopin have to do with it?

She played the piano. Chopin.

Do I have to worry about this Sieglinde?

No. You don't.

I hope not, May said. That was certainly a surprise. Not a welcome surprise.

Everybody has a past, Harry said.

Not everybody, May said.

They met on a wet afternoon in April 1969, in a seminar room of the small college near Denver, the alma mater of a deputy assistant secretary of state. Harry was on home leave from Asunción. The chairman of the history department at the college had asked the deputy, the alumnus, to send someone to talk about the war—someone young, good on his feet, attractive, someone who could *relate*—and helpfully added that the class was composed mostly of the children of middle-class parents who lived nearby, a few ranch kids from the high country, a distinctly nonpolitical group, and that was the trouble. The chairman wanted someone who could stir them up a little. Harry protested that he had not been to the war zone in two years. What he knew about the war he read in newspapers. In any case, he was not an advocate and the war was on its way to being lost. Sorry, the deputy said, everyone else in this shop is busy. You're not busy, so you're nominated. Give them a good spiel, Harry. Put a good face on it.

The students seemed to him from another world. The boys had the fresh faces of American infantrymen. But they were not infantrymen, though some of them soon would be. Harry stood at a lectern, and on the wall opposite was a drypoint print of bearded, weary Herodotus, who had traveled the known world in search of unheard-of civilizations. Wherever he went, Herodotus insinuated himself into the fabric of life in foreign lands. Harry had always thought of him as the first foreign correspondent, moving hither and thither on someone else's dime. What would these students think if Harry were to tell them he was out-of-date. The war had been going badly when he was there and it was worse now and would be worse still next year and the year after. Harry tried to gather himself for the task at hand, the American mission, its causes, its ways and means, its prospects, its objective. War aims. The war was misbegotten, that was the truth of it; and his memory wound back to his trek through the jungle and the pockmarked face of the enemy soldier soon to be dead. He paused somewhere in the middle of his discussion of war aims, quoting the secretary of state as saying they were nothing more or less than "to stop the North from doing what it is doing." A formulation perhaps not fully thought through. A reductio ad absurdum. He wondered if he should tell them that when he was in the war he lived there as easily as they lived in their dormitories, except that nine-tenths of his world was below the surface, life an enigma; and it was likely the same was true for them in suburban Denver. They were very young after all. Harry watched them nod off. In the rear of the room two girls passed notes as they looked out the window. This war defeated lan-

183

guage. He caught his breath when he realized that he was looking at the dead and wounded of next year and the year after. He owed it to them to suggest Canada, an altogether pleasant country, easy to get lost in. But there were consequences to Canada, too, a reckoning down the line. All in all, Harry's appearance in the seminar room was a wasted two hours, and late in the afternoon, when he could decently excuse himself, he went at once to a bar near the campus for a drink before the ride to the airport, thinking all the while that he was not an outside man. He was not a Spokesman. Harry preferred the privacy and infinite subtleties of inside work.

May and two friends were at a corner table. Harry recognized them from the seminar, the two note-passers and a pretty girl who sat behind them, attentive. When May approached and asked if he would join them, Harry said he had only a few minutes, and when she pressed him he said all right, because she was the attentive one, most attractive, with pale gray eyes and an open smile, a mellow voice, freckles, a face with a rosy glow. She said, My friends and I want to know what it's like for you in the war. How do you get on? Do you like the people? Do the people like you? Do you have a so- cial life? Harry sat drinking with them for two hours and finally the friends wandered off. He rebooked his flight. The bar filled up. When Harry asked May why she was interested in the war, she said she wasn't that interested but thought she ought to know something about it, and besides, she had seen his photograph in the school newspaper and liked his looks. She was an art history major, Angelico to Zurbarán. All day long she looked at faces. Dürer faces. Rembrandt faces. Hopper faces. Why do you suppose there are so few female painters? Harry said he didn't know but it was worth thinking about. He and May sat talking until near midnight, when they went together to her apartment. Harry stayed on another day and night, and then he was back in Washington, receiving a final desultory briefing before returning to Paraguay. Paraguay was not on their minds. The nation was at war and the State Department had become a war department.

Harry and May wrote each other often, long colorful letters, May of her afternoons on horseback, Harry of his journeys to the Paraguayan interior. That was where some Nazis supposedly were, but he never saw one. May had taken a job at a country club stable teaching the fine points of horsemanship to teenage girls, and when the lessons were done she took one of the horses into the countryside, riding until dusk and beyond, moonlit fields and hills, riding breakneck all the way. And at night she had a new enthusiasm, Francisco Goya, painter of kings and queens, the vicious and the prey of the vicious. Harry could not resist quoting a letter he received from a friend in the war zone, Franz, whose most immediate problem was a sixteen-foot python, the python ineffectively imprisoned behind chicken wire. Its name was Wormwood, an indolent creature but ever poised and spiteful. The python put Harry's friend in mind of the war itself, slow-moving but dangerous and sinister. Treacherous, Franz said, long periods of immobility and then a slow Wormwood uncoiling, a kind of shudder. Wormwood was heedless, a heartless mass of willful muscle with an appetite that came and went according to whim or some mysterious snake-rhythm. When a neighborhood cat went missing, no need to ask where it was. The python seemed to be most active in the evening hours. No cage could contain it and night was its friend and it always returned in the morning, sluggish and distracted. Franz wrote that he, too, lived in a shadow world where much transpired in the dark. The American occupiers were the veneer of the earth, its visible lakes and oceans, its rivers and mountain ranges and deserts and forests. Everything subterranean belonged to the communist enemy. Reading Franz's letters gave Harry the awful premonition that this was to be the way of things for years to come. And Franz had an inquiry of his own. What in God's name do you do in Paraguay? What are the women like? Harry replied that he thought he had found a Nazi in the hills of Curuguaty, close by the Brazilian border, but alas he was but an old infantryman from the Great War whose memories of the Somme would not go away. He'd lost an arm there, at either Ypres or Thiepval, he could not remember which. Really, there was no difference between them. He was not right in the head in that year, 1916. A pig of a year. He left Germany for good after the war, immigrated to Paraguay, and now managed an estate. Harry met the old man in a bodega and listened to his tales of the Somme, scarcely imaginable. He countered with tales of his own war but they did not measure up. He did omit the boy with the carbine. He was talking arithmetic to a man skilled in quantum mechanics.

Harry completed his tour in Paraguay. His apprehension of the future did not abate. He and May married in Paris, a civil ceremony in the *mairie* of the Fourteenth Arrondissement. Friends from the embassy were the witnesses, Harry and May having decided that a *mairie* wedding with both families present would be a catastrophe. A month's honeymoon in sunny Provence and then to a central African nation where Harry took up his duties as ambassador, supervising a staff of eight.

Along with Harry came the foreign service, its traditions and customs, its rules, its hierarchies, its formal pace with continual changes of venue. Time was measured by "tours" and "postings." Harry liked the idea of a fresh billet every few years, fresh faces, a fresh terrain, and another language. He liked getting out of the office, and naturally each country had its own history and set of circumstances and constellation of personalities who often enough controlled events or thought they did. May liked to say she came from a long line of people who had stayed put and she had broken the mold. Mold-breaking was not her family's way, either. She grew distant from them. Letters between May and her family became less frequent as time went on and finally ceased altogether. In due course her parents died. Her sister died. She and May had had a vicious quarrel when May married Harry—by no means the first in their long and contentious life together but the most consequential and unforgettable, and that quarrel had never been resolved.

Five years separated them, May and May Belle, called Belle. Belle did not like the idea of Little Sister. Subordination was not in her makeup. The sisters had never been close, although May looked on Belle as a second self, the doppelgänger who was forever out of reach, willful on the outside and chilly within. The five years might have been a century. They did not resemble each other but anyone seeing them together knew they were sisters, something subtle, a way of walking perhaps, a certain tilt of the head and particular gestures. Belle was a tomboy and indisputably her father's favorite. He called her Bill, taught her the ropes, taught her to drive a tractor when she was ten years old, took her to the rifle range. They were a closed circle with no entry for May. When May got her period, Belle was furious and refused to speak to her for a week, and when she did, her voice was an insinuating sneer, as if some cherished rule had been broken. May had cheated.

Each sister had the ability to read the other's thoughts, not always but at specific times and places. The thoughts May read she did not like, Belle continually weighing and measuring with May coming up short. May often heard her sister and her father snickering over the breakfast table, then falling silent when she joined them. Belle was high-spirited, her father's darling and her mother's worry. Belle had the looks and bearing of an actress and a temperament that stole the oxygen from any room. May was the shy one, good at school, often with her nose in a book, happiest when alone on horseback. However, she did not ride like a farm girl but like a Denver debutante at a horse show. No fun to be around, her father said. May was cut from strange cloth. Who did she think she was? May herself did not know, but she was determined to find out in someplace other than Slother, Vermont, with its monotony and subservience to weather. She called farm life weather-beaten, as if it had an ancient face, lined, raw-boned, and morose. She had no interest in farm animals or wildlife generally, although the howling of coyotes late at night had a certain primal attraction. May's health was delicate. Always around the ides of March May took to her bed with bronchitis and a high fever that would last for a fortnight and sometimes longer. She did not appear to require attention, so her mother brought her meals and the prescribed medications and left her alone. When the fever was at its height May would hallucinate, crying out in an anguished incoherent tongue. In some inevitable thoughtless way May slipped to the margins of family life, an unwelcome guest in her own house. Her family thought it was her own choice, a willed distance, but that was not how May saw it. She saw her family as a nation with a fault line, America and slavery, the French and their bloody revolution, the Spanish Inquisition. She was the Other. And when May went off to her Denver college on a generous grant-in-aid everyone breathed easier. No member of the family had ever been to college. There had been no need of it.

May had been an unhappy inhabitant of God's country but that did not mean an absence of grief when her family disappeared, all within two years. When her parents died she and Harry were in Washington for the obligatory home posting. The news came in a letter from Belle some days after the funeral. They died in a fire at night, the farmhouse consumed, burned to the ground. All that remained was the land itself, deeded to Belle the year before. The funeral, Belle wrote, was a simple affair but everyone in the village attended. The letter ended there and was signed simply "Your Sister Belle." Two years later Belle died of cancer, but by the time the news reached May, the funeral had already been held. The funeral director had thought to contact the State Department, but by then a week had passed. May and Harry were in Oslo.

May was shaken by this news. In fact, she was surprised at her distress. Her family came back to her in dreams, especially her father and Belle. No more agreeable in dreamland than they were in life, but poignant still. She knew in her heart that reconciliation was impossible. She had chosen one sort of life and they had chosen another, and when May looked back on it she wondered about the word "chosen." She was not conscious of having chosen anything. She was born into one sort of life and that had led to a college near

Denver, and one afternoon she had gone to a lecture, dreading it actually, and there was Harry Sanders, foreign service officer. And her life changed utterly. She wished she had known her mother better. They might have been close, been able to confide in each other, but her mother had not wanted that. May had not seen them in many years and always remembered the family stonefaced when she and Harry drove away in their rental car after the disastrous weekend at the farm. Her family had been rude to him and rude to her. May did not care if she ever saw Vermont again, though she knew it would always be with her. You could never avoid your birthplace. It was where your memories began and if many of those memories were unhappy—well then, all subsequent memories were contaminated. The subsequent memories were shadowed by the early pentimento. Americans were supposed to be born free, but the truth was that they were no more free than anyone else. Canadians. Mexicans. The idea was that Americans were in a constant state of reinvention, but invention and reinvention did not liberate but only brought you closer to your essential self and that was governed by the childhood pentimento. May brought those scattered thoughts, much edited in her telling, to the family table one night. They elicited only silence until her father said, Well, I don't know, May. Look at the Eskimos. One igloo is pretty much like another, wouldn't you say? And Belle howled with laughter. May shrugged them off; her father's comment made no sense to her. She herself hoped to God her inference was not correct, because the north country was a blight on her spirit. The woods were a barrier as formidable as any ocean or mountain range, a prison for its inhabitants, a narrow slice of life in a narrow part of the world, where even a desire to ride a horse was looked upon as condescension. The region was an ice palace with no possibility of thaw. She wanted to make something of herself. What that something was, she had no fixed idea. So she would fly away with Harry Sanders and that would be that, put paid. Her family would be rid of her and she would be rid of her family. Their hearts were closed to her and, she knew now, vice

189

versa. Of course dead or alive they were still her family—and what they saw was that May didn't care. Didn't care for the farm. Didn't care about livestock. Didn't care about the northern lights or winter blizzards or the hunt. Didn't care that the farm had been in the Huerwood family for a hundred years. Was sick each March. May believed that her nonconformity was essential to her self, her way of getting on in the world. Her own destiny. No one ever said that the north country was easy.

May wished she had put a simple question to her family.

What is there about me that you dislike so?

She was ill at ease in Africa. She reminded herself of the tourists she saw in Slother, arriving in their German cars, always well turned out, bound at once for the three Victorian houses on the town green, beautiful houses with wide porches and narrow windows. The Congregational church, built in 1790, was badly in need of paint but its lines were as chaste as a Puritan's sermon. The tourists would stop at curbside to look at the church and the houses before leaving in a hurry, bound for Canada or the resort hotel to the southeast. In Africa May felt like an ill-mannered tourist or an amateur sociologist come to inspect the culture of the natives. In these endeavors chaste was not the word that came to mind. By contrast Harry seemed quite at home. He explained to her that his task was to understand the problems, but in Africa understanding did not lead to solutions. It led to discouragement because the facts were brutal. Poverty, disease, ignorance, corruption, violence, and an absence of law. The war had given Harry a cautious approach to intervention. He said to her that one of his specialties was the problem that had no obvious solution. This was not an excuse for inaction, only a reason to avoid the wrong kind of action. He said, We are not a colonial power despite appearances. I am doing what I can to avoid a colonial attitude. Also, revolution was in the air but revolution never came. Breakdown came. Nevertheless, May said, I will do what I can for children and their mothers. That will be my task.

Easy to call Harry cynical and May naïve, and easier still to say that May had the larger heart, but that was closer to the truth. Harry believed that his wife needed a period of adjustment. She had never been outside the United States and was unprepared for the tumult of central Africa, its noise during the day and its deep silence at night—deep silence unless you listened carefully and heard the feral rustle in the bush. Harry realized eventually that the daytime noise and nighttime silence were what May was prepared for, and they were not consoling. The capital was disheveled, a knot of streets with crowded concrete buildings and an open-air market, soldiers lounging nearby. The food stalls were filthy. Soon enough May chose to shop at the commissary like the other embassy wives. The French, Italians, and Spanish had small missions with ambassadors. There were half a dozen others supervised by a chargé d'affaires. The Soviet Union had a suspiciously large mission, including a technical office with a team of geologists said to be in search of uranium deposits. The embassy residences were located in a cul-de-sac, entry gained through an iron gate overseen by two soldiers in dusty white uniforms. No expatriates, because this was not the sort of country a man expatriated himself to, unless he was on the run. What would be the point?

On weekends Harry and May often drove into the countryside, miles and miles of stunted trees and shrubs. They looked for game but there was no game. Once they saw an elephant by the side of the road. May had never seen terrain as monotonous as this African terrain, few dwellings, few people. Late in the afternoon the security car that followed them wherever they went honked twice and pulled over. The command sergeant alighted and suggested, most politely, that they return now to the capital.

It is not good to travel at night. Bandits come out at night.

Dangerous bandits? May asked.

Not dangerous, the sergeant said. Unruly.

He means drunk, Harry said.

That is correct, the sergeant said. Drunk and unpredictable.

Their social life, such as it was, centered around the other foreign diplomats—though the Russians kept to themselves. Each weekend there was something festive, a cocktail party or dinner. Now and again one of the senior government officials, the vice president or the foreign minister, would have a reception. The country was at the far margins of significance and Harry questioned more than once why America bothered except to keep an eye on the Russian geologists. In time May involved herself in relief work, distributing food and medicines, opening a U.S.-sponsored clinic, donating books to the few schools, trying to be helpful. Meanwhile, Harry kept his eye on the Russians and cultivated sources inside the government. They did make side trips every few months, to Cape Town and Salisbury, Nairobi once, thriving cities with decent hotels and restaurants. And then, deep into their second year in Africa, May discovered she was pregnant. Her mood brightened and in some deep-felt sense her period of adjustment came to an end. She threw herself into her relief work, stopping only when she reached the seventh month of her pregnancy. She sent away for a bassinet and other newborn paraphernalia. She painted the spare second-floor bedroom that would now be the baby's. The doctor said that all was proceeding quite normally. He gave May a brilliantly colored lambswool sweater with a front pouch for the baby. It was knitted by the doctor's wife, who wished for a boy child. The doctor said, I hope you have the baby with us.

May shook her head, embarrassed.

You will go to the English hospital, then.

Yes. I'm sorry.

We deliver babies here every day, the doctor said in a low voice.

My husband insisted, May said.

The ambassador insisted?

Yes, May said. It is my first child. He worries about me.

I see, the doctor said. I wish you good fortune.

Thank you, May said.

It is a fine hospital, the English hospital. It is immaculate. They have equipment . . . He did not finish the sentence but said instead, Of course you will fly there.

Yes. It's not so far. Two hours, they told me.

Drink plenty of water on the airplane.

Thank you for all you have done, May said. You have been very kind. We hope you will look after the baby when we return.

I will be happy to do so, the doctor said. I feel I already know her.

How do you know it's a girl?

Things like that I know. I always have.

Instinct, May said with a smile.

Experience, the doctor said.

They thought they had left in good time, two weeks prior to the delivery date. But May went into labor on the airplane, with pain such as she had never experienced in her life, wave after wave. They took a cab from the airport because the ambulance was engaged. May was in and out of consciousness and half crazy with pain. She lay with her head in Harry's lap, remembering him handing money to the cabman and saying, Drive! Drive! The traffic was terrible at five in the afternoon. When they arrived at the English hospital she was taken at once to the emergency room, two doctors and a nurse assisting. They gave her something and she fell unconscious at once, knowing her baby was gone, had been gone for some little while. She came awake in a room with white walls and an overhead fan. She required a moment or two to locate herself, surprised at her shrunken belly. The air was warm, the windows thrown open to the African night. Harry was snoring in the bed next to hers. She wondered if he was dreaming of the Chopin girl and then thought not. His face was tight and his expression sober. A bat flew into the room and out again. She heard noises in the corridor and when she turned to look out the door the pain almost made her faint. Her forehead was clammy, slick with sweat. May reached for the call button but decided against it, and the pain subsided, drawing back like waves on a beach. She did not want to talk to anyone.

How could such a thing happen?

She had followed instructions to the letter.

She had done everything they told her to do.

Everything will be fine, they said.

In the corridor someone giggled, no doubt one of the young nurses. The doctors were brutes but the nurses were kind. Their voices rose in a British-accented lilt, asking if she was better, if the pain was manageable, giving her pills and a damp cloth to wash with. One of the nurses did May's hair, washing and combing and giving her a mirror to see the result. Day and night she sweated in the heat. The doctors wanted to discharge her after four days but she resisted, and Harry told them she would stay an extra day, two or three days if necessary. She could not bear returning to the embassy residence, "home" as Harry said, but no longer home to her. The doctors told her quite bluntly that she would have no more children. Why in God's name did you wait so long before coming to us? Sensible people did not wait so long. Americans especially were impatient. Unwilling to take precautions. Finally May told them to shut up. She found disease and death all around her, her days saturated with them. She did not know how she would resume her former life, one that now seemed to her pointless, almost a sham. She did not think it possible to resume her former life. She looked out the window at a flowering tree and burst into tears. Behind the tree somewhere were children roughhousing. Harry came into her room with a cup of steaming tea and she turned her face and waved him off. She did not want tea. She wanted to go home but was not strong enough to move. Harry put a cluster of flowers in the vase next to her bed and tiptoed out as he had tiptoed in. She called him back but her voice was too weak to carry. They had planned to call their daughter Josiana, the name of a character from one of Hugo's novels, the one about the smiling man. May said the name out loud and was tormented. Near dawn, the day's heat already beginning to build, May began to think more clearly. She had counted so on the baby, had thought of little else for months and months. The second-floor bedroom was fixed up with a crib and bright pictures on the wall, animal pictures, cats and cocker spaniel dogs, deer, raccoons, a Shetland pony. Harry's secretary had given her a charming recording of verse, *Jim Copp Tales* it was called. Helen Sanders had sent box after box from the baby department at Saks, duvets and pillowcases, stuffed animals, teething rings, and little hats, and from Tiffany a silver spoon and matching cup. Harry Sr. sent her a check for a thousand dollars with instructions to buy something frivolous, and that caused her to laugh because there were no frivolous things in central Africa; few enough essentials, nothing trifling—and then at a stall in the market downtown she found a beautiful ebony sculpture of a bird and bought that and put it on the mantel of the second-floor bedroom in the baby's line of sight; cost, fifty dollars. She would have it always, a souvenir of central Africa. May knew she was carrying a girl. The doctor guaranteed it.

Josiana's room was air-conditioned. Of course for the first month she would stay with her mother. Not too long, though; sooner rather than later she would sleep by herself in the crib, the better to learn self-sufficiency. May would not raise her baby as she herself had been raised, willy-nilly, and later, when Josiana could walk and speak and think for herself, she would be encouraged. She would be loved unconditionally. Every night May would read to her and soon enough she would begin to read by herself. And then they would be long gone from central Africa, no place for small children. She and Harry would protect her always. They would be a real family at last. Their daughter would be surrounded by love. That was the main thing. Now all that, everything, was lost. May thought of the baby's room as an installation in a museum, static, lifeless, and curated. And it would always be there, a snarl in her memory, and Harry's, too. She hoped this snarl would unite them but she was not certain of that. She was not certain of anything except the ache of loss.

May saw the future as a void, formless, without boundaries, without context, without—beauty. She could not see the next step. She was torn up inside, and that, too, was void. What had she done to deserve this? Nothing at all except to take an airplane ride on the wrong day. Perhaps to take an airplane in the first place instead of trusting the kindly doctor who was so disappointed that he would not assist at the birth of her child. He was insulted, scorned. May was embarrassed to tell him that they were trusting the English, the white people. As if he were a clumsy back-alley practitioner. But everyone said that was what she must do. Harry insisted on it and she had gone along without complaint. It was inconceivable to her that anything could go wrong. Such a thought had never entered her mind. She looked to the window, the sun streaming through; it hurt her eyes to look at it. The heat continued to build and she remembered her father's word for such days: scorchers. She heard noises in the corridor and then the door opened. She closed her eyes, pretending sleep, and whoever it was went away. May wanted to believe in a future with promise, she and Harry happy together in a pretty house somewhere, a home as opposed to a residence. She feared her own life was disappearing into Africa, and Africa never yielded. You accommodated yourself to it like an aerialist on a high wire, watchful every minute. The void was unforgiving. Yellow sunlight advanced in the room. She closed her eyes once again and tried to sleep. She was weary of enigma, realizing that she knew so little about them, what they believed in, their hopes for themselves beyond food on the table and a bed to sleep in and protection from hunger, disease, and gangs of armed men, usually drunk. Probably the people would want a grade school within walking distance and qualified teachers and books to go into the classroom and some sense of what was in store when the children could read and write. The rule of law would count for something. She had no idea what was required actually.

Sleep approached. The silence was strained, something sinister about it, a held breath. May turned toward the door and saw it was open a crack, and as she watched, the door eased shut. The window curtains closed and the room was abruptly dark. She did not wish to speak with anyone. She was exhausted but sleep would not come.

The room's heavy atmosphere closed in around her. The medicinal smell went away, replaced by something else. She felt crowded so she screwed her eyes shut and wondered what to think about. What would bring sleep? She willed herself not to think of Josiana or anything to do with Josiana but she found Victor Hugo in her thoughts, his huge heart and vast knowledge of the good and the corrupt. Maybe when they left this place she would give her Hugo books to the school, if there was one by then. Hugo had a fine eye for corruption, perhaps too fine for an African child. Parisian corruption was on a special scale. It required a highly developed civilization and a government to go with it, that is to say complement it. What need for a Kalashnikov when you had a learned *notaire*? May wondered if Victor Hugo had ever seen Africa. Surely not, unless it was North Africa, another milieu altogether. Hugo would not have trouble sleeping. He rarely slept. Instead, he wrote. She remembered then that Hugo was born well after the French Revolution. Her forehead was damp. The smell of the bush was in the room, but how could that be? She felt a slight breeze. She was covered by a single counterpane but felt its weight. She forgot about Hugo.

She said, Go away.

I must sleep.

Sleep crept closer, then backed off. She heard the door open and close. She believed she was hallucinating and tried to put the hallucination to good use. She was riding horseback in the desert when she came upon an ancient house, a house centuries old, uninhabited. She drew near but had difficulty controlling the horse. At the horizon the sun began to set and then above the sun an enormous blue moon. The desert was flooded with light as her horse moved off at a trot. She was having trouble with the saddle, and then she floated free, wrapped in the counterpane. Her body pain seemed to ease. Sleep came at last, accompanied by a kiss on the forehead. Harry.

May told Harry she was self-conscious every day. She said she didn't feel she counted for anything, and she wondered if that was one reason she had counted so on their child, perhaps in the way a composer counted on producing a beautiful piece of music, unique in all the world. Once born, the music would find its own way, the composer a bystander. That was how she thought of their little girl and was consoled, partly. She said, I had a child and I lost her. I lost her because we stepped on an airplane a day later than we should have. And my life changed forever. Your life, too. And when I was told I would never again have a child, that the music had stopped for good, I realized I was living in a shadow world where I am a visitor and not a very welcome visitor, anyhow no more than a visitor. I am that anonymous woman you see in the railway station looking at the arrival and departure signboard. You look away. Minutes later you look up again and see that I have not moved. You look away once more, as you have no wish to become involved with one who is so plainly distressed. And when next you take a sidelong glance I am gone, God knows where. Your first thought is relief. Your second is chagrin because your natural curiosity will never be satisfied. I am gone, vanished. Often arrival and departure are different words for the same thing. And what I am wondering is whether it was wise for me to leave the Northeast Kingdom, dreadful as my life was with my family. Perhaps some people are meant to remain where they were born. Not an American thought, I agree. I wonder sometimes if I do not have the mentality of a European peasant, fearful of the outside world, suspicious of it, frightened of it, knowing that it is not my place. I am not an ambitious person. I do not wish to be a senator or a film star or a corporate executive. I wish to live at peace, find my own life. Read my books. Did I tell you I bought a camera? I intend to photograph the things that are in my vision, the life around me, the surroundings that appear to me so alien.

Give it time, darling.

I have. I will.

You didn't tell me about the camera.

I did. You weren't listening.

When was that?

Months and months ago. When I was pregnant.

I'll be damned. I don't remember at all.

It was late at night.

Maybe I was asleep.

Maybe, she said with the beginning of a smile.

I'm sorry about all this, Harry said.

Then May said, Do you know who I met the other day? A girl reporter.

Harry said, Which one?

She worked for one of the American magazines. She was the first female reporter I've met, not that she had any interest in talking to me. She was all over the place, interviewing people, getting their names and ages, listening to their complaints. She was tireless. She never shut up. And after she'd loaded up her notebooks with the complaints she went to the village chief and his deputy and your man Axel and demanded that something be done. Where was the food that was promised? What about the medicines? She was in their faces writing down what they said. Their excuses. She kept saying that she had a "hell of a piece, just a hell of a piece" and that she would try to put things right. She was very aggressive. She was a dervish, that one.

I know the one you mean. She's a pain in the ass. She thinks everything should have been done yesterday if not the day before. She's smart, by the way. Watch yourself when you're with her.

Are there many of them?

More all the time, Harry said. Thank God we don't attract much attention here.

She was remarkable, May said.

On the other hand, she has been helpful to me once or twice.

What do you mean?

Publicity at the right time can grab the attention of the State Department like no cable ever does.

She never gave up. She'd ask a question and refuse to shut up until she got the answer. I can't say I cared for her much. She walked in a kind of strut. She was like an actress. Your eye went to her.

She takes some getting used to, Harry said. Her name is Zoe.

I suppose she's younger than me by ten years. Not an especially attractive girl. She wore a bush hat and a safari jacket. Rolex wristwatch, by the way. Sandals. She'd painted her toenails pink. But we were so different. She loved what she was doing. Loved it to death, Zoe. She fit right in.

That's their specialty, Harry said. Fitting in. They want you to forget they're writing everything down.

I don't fit in, May said. I am unmoored except to you. Is that a burden? I imagine it is. My efforts here are provisional. Cosmetic, I would say. Validated only in the photo opportunity at the orphanage or clinic. Ambassador's Wife Dedicates Child Care Center. And that's me, wearing a pair of sensible shoes and a smart American smile, a mannequin in a shop window.

Oh, come on, Harry said.

You try it sometime.

I do it all the time. It's part of the damned job.

You'd be better off with Zoe, with her bush hat and her Rolex. Did you find her attractive?

May, he said. Don't say that.

Thing is, May said, I'm not certain we belong here at all. I'm not certain that the people wouldn't get along better if we were gone. They got along fine without us for hundreds, thousands of years.

They did not get along fine without us.

They're still here, aren't they?

What we do here is valuable. We should be doing more, not less.

I wish I could be convinced. I'm not.

They depend on us, Harry said.

That's another problem. Dependency.

You have a point there, Harry said.

May did not reply to that.

We have a year to go, Harry said. Can you bear it?

I can bear it.

Later this month we'll go somewhere.

I'd like that, she said.

You choose, he said.

All right, she said.

You can forget about the photo opportunities. I'll put a stop to them.

Thank you, she said.

Christ, he said. This place. It's so—

Strenuous, she said.

Strenuous, Harry agreed.

Thank God we're together, May said.

As spring turned to summer, May's mood improved and once again she pitched in, organizing relief efforts, volunteering at clinics and schools and the other places where there was need of the ambassador's wife. She tried to set herself apart, recognizing the limits of compassion. Her new attitude was successful at first, then less so. She did not thrive. She grieved for the victims, and there were so many of them, children especially, most of them famished, some of them suffering from diseases too exotic to treat with any confidence that the medicines would actually work. She was astonished at the forbearance of the mothers. One afternoon a child died in May's arms and she did not know it until a pair of ragged hands tore the child from her and disappeared into the bush, leaving May aghast. How could she not have realized that the child was gone? But the very young children were so small, scarcely larger than dolls, with a doll's eyes and a doll's rubbery skin and unnatural hair. The rose-bud smile was missing. They were passive like dolls and often when they opened their mouths no sound came forth. The act of speech was too much for them, and each day word came of a fresh disease that turned healthy men into skeletons. Nothing had prepared May for this experience—and then she remembered the doctor at the

English hospital asking if she wished to see her stillborn child, and she recoiled in despair and turned her face to the wall. Words failed her. If you asked her, as Zoe did one day, if she felt she was effective in her rescue work, she would have replied, Yes, within limits. Within the bounds of what she was called upon to do. Yes, in the sense of an amateur mariner successfully navigating a rowboat on the open ocean. Within the boundaries of time and tide and the weather and God's will and her own morale. She asked the reporter Zoe, Is it true that conditions are much worse in Ivory Coast? She opened her mouth to say more but her escort Axel, the embassy's aid administrator, observing her distress and finding trouble ahead, cut short the interview and hustled her into the embassy van. One more clinic to visit.

Home at last, May stepped through the front door and into the foyer. She heard the servants rattling plates in the kitchen. Through the porch door she saw Harry having a drink beside the pool. The water was a soft turquoise. The day's heat was beginning to lift. Harry wore a planter's hat, its wide brim casting his face in shadow. His skin was brown from the sun. May stood a moment watching him. Harry had an open book in his lap but he was not reading. He was staring into space and smiling, preoccupied as he so often was. May was exhausted, and when she looked at the pool she thought it could have been a suburban pool anywhere in America, a low board at the far end, wooden tables and chairs here and there, a portable bar under the awning. Then she noticed a copy of *Newsweek* at Harry's feet. May had a sudden desire for a swim and went at once to their bedroom and pulled on her bikini. Downstairs, she ran through the door and dived over Harry's feet into the pool. She swam one lap and another and gave it up after four laps. She hung on the side of the pool and Harry handed her a gin and tonic, the lime bright in the failing sun.

Harry said, You ought to check out the water before you dive in. They found a cobra in there the other day. Little one.

She said, I. Don't. Give. A. Shit. About. Cobras.

That's what I told Gamal. Let the cobras flourish, I said.

We had timber rattlers in Vermont. Seldom seen, but once seen, never forgotten. Nasty brutes.

They say the same's true with cobras.

Do they now? May said.

They surely do, Harry said.

She dipped her head underwater and remained there for a count of fifty while she rubbed her forehead and cheeks, feeling her sweat dissolve. The dead child at the clinic was still on her mind. When she rose from the water, shaking her head like a sea lion, she felt better. The gin helped, too, and she took another swallow, the glass cool and slippery in her hand. She stared at Harry's feet and legs, brown and taut as a lifeguard's. Under the brim of his planter's hat she saw curly locks of hair, hints of gray here and there. He looked ten years younger than his age, a curiosity because he rarely exercised. And then he moved and she saw the scars on the soles of his feet, ugly ridges with suture marks still visible. She gave his foot a soft squeeze. She asked him if he wanted another gin and tonic; she certainly did. Don't bother, she said. I'll get them.

May said from the bar, Did you have a good day?

He said, The usual.

I wish I could say the same.

What happened?

A baby died in my arms. I didn't even know it.

My God, Harry said.

Little thing. She'd fit into a shoebox. Her heart just stopped.

My goodness, Harry said. His memory stirred, conjuring the dead woman in Village Number Five. He opened his mouth to say something, then decided not to.

I hated it, she said.

You don't have to do that business anymore. I told you that.

You know something? I think I won't.

Good idea, he said. Bravo.

Do you think this place is cursed?

Harry shook his head, giving no direct answer, unless the head-shake was a direct answer.

A week later, he left for an ambassadors' meeting in Dakar. The envoys were to appreciate the situation in Africa for the benefit of an assistant secretary of state. On Friday evening May went alone to the French embassy, a reception for the traveling foreign minister, an ocean of champagne and platters of foie gras with toast points, two wheels of Brie and wedges of bleu and Camembert and, so incongruous she had to look twice, a plate of Ritz crackers. She had been introduced to the Belgian chargé d'affaires, newly arrived and finding his way around. Andres spoke an elegant French-accented English acquired, it turned out, at the University of Colorado. So they reminisced about Colorado, hiking and skiing, fishing in the mountain streams, and Denver restaurants, where the beef was sublime. Andres had been an exchange student and May said she was, too, in a way. She described the Northeast Kingdom, which, oddly, he had heard about, though he seemed to think it resembled Switzerland. Not Switzerland, she said, more like East Prussia with the Masurian Lakes and tiny hills and forests of fir and strict codes of conduct—well, maybe not strict codes of conduct; the Northeast Kingdom was loose so far as conduct was concerned. She had never before thought to compare Vermont with Prussia but Andres had laughed and laughed. They did not move far from the buffet table except to fetch shrimp when it came by. This was Andres's first embassy reception but he seemed to know many of the guests, who invariably greeted him as Monsieur le Comte, and when May asked him about it he said yes, he was a count, but it didn't mean anything and he didn't care about it. That was one of the things he liked about America, none of that titled rubbish. He said this was his first posting abroad, not very promising but you had to start somewhere. The Belgians had been terrible in Africa—not that anyone in Belgium cared. Probably the best thing he could do was stay out of sight, become the invisible Belgian. Really, he said, we Belgians were criminals. Criminal behavior, including the king. The king most of all, fooking war criminal. Kings should be outlawed, imprisoned, or sent into exile. May was charmed by him, this Count Andres, his wit and ready smile and denunciation of his own government. May had but scant knowledge of the Belgian record in Africa. Andres was light on his feet, graceful as a dancer, and he surely did like champagne. She had the idea that, for Andres, life was not to be taken seriously. Central Africa did not seem a good choice for him.

She said, Do you like to ride horses?

Of course I like to ride horses. I am riding horses my entire life.

Find two and we can go riding.

There are no horses here. I checked.

They say the president has a stable.

I will present my credentials next week and ask him.

Good, she said. I understand he wants an air force. He claims he has enemies in the north and they can only be subdued from the air. That's what I hear.

I will promise him a jet fighter if he will let us ride his horses.

That should do it, May said. Throw in a couple of battle tanks.

Washington has probably already given him his air force and the battle tanks, too. I am sure I have been outmaneuvered.

Try anyway, May said.

Rest assured, Andres replied.

He asked her about Harry, how he got on with the government. Were they cooperative? May's answer was noncommittal, though she knew Harry was at odds with the Pentagon over the air force issue — grotesque, as Harry said. She was only having fun with the horses but thought now that she had gone too far. In the brittle silence Andres asked her what she did in her spare time. She replied that she did relief work. She visited medical clinics and schools. Once she dedicated a village well. Andres seemed to sense that she was uncomfortable talking about herself, so he turned the conversation back to horses, where they might be ridden and when. Finally, as the reception was breaking up, he asked if she would like a nightcap at his villa, only a few steps from her own. May said yes, that would be nice, a glass of wine at the end of the evening. Andres said they should take his car, and she agreed. She had dismissed her driver knowing that someone would offer her a lift home. They all lived within six blocks of each other.

Andres drove a green Karmann Ghia convertible, the bucket seats so confined their shoulders touched. He drove at speed but knew what he was doing behind a wheel. She was not alarmed as she often was with Harry, who had no love of automobiles and drove slowly and without enthusiasm. He often took his eyes off the road. Harry looked on cars as an opportunity for sustained conversation, no telephones or meetings to break things up. Andres hardly spoke except to comment on the softness of the night, the many stars overhead, and the aroma of lilacs. Were they lilacs? Jasmine, May replied. They were two minutes from Andres's villa, a modest bungalow hidden behind an enormous hedge. He parked in the carport and they entered the kitchen. He opened the door to the pool area and indicated chairs gathered around a table. He said he would drink beer and May said she would have beer, too. Belgian beer, Andres said, the best thing about his country. May took a seat, stretched out her legs, and looked at the stars, searching for the Southern Cross and not finding it. Things were not in their places in Africa. Untamed Africa had its own rules, ill-defined boundaries with chaos on both sides. She was drowsy, thinking that Andres brought a measure of civilization to the night. May kicked off her shoes and rubbed her toes on the flagstones, still warm from the day's heat. Suddenly a bottle of beer was at her elbow and Andres was stepping into the pool, his own bottle held aloft in his right hand, Mr. Statue of Liberty. A moment later his head appeared at the edge of the pool, his hair slick as honey. He said, If you're looking for the Southern Cross, it's over your right shoulder. She looked up and stared at the Southern Cross. Andres described the prophetic properties of the Southern Cross, something he claimed to have heard firsthand from an astronomer. He turned his back on her then, allowing his legs to float. Andres was well muscled, the long muscles of a swimmer. He had not bothered to put on swim trunks. She reached out and touched his honeyed head, not slick but coarse. He wore his hair long, curling over his ears. Andres did not look or talk like any diplomat she had met. His behavior did not fit the norm either. Yet here she was at one o'clock in the morning having a party-after-the-party, so to speak.

She wondered what it would be like if she went away with him, only a few days. But where could they go? There was no place to go in this wretched landlocked country, not a hotel, not even a rest house. She put her hands on his wet shoulders. He appeared not to notice. Andres said, I have always wanted to live in Africa, not forever but for a time, see it up close, try to fathom it. Of course that was an impossible objective. You didn't fathom Africa, you got out of its way. You did not in any case interfere. He had always been a trekker, traveling in much of Asia Minor, once to Peru. Did you know there was an opera house in Iquitos, in the back of beyond up the Amazon, an opera house as handsome as any opera house anywhere? Trekking, you moved at your own pace and when you felt like it you stopped. If the country was banal or uninteresting you hopped a train until you found something agreeable. That's why I joined our foreign service, he said. Though that was probably a mistake. A failure of foresight. Andres laughed then, genuine mirth. I don't think I like diplomatic work, always saying what you mean in a tone of voice that casts doubt. It's a gentleman's job certainly, and that's what's wrong with it. The fact is, there isn't much to do here, this playground for idle hands. The reason I'm here is that Belgians have some mining interests in the east. I'm supposed to look out for their interests, let them know if the Russians are poaching. We have concessions and they must be kept up-to-date. Now that I think about it, my diplomatic work has nothing to do with being a gentleman. More like a fly on the wall. A fly with a fax machine.

I think I'll go back to trekking. Want to come along?

God, no, she said.

You'd like it. We could go away on horseback.

Not on your life, she said, wondering what there was about the men she knew that led them far afield, into regions scarcely inhabited, and even when inhabited, a wilderness. She thought this Andres a lonely soul and said so.

I don't mind my own company, if that's what you mean. I can look after myself, always have done. I have money of my own. I can do what I want. I am unleashed. Also, I am irresponsible. Do you see the irresponsibility, May? You have only to look. I do not hide my irresponsibility. What would be the point?

She said, I didn't know irresponsibility had a look.

He said, The eyes are a giveaway.

She said, They are? What exactly do they give away?

He said, They give away the future. I sense you are irresponsible too, except you don't like to admit it. There's nothing wrong with it—it's only a way of life like any other. The trick is not to let irresponsibility slide into the unreliable. Unreliable is no good. Unreliable brings you grief along with excitement. Andres went on to elaborate the irresponsibility-as-a-way-of-life-like-any-other but May wasn't listening. She had gone off into one of her many dream worlds, this one voluptuous, a dream world of the moment. A dream world such as Renoir might render it. Andres's chatter did not interest her enough to go on listening to it, though she did like his voice, somewhat hoarse, French-inflected, seductive. By then she had removed her clothes and eased herself into the pool's tepid water. The vast African night enclosed them, a velvet cap, the stars and half-moon giving them as much light as they needed. She felt she had a continent-sized oasis to do with as she pleased. The night shadows on their bodies were erotic. Andres said something funny and she laughed. They stood in the water, kissing in a pool of starlight, and then drifted away toward the deep end, submerging themselves for a long minute. May closed her eyes, they were both so slippery, slippery as she imagined eels were slippery. She stayed underwater until she thought her lungs would burst and then remained a while longer, rising finally to find a handhold at the edge of the pool, submerging once more and remaining. He never let go of her hand until they surfaced for keeps and by then the present moment was what she had, all else of no account, out of sight and unremembered. The force of the moment carried her away.

They were together later in his study, and later still in his bedroom off the study, until morning came and they found the pool once more, the sun rising as red as an apple. They ate breakfast together, both of them ravenous. They returned to the study and his bedroom off the study and then he drove her home. He did not linger. May fell into a dreamless sleep that lasted until late afternoon. She awoke in a state of confused lethargy, the residue of desire. She lay there awhile in a state of incoherence until she heard the front door slam, Harry downstairs, Harry returned from wherever he had been. May left her bed for the shower, as hot as she could stand it, and the hours with Andres were with her still, as was the residue of desire and a thin mist of forgetfulness.

Are you here? Harry called.

I'm here, she said.

Come down, he said. We'll have a swim.

Right away, she said. How was your trip?

Uneventful, Harry said.

Nine

WITHOUT REGRETS HARRY and May left Africa for two years in Washington, the Africa desk. They rented a row house in Georgetown and a cottage out near Middleburg where May could ride. Life was pleasant enough in Washington, the restaurants good and the company congenial. Nearly every weekend they went to Middleburg. May later described the tour as routine, which it certainly was. Harry was bored and eager to return abroad, any country would do. In good time, and thanks, he believed, to Basso Earle, Harry was sent as ambassador to the eastern Mediterranean, to an island nation that had horses galore and an atmosphere of violence. Harry earned a commendation from the Department. All in all, a successful adventure for Harry, and for May too, who liked the horses and beaches. They returned to Washington for three years and in due course arrived in chilly Oslo. Wherever they went May looked for a retirement villa, somewhere quiet, a place where they could unpack for good. A friend suggested North Carolina, perhaps the Outer Banks or the golf country around Asheville. Harry said he was a Northerner and did not care for the comforts of the South. Someone else suggested Seattle, the city of the future. Providence, Rhode Island, earned a mention, as did Burlington, Vermont, at which both Harry and May laughed.

Harry was unenthusiastic about settling in America, so somehow they never got to North Carolina or the rainy state of Washington but toured again and again in Tuscany and Provence, the Low Countries, the Frisian Islands, Scandinavia, and the south of Spain. Once to Sardinia, twice to Tunisia. May thought they ought to take a look at Cambodia, but Harry said alas no, not Southeast Asia if she didn't mind. He added, Cambodia did not have amenities. Instead, it had an appalling history of violence. To which May replied, So did the Northeast Kingdom. She did see possibilities wherever they went. Wasn't Lucca lovely? Ronda was a jewel. But the possibilities never quite added up. What May wanted was to be free of embassies, the bodyguards and the protocol, a fresh language for each tour; and that was Harry's life, the one he had chosen long before he met her. To Harry, the embassy was a world of its own, its own face, its own secrets, unique complexities, unique personalities. May wanted to be rid of traveling because she had come from a long line of people who stayed put. She wanted to stay put and she didn't much care where, except she did prefer America. She asked Harry once if he wanted to return to Connecticut, near his family's house in the hills around Salisbury. Oh, no, he said, I don't know anyone there, not anymore. I like to stay in touch. A man is not in touch in Connecticut. I am not a gardener. I do not play golf. What would I do in Connecticut? To which she replied that if he rode horses he would find Connecticut congenial, a paradise. And if not Connecticut or Tuscany or Andalusia or Provence or Sardinia, well then, where? We'll know it when we see it, Harry replied. That answer did not satisfy May and she went away in a snit. The truth was, Harry refused to think about retirement and May could think of little else. She had come to think of the foreign service as a bespoke penitentiary.

Many in their community said that May was filled with grievance and self-pity, a most unsuitable, perhaps unstable personality for the work she was called upon to do and the places she was obliged to do it in. Entertaining was a chore, the conversation always swirling around government and politics. She had a fixed idea that Harry could not forget the war, as she could not forget the English hospital. Wasn't it tragic to see a woman so out of her depth, so unsettled in her own skin? Yes, she had lost a child owing to a simple mistake. No one would wish that on any woman. But when her friends suggested adoption, May shook her head and refused to discuss the matter except to say, I wanted my own child, not someone else's child. The more exotic procedures, just then coming into practice, did not appeal to her either. She believed that fate had taken a hand and voguish procedures would not stay the hand. And yes, the diplomatic life was strenuous and not to everyone's taste, but wasn't the essence of service an appreciation of complexity and compromise and simply soldiering on? What did Harry see in her? She was a pretty woman, yes, but pretty women were a dime a carload and this one was eternally discontented whereas Harry was cheerful, an optimist, good-humored and determined to make the best of things. He was very good with staff. A superior diplomat in all respects, the country was lucky to have him. Wasn't that the point after all? The foreign service rewarded savoir faire, and savoir faire was not May's long suit. One caveat: No one ever criticized May to Harry's face. If asked, he would have said he loved her from the moment he saw her. They were destined to be together forever. How were such things explained? Answer: They were not explained, at least not explained to anyone's satisfaction. Still, May was kind. She was courageous in her own way and resourceful. She felt things deeply, hence her moments of near-crippling melancholy. That she had survived her harsh Vermont family was a miracle. What others saw as restiveness and indecision, Harry saw as thoughtfulness and grit. Not that the grit did not, from time to time, turn to putty. Not that she wasn't, now and again, overwhelmed. A life inside the government had its own special demands. A foreign service officer felt he owed best efforts at all times. He took an oath to defend the Constitution of the United States no less than the president. Harry believed that May was included in the oath, and if the situation were reversed, the same would apply. May said to him once that she was living half a life, and when he asked her what that meant she said she wasn't sure, only that what she said was true. Then she thought a moment and said that half her life was missing, gone away somewhere out of reach. She was driven to take refuge beyond the government's reach. Twice she left him, twice she returned.

I'll always come back to you, she said.

Who else would I come back to?

Then one time she didn't. Harry was alone in his office on a Sunday afternoon drafting a cable to Washington, a tiresome economic matter. He wrote two drafts, neither one satisfactory, and then gave it up, deciding instead to write his father a birthday note. The old man had lived to great age, long a widower. Harry wrote a letter describing conditions in the Balkans, his present post, an impossible post because he was dealing with impossible people whose sense of grievance was seemingly limitless. He proposed a Christmas visit, perhaps a Sunday lunch to go with it, a reminder of the old days. When the telephone rang he almost didn't answer it, then in a fit of irritation he picked up the receiver and said only, Where are you? It had to be May. But the voice, hesitant, almost timid, most un-Balkan, belonged to an inspector of police.

May was dead in her car at the bottom of a ravine only one hour distant from the capital. The guardrail had snapped like a matchstick. Police at the scene speculated that she had suffered some sort of seizure at the wheel, perhaps a cardiac event. There were no skid marks. The weather was clear. There were no witnesses to the accident, at least no one had come forward. She might have been in the ravine for a day, possibly longer. The area was desolate but the road was in good repair, perhaps madame was speeding . . . Wait one moment, Inspector, Harry said and put the phone down. He sat quietly a moment staring at the telephone. He was trying to understand fully what he had been told. Yes, he said finally, go on. Tell me what you know.

We are most sorry, Excellency, the official said. Was your wife in good health? Harry did not reply, wondering if this was a case of mistaken identity. The car was a common model, but it did have diplomatic license plates. So it was not a case of mistaken identity. He was so shaken he did not hang up the telephone but sat in a lethargic state until he heard another voice, heavily accented, gruff, explaining something about the fine condition of the road and the rescue efforts. Rescue of the car. May would be taken to the hospital in the capital. What sort of funeral arrangements would the ambassador prefer? Of course an autopsy would be undertaken at once, that was the law. And then Harry said an automatic goodbye, and still he did not move from his chair, becalmed like a vessel at sea, the only sound the creaking of rigging, in actual fact the tick-tick of his desk clock. He reread every word of his longhand letter to his father and then folded it twice and threw it into the burn bag. His eyes filled with tears. His strength drained away, leaving him limp as string. He was breathing heavily. How had this come to pass? The telephone receiver was still in his hand. He stared at it, willing it to ring once more with different news. A ghastly mistake. He stared at May's photograph, imagining her little red Honda crumpled like discarded tissue paper. He had not asked where she was precisely and the official had not said. Surely it was the mountain road heading south, a treacherous passage under the best of conditions. The official said something about returning to the capital with "the remains." The ambassador thought to hang up the telephone and then stood and stepped to the window that gave out onto the square, the one with the iron sundial next to the general on horseback. The square was filled with people, couples, families with children. There were fewer of them than usual on a Sunday. When he heard a knock on the door he said, Go away, probably not loud enough to be heard. He looked at the cable on his computer screen and could not remember its subject. He was appreciating a situation, no doubt important because Sunday afternoons were reserved for May.

An hour later, the ambassador left his office and took the back stairs to the embassy lobby. He said good evening to the marine guard, who looked up from his paperback, startled. Will you take the car, sir? Harry shook his head and walked out into the night, chilly, with a stiff wind. The square was almost deserted now. He walked slowly, leaning on his cane, indifferent to his surroundings, one more foreign boulevard in a lifetime of foreign boulevards. A taxi passed slowly by and he wondered if he should take it, then thought no. The walk would do him—not good, but something else. He would have time to think. Alone, he would not be obliged to speak. He reached with his right hand to scratch his ankle and the image of the boy enemy came to his mind, remaining a moment before he vanished, an occurrence so common he did not dwell on it. The wind picked up and he drew a scarf from his overcoat pocket and wrapped it around his neck. Hard little snowflakes brushed his skin. One more miserable night in the Balkans. She was gone, that was the fact of it. There were arrangements to be made. They had never discussed arrangements, where the funerals were to be held and where the bodies were to be buried. They had agreed on cremation. Harry tried to think where they had been happiest. Not Africa. Perhaps the Mediterranean island. Norway had been all right. They had been very happy in anonymous Colorado. Harry put the arrangements problem out of his head. She drove too fast. She had always driven too fast. She rode horses at a gallop and drove the same way. That was what they learned in Vermont, exceed the speed limit and dare the Highway Patrol to catch them. In Vermont drinking and driving was a way of life. Harry pulled his hat down around his ears because the wind had picked up again. He was alone on the sidewalk listening to the click-click of his whalebone cane, May's gift. He was almost home. To his right was the residence of the French ambassador, a former admiral with an admiral's bearing and an admiral's voice; he gave the impression he was forever standing on a bridge ordering flank speed. The house was brightly lit, a Sunday soiree. Harry paused to hear the sound of violins, and behind

215

the violins laughter and the buzz of conversation. Perhaps he was imagining that. His own residence was just ahead, the porch light on, the house itself in darkness. He had given the servants the night off because he expected May and planned to go out somewhere to dinner after the reception at the French embassy. Harry's hands were numb when he reached the front door. He walked through the house turning on lights. His study was chilly but he noticed that Ramon had laid wood for a fire. He opened the liquor cabinet and rummaged among the bottles for the scotch and made himself a drink. His hands were steady. He did not feel steady but his hands were all right. His feet hurt. He was cold all the way through. Ramon had left a plate of lemon peels and a dish of peanuts.

Harry poured a large whiskey and stepped to the fire. He lit the kindling but it failed to catch. When he lit it again he managed to coax a weak flicker of flame. He sat in the big chair next to the fire and waited. He wondered how he would regain his balance, his thoughts turning every which way, now thinking of May in her Honda, now of the unfinished cable on his computer at the embassy. He tried again to remember the subject but could not. These thoughts were as slippery and fleeting as fish. He stared into the smoldering fire and noticed on the mantel a stack of yesterday's mail. He leafed through it, half a dozen invitations and a postcard in an unfamiliar hand. It took him a moment to decipher the signature, that of his aid administrator in Africa years before, Axel Brown. He had not heard from Axel in years. Axel had resigned from the foreign service and gone to work for a foundation, and now he was writing to say that he and Zoe Aaron were returning to the United States after so many years in Africa, inside work at the head office in Washington. They hated to leave Africa but their twin daughters were enrolled at Georgetown and they wanted to be nearby. Besides, it was time. The postcard was signed by Axel, "Most fondly," and a P.S.: "Give love to May." Harry tapped the postcard on his fingernail, remembering Axel and Zoe, Axel so quiet, Zoe a dynamo, more energy than was good for her. He and Zoe had had a brief fling—well, any fling was by definition brief—those many years ago, nothing serious. However, he had not forgotten and now the memory returned in fragments. It was an incoherent memory. Incomplete would be the better word. It had happened at one of the aid stations deep in the interior. Soon after, Zoe and Axel were together. And now they had twin daughters in college. Harry remembered Zoe coming to him for advice. She was weary of magazine reporting and wanted a change, something more—active. Would the foreign service be a good idea? It would not, Harry told her with a smile. Diplomacy is not your long suit, Zoe. He suggested instead one of the relief agencies or a foundation; there were many good ones.

I love Africa, Zoe said.

I know, Harry replied.

I could stay here forever.

I know that, too. Good luck to you, kiddo.

Things are alive in Africa, Zoe said. So much to be done.

And all the time in the world to do it, Harry said.

Harry took off his shoes and massaged his feet. His toes were like ice. Those three years in Africa. How had they managed it? Zoe and Axel slipped from his mind and when he took a swallow of scotch he thought of his father. He would have to tell his father about May, find a gentle way to do it. The old man was very old, an antique, but in good health and of sound mind except for occasional blank episodes, when he drew a curtain and went away. His mother had died years back. Harry and his father were the last of their line. He would have to go to Connecticut to see his father. He had not been back in almost a year, and it was time.

Harry sat listening to the clock tick and then caught sight of a photograph of May on the mantel. They were having lunch at the harbor restaurant in—and at that moment he could not remember where it was, only that the surroundings were charming. It was April, the day balmy, ships moving idly at anchor. The harbor was very old, dating to antiquity. She wore dark glasses and smiled for the camera. He remembered the meal, bouillabaisse and sorbet to finish, coffee medium sweet. They were reminiscing about Africa, something they did not often do. We were lucky to get out alive, she said. Remember the cobra in the swimming pool? Harry was looking at her photograph and trying to remember her voice, its timbre and rhythm. He was searching for it now in his study, as quiet as a desert, but nothing came to him. Her words returned but not her voice. He was unnerved at this thought and pushed the button on the CD player and waited for whatever was there — as it turned out, Brahms's *German Requiem*. He sipped whiskey and devoted himself to Brahms, thinking now of the German dead in two wars. Brahms composed the *Requiem* after the death of his mother; the world wars were many years distant. May had always wanted a posting in Berlin, but he told her that Berlin was not in the cards. He had no special expertise, not even the language. Germany required total commitment, like a marriage or a war. Berlin was filled with ghosts; turn any corner and you were face to face with the Third Reich. Germans frightened people, themselves most of all. But they were also hospitable and fiercely intelligent. Their diplomatic corps was first rate, good at staying out of trouble, good at lengthy explanations of complex moral questions, very good at defending their commercial interests. Their security services were exceptional inside their country, thin on the ground elsewhere. Their diplomats had surprising latitude, but of course they did not have a Pentagon to worry about. Harry closed his eyes and thought about Germany and its immense capacity for delusion. Perhaps that was the source of inspiration for its composers. The sublime melodies of Brahms and Mahler could come only from some German-speaking magic garden of the soul. Whatever the source of German romanticism, Harry wished he had seen it up close, listened to it in conversation, negotiated with it. American delusions, mostly of grandeur, often of the evangelical variety, the Good News of democracy, also frightened people. Americans lacked modesty. Americans did not set a good example. Americans cast a long shadow of self-righteousness, and if you didn't like it they sent the Sixth Fleet and a squadron of warplanes. That was what the ambassador's years of diplomacy had taught him. The shrill ring of the telephone startled him but he did not move from his chair and eventually the caller gave up.

Go away, he said aloud.

I do not wish to be disturbed.

What on earth had caused him to think about Germany?

Harry rose heavily from his chair and limped to the cabinet and poured another whiskey, this one not so large. He paused to listen to the third movement of *Ein deutsches Requiem*, thinking that he would have been a good choice for embassy Berlin. He had a high appreciation of forgetfulness, a constant struggle. Germany was only trying to stay calm and out of everyone's way and be left alone to build a durable republic and an export economy, a mighty engine that would prevent another Weimar or Third Reich, and that was Harry's preference, too, had anyone asked, and no one did. There were temptations on every continent. Still, the less meddling the better, one more lesson learned from his own war.

He would have liked Moscow, too, or Paris. Naturally they were not in the cards either, those embassies being reserved for specialists or friends of the president or retired politicians or industrialists, people who thought they were owed a favor. He was certain that May would have liked Berlin and Paris. There were horses aplenty in both capitals and good places to ride them. She would have hated Moscow, the constant suspicion, the bad food, the trials of ordinary life.

Harry pulled his chair closer to the smoldering fire, sparks here and there but no flames. He hunched his shoulders and listened to the sizzle that meant the wood was soft, wet with rain. He heard the wind against the windows. There was nothing more dispiriting than a cold fireplace. He pulled his jacket around him. No doubt he should go to bed. There would be much to do in the morning, telephone calls, messages from the Department. As if on signal the phone rang once more and Harry did not move, counting ten rings before it stopped. Probably he should have a few people in tomorrow night or the next night. He was not especially close with the diplomatic community, unlike other places he had served where casual dinners were frequent. Perhaps something for the embassy staff, all of it. Harry looked again at the fire, a wan affair providing neither heat nor light. The room was cold. But he was not ready for the climb upstairs, the rooms dark, the bedroom empty. He sat alone in the cold a while longer, wondering to himself why he had gone on so long about Berlin. Surely it was listening to the *Requiem*. Brahms had written it for his dead mother but Harry could not listen to it without thinking of Germans and their wars, in the way that listening to Cole Porter made him think of young American expatriates dancing on tabletops at two in the morning. He had never heard of an American diplomat retiring to Germany. He had friends who had served in embassy Berlin and had loved it, but when retirement came they went to Tuscany or back to the row house in Georgetown, or to Maine or Florida. He did not want to return to America, that was for sure. He would take his final tour at the Department in Washington and then say bye-bye. He had no idea where he could live in America, certainly not Connecticut or Washington or any of its suburbs. He had sent some money to Clinton's campaign but not enough to buy a retirement embassy—Jamaica, say, or Malta. Not even Burundi. He was too old for Burundi. Burundi required stamina and a high tolerance for disorder and an idealism that had left him long ago, and he had never been generously endowed anyhow. Idealism was an acquired quality, one dependent on circumstance, the facts of the matter, meaning successful outcomes. Harry thought of diplomacy as Sisyphus thought of his wretched stone. May had objected to that, arguing that nothing was more idealistic than the pursuit of a doomed objective. They had argued about it for most of an evening, the evening ending in peals of laughter and Harry promising to write a check for five thousand dollars to the local Red Cross; that was in Africa. Certainly idealism could return at any time, arriving at the door in a top hat and a white tie, energy to burn, and an impossible task at hand. But it would not return for him, and if it did he would not recognize its face. Go away. I do not wish to be disturbed.

He heard a soft knock at the door and said, Yes?

Ramon appeared with a plate of cold cuts. He said, I am very sorry.

Thank you, Ramon. It was so sudden. How did you hear?

He said, From the valet next door.

The French?

Yes. They are very upset. They called your private line but you did not answer.

No, I didn't.

They said you are welcome at any time. They would like to help.

I'll call them tomorrow.

Ramon put the plate on the sideboard, along with a napkin and flatware. He said, Will there be anything else?

No, thank you, Ramon. Harry stared bleakly at the sticks of wood in the fireplace, stone cold at last, not so much as a wisp of smoke. He reached to massage his feet. He had walked longer than he intended, at any event longer than was good for him. His whiskey was tepid in the glass and when he looked up he saw that Ramon had left the room as silently as he had entered it. He began to quarter the cold cuts, ham, salami, a German sausage. Ramon had brought mustard also. He quartered once, and again. Ham, salami, sausage. Finally the slices were child-size bites. He ate a morsel of ham and stepped to the sideboard and made another whiskey. Across the lawn the French embassy was ablaze with lights. He sipped whiskey. It had had no effect so far. He ate a slice of salami and pushed the plate away. Then he shook his head as one does when baffled by events, a telephone call from a stranger, a road accident, and life collapsed utterly. This happened all the time in his professional life, an assassination, a border incident, a sudden change in American policy, a scandal. Bad news so often came by telephone.

Harry lit a cigarette and blew a smoke ring that held its shape for the length of his arm before it broke apart. He stepped to the window that looked onto May's garden. He heard the click of hydrangea stalks in the wind. The garden was dead. Beyond it through the high hedge he saw a faint yellow glow. The party was over. A smart gust of wind rattled the hydrangeas. The garden was dark but he could make out the shape of the heavy wooden rocker where in warm weather May would sit for hours reading. She always seemed to know when he was at the window. She would look up and give a little wave, wiggling the fingers of her right hand, and return at once to the page she was reading. Later, when he peeked out the window once again, she would be on her hands and knees weeding the garden. Clearing it, really. Giving symmetry, meaning order. Or flavor, she would say, a complex flavor like a good French stew. A tangled garden was worse than useless. Enough chaos in ordinary life. A garden was meant to be a place of repose, a delight to the eye, don't you agree? He did agree. Even so—what was a garden without a weed?

She had left him a note, on his desk when he returned in the evening from the embassy. *I'm off for a few days, back Sunday morning. XOXO, M.* He had a hint something was in the wind because the night before she had commenced a long reminiscence about her life in Slother, affairs of the family, the time her father broke his wrist arm-wrestling at the August carnival. She was a small child, six, seven years old. The broken wrist did not stop her father, who continued on, seemingly oblivious, until he fainted. He never complained about it then or later. The family generally was subject to injuries, and of course she herself had fevers around the ides of March. We were often in a state of crisis, May said. Was your family in a state of crisis? Not that I remember, Harry said. Perhaps we were distracted by world crises. I had the usual childhood diseases. Injuries were not common in my family. The ides of March did not figure on our calendar. Lucky you, May said. We had all the childhood diseases and more, except for Belle, who was the picture of health. She was proud of it, too, her clean bill of health.

My father worried about money, Harry said, which was absurd. He had plenty of money. He had a trust officer at a bank in New York who was supposed to do the worrying. How did that work, exactly? May asked. Harry explained about trusts, how they were established and who was responsible for the investments and so forth and so on, a vague answer because there was an edge to May's voice. So, she said, your father asked the trust officer for money and he sent some? I suppose that was it more or less, Harry said, in a manner of speaking.

That's the way to go about it, I suppose, May said.

My father worried anyhow, Harry said.

When your father goes, does the trust come down to you?

Yes, Harry said.

How much? May asked.

I have no idea, Harry said.

There wasn't much talk about money in our house, May said, probably because there was so little of it. Just enough to get by. We were never hungry or anything, but every few months we went on short rations. That was what my father called it, short rations, and that meant soup for dinner on Tuesday nights. I don't know why he chose Tuesday. Of course the pot garden helped. Harry said, What's a pot garden? May looked at him sideways and said, The garden where we grew pot, for God's sake, Harry. We sold some of it in the neighborhood but kept most of it for ourselves. Or themselves, I should say. As youngsters Belle and I were not allowed to smoke, even cigarettes. In some ways our parents were strait-laced. But you know Vermont. Always on the cutting edge.

They were taking an early-evening stroll in the park around the corner from the residence, an orangey light still strong from the west. They could have been in a remote country forest except for the industrial hum nearby. There were only a few other couples about. Harry was contemplating the pot garden in Slother. That was new. May had never spoken of it before and how many years had they been married? Another of her buried memories that from time to time went off like a tiny time bomb. Harry had never thought of Vermont on the cutting edge of anything except self-satisfaction. They did think well of themselves in Vermont.

I miss it sometimes, May said.

Do you?

I miss evenings on horseback. We had wonderful trails.

You do that here, Harry said.

It's not the same, May replied.

Why not?

It's in America, for one thing.

Oh, yes. That's certainly true.

Uncrowded, May said.

Except for the pot gardens, Harry said.

Those, too, May said.

Harry yawned deeply. He had had a tiring day, two meetings in the morning, three in the afternoon. A congressional delegation—"codel" in the parlance—was due at the end of the month, wives included, and the embassy staff was busy with addresses for museums and art galleries, boutiques, decent restaurants, and journeys of a historical nature away from the capital, a dossier for each congressman. It had been a while since the last codel. There was also a schedule of meetings with government officials, Harry the guide. The defense minister was giving them lunch. At the same time, Department security specialists were arriving to conduct an examination of the embassy's security procedures to assure themselves that the new protocols were being observed, and if they weren't you got a demerit on your report card. At that moment Harry considered himself the principal of a second-rate high school that had unaccountably lost its accreditation, or was about to.

I miss its simplicity, May said.

Harry had not been listening. He said, I beg your pardon?

Vermont, she said. I was talking about Vermont.

Yes, of course. Sorry. What did you say?

I miss it sometimes, May said. I wish you'd listen. May was silent then, her hands jammed into her armpits. A wind had come up. Harry was conscious of the click of his cane. She moved a little ahead, then turned to face him.

She said, You're being tiresome.

I've never heard you express nostalgia for Slother.

It wasn't all bad, she said.

I'm sure it wasn't.

I wish I'd been able to patch things up.

I know, he said. I don't want to be tiresome. I had a lousy day.

I don't even have a memento of those years, only a few photographs. Belle took everything. I suppose her children have them now, stuff that was around the house. Prizes won at Carnival. My mother's needlework. Odds and ends. I've been thinking about them for days. When the house burned down everything was lost except the things Belle had. May was silent a minute and then she said, So you had a lousy day.

I did, he said.

The codel?

Among other things.

You must learn to delegate.

I'm trying, Harry said.

Try harder.

They walked back to the residence quite out of step.

That was Thursday. When they reached the residence gate Harry thought to look at his watch, a premonition, and was startled to see the date, March 13. He opened his mouth to say something but thought better of it.

Harry turned from the window and made a fresh whiskey. Seated once again, he was annoyed by more questions. Was she speeding? Did she fall asleep at the wheel? What would he do now? He had no idea and tried to dismiss the thought, a nagging voice. He shut a door on it but the door refused to stay shut and the voice went on, sentence fragments. Resign from the foreign service. Move to

France. Visit his father in Connecticut. The standard advice was to do nothing, wait for the dust to settle. Harry could not corral these thoughts that bucked and quartered in his head. He blew another smoke ring in an unsuccessful attempt to find repose. He was tired but not ready for the bedroom. He sat quietly waiting for things to settle. He did not know why he had gone on so about Berlin, one pessimistic thought after another about a city he had visited only a few times. Berlin was divided then, and when he and May made the passage to the East via Checkpoint Charlie they were followed by a goon in a black leather coat, little wire spectacles on his nose and a black beret on his shaved head, a sneer from the atelier of George Grosz. May was amused by him, his clumsy attempts at intimidation. She said he reminded her of the biker boys at the Slother Carnival except for his Baltic-blue eyes, lady-killer eyes. He did remember East Berlin, as grim a city as he had ever seen, worse in its way than the broken-down cities of central Africa because here and there were mementos of what it had been before the war. A few buildings from that time still survived, even Schinkel's buildings, shrapnel-pocked. A few damaged people also, stooped as if they bore heavy burdens, unspeakable burdens. They looked as if they still lived in the war's context. The city was gray. The people were gray. The sky was gray, too, and spitting down rain. Even the rain looked exhausted, as if it were, like him, the last of its line, the final shower before the flood. The goon in the black leather coat was replaced by another goon in blue leather, his yellow hair reminding May of a Vermont haystack. They strolled for an afternoon, visiting the Pergamon, eating a dreadful lunch, trying and failing to find a souvenir. Harry suggested they kidnap one of the goons, take him home and civilize him like Huck Finn. They hurried back to their hotel in the West, enjoyed a tumble, arrived on time for the Berlin Symphony that night. Grieg. Mahler. Solti guest-conducting. They had one more day in Berlin and remarked to each other what a fine weekend it had been, despite the rain and the goons. The music had been sublime. And how happy they were to leave.

The room was silent except for the March wind, and Harry considered reprising Brahms, then decided against it. To repeat the *German Requiem* would be an indulgence, and there had been enough of that for one night.

The ambassador arranged a brief ceremony at the embassy, staff only. The ground-floor reception room was filled with flowers, the arrangement by the press attaché and her husband. Harry had never liked the room, its wintry atmosphere, low ceiling, narrow windows, Balkan art on the walls. The pictures were nineteenth-century rural scenes, a country wedding, happy peasants at work in the fields. Harry and May had planned to replace the art but never got around to it. But the flowers transformed the room into something almost elegant. Harry said a few words of welcome, as did his deputy chief of mission and the head of the political section. May and the station chief were great friends, and he would have spoken too, but he was scheduled to brief the codel, arrived from Trieste that morning. He knew several of the members personally and wanted to spare Harry the chore. The wives of two staffers spoke, remembering May fondly. The cook and the housekeeper chimed in. Ramon read a sentimental poem in his own language, beautifully spoken. Listening to them, the ambassador was certain that May would have been pleased. They all spoke of her as a free spirit, a thought not quite true but affectionately meant. Harry rose again at the end to mumble a few short sentences, something about chance and misfortune, something more about finding a safe place in the world, the difficulty of it in a business where your destinations were directed by others. Where you were, for the most part, at the mercy of events. May had seen many distressing sights in Africa. Nothing had prepared her for them. An ambassador and his family were sent somewhere and they went, conscious always of the responsibility, and the honor, of representing their country. Harry told an amusing story about May on horseback some years ago, the horse spirited but not as spirited as she was. Another story of a reception in an unnamed country, May presiding with aplomb until the foreign minister, filled with whiskey, stumbled into a potted palm and collapsed into May's arms. Fortunately he was six inches shorter than she was, so May was able to catch him unassisted and lay him out on the couch until his driver could come fetch him. Four dozen roses arrived by courier the following morning, along with an antique cup said to originate in Carthage. Harry concluded with a mystifying reference to the painter Goya, his superb understanding of grief. His compassion. His loathing of cruelty and indifference. The company was silent for a long minute, uncertain how to respond. The ambassador seemed at a loss. Then everyone gathered for drinks and hors d'oeuvres and by nine p.m. the ambassador was alone in his silent office once again, undone.

Some mysteries were inevitable and more or less bearable, others not. One had a responsibility to clear the fog of doubt, the loose end left dangling. To do otherwise was careless. The next morning Harry summoned the station chief and described May's accident, its approximate location, and the few facts he had in hand. He wanted to know what happened to cause his wife's car to plunge off a road in clear weather. The car was at the bottom of a ravine, all but inaccessible.

He said, Can you help me out?

Of course, Herb Schroeder said.

Can you do it now?

Not with the team I have here, Herb said.

Harry said, Shit.

But I can get a team together from our European stations. Take a few days.

Any way you can stop the locals from tainting the evidence?

I've done that, Harry.

How did you do it?

I've had two of my lads at the car since the accident. Every hour or so they're running off some local thug who wants to steal the battery, the windshield wipers. The tires. How they thought they would get tires out of the ravine is something else again. The slope is almost vertical. But, you know, their plans are not fully thought through. They don't think much beyond the theft itself.

Thanks, Herb, I appreciate it.

What's to be found, we'll find. How about you? Are you all right?

I'm all right.

You look like hell.

Harry's eyes strayed to the leaded windows and the garden beyond. He said, Does Alice like pearls?

All women like pearls, Harry. Pearls are the coin of the realm.

May had a pearl necklace—

No, Harry. Out of the question.

Not out of the question. Very much in the question. Ramon will bring it over this afternoon. My thanks. May didn't wear them often. I don't know why.

Two days later Herb Schroeder was back, a thick file under his arm.

He said, How much do you want to know?

Harry said, Everything you've got.

Herb smiled at that and began with the condition of the road, good enough, and the weather, also good. There were no skid marks on the road and the car appeared to have hit the guardrail full force, a direct hit. He described the condition of the car. There was nothing to indicate mischief, meaning foul play, an arranged accident, but the car was so torn up that nothing could be ruled out. Nevertheless, Herb said, I am ruling it out. He went on to describe the interior of the car, May's leather purse stuffed under the passenger seat, money and credit cards intact. Nothing suspicious. Herb handed over the purse.

Let me ask one question. Did May smoke? I never remember her smoking.

Once in a while, Harry said. She liked to smoke while she was driving, as a matter of fact.

What brand?

Pall Mall, Harry said.

Only Pall Mall?

That was her brand.

There were two Gitanes in the ashtray.

She never smoked a Gitane in her life.

A workingman's cigarette for sure. Filthy stuff.

No Pall Malls?

The Gitanes appeared to be at least a week old, maybe more than that. My people are working on it but, frankly, there won't be much more to learn. The Gitanes were smoked all the way down to the filter.

Harry was silent a moment. Wasn't life full of surprises? And one mystery so often led to another. He said, What do you make of that?

I don't know what to make of it. Would she pick up a hitchhiker?

Very doubtful, Harry said. Unless the hitchhiker was a woman. Then she might.

We have only the cigarette stubs, not the package they came from. No way to find the provenance, a tax stamp to show what country they came from, for example. Do you know where she was driving to? Or from?

No idea, Harry said.

Herb paused a moment. She go away often?

From time to time she would go away, Harry said. He said nothing more, uncertain how far to go with Herb Schroeder, who was a friend but not a close friend. They were colleagues more than friends but he had gone out of his way to help. Harry said, Usually two or three days. She always came back to me. It's only happened a few times. This was the third time. Sometimes she needed to get away from the embassy. Me.

We're checking the hotels in the vicinity, Herb said. There aren't many. Nothing has turned up so far. The locals are cooperative, by the way. And that's what I know. Sorry. It's not much.

I appreciate what you've done, Harry said. Anything turns up, let me know. Otherwise—and Harry let the thought hang. Otherwise what? He stepped to the window and looked down into the embassy garden, the plants wilting in the cold. The trees were barely coming into leaf. Beyond the trees he could see Christina Noiret standing in the doorway of her house, pulling on her gloves. She was dressed in slacks and a fur coat and in a moment disappeared into the open door of the ambassador's car. The driver eased the door shut and the car purred away, trailing a little plume of exhaust. Harry watched this ceremony with a smile. He knew he was through with the diplomacy business.

I don't think there's anything sinister about it, Herb said. That's my instinct.

Your instincts are good, Harry said.

Have been in the past, Herb agreed.

Still, Harry said. The Gitanes—

There's always a loose end, Harry. Always. No exceptions.

He looked him in the eyes. None?

In my experience, Herb said.

He slept badly and was listless in the mornings as if his circulation were laboring in first gear. He was asked out every night but usually declined, pleading work, and after a few weeks the invitations stopped except for Henri and Christina Noiret, the French ambassador and his young wife, the invitations arriving by hand from the embassy next door—come for lunch, come for drinks, come for supper, come any time but do call ahead, Christina wrote. We miss May but we miss you, too. You should not be so much alone. Harry went once, taking supper with them in the kitchen, Christina's succulent rabbit stew, remaining until midnight drinking a superb marc de Bourgogne. The ambassador was reminiscing about his naval days, the various ports of call. In thirty years he had never had occasion to fire his cannons in anger. Made him wonder if the country actually needed a navy. But it had the *force de frappe* with its airborne missiles and it didn't need those, either. Yet there they were, a source of pride to the nation, when the nation thought about them, which it seldom did. Harry thought the admiral was leaving something out, he was a highly decorated sailor. You loved your boats, Christina said. Admit it. Of course I loved my boats, the admiral said. Who wouldn't?

Seaborne Potemkin village, he said.

You had to show the flag, Harry said.

Of course. Charles de Gaulle insisted on it. As did his successors, not quite with the same panache. We had to keep up with the Anglo-Saxons. Or appear to try to keep up.

Harry laughed, the admiral so loquacious. He said, How did you get into the diplomacy business? The admiral smiled broadly and commenced a long story involving a friend who lobbied the Élysée on his behalf, arguing that a retired admiral was owed a billet in the diplomatic service, perhaps envoy to a country that desired a navy. And France had boats for sale, beautiful boats just north of obsolete, boats waiting for a customer.

And that was successful, Harry said.

Yes, the admiral said. They gave me the Légion d'honneur.

You were a good salesman, Harry said.

Yes I was, the admiral said. And you. What was your moment of success?

Harry waited a long minute, weighing the answer.

He said, I killed a man.

Christina's hand went to her mouth, an audible gasp. The admiral refilled their glasses. Neither spoke.

During my war, Harry said. I was very young. My first serious assignment. I was sent to a remote part of the country to meet with a representative from the other side, see if they were interested in a negotiated settlement. They weren't. The rendezvous was a failure all the way around. I was obliged to find my way home, and during the trek I came upon a militiaman. Or he came upon me. I knocked him down, took his carbine, and shot him. I think about it all the

232

time. I wonder if there was another solution. However, at that moment, none presented itself.

The admiral cleared his throat. That was a success?

I survived, Harry said. He didn't.

How awful for you, Christina said.

Yes it was, Harry said. For him, too.

And the consequences, the admiral said. Your ambassador—

I can't go into that, Harry said.

We will not speak of it further, the admiral said.

They went on to talk of other things, good postings, bad postings. The air in the room was heavy. Harry told them the African story, May's miscarriage, the utter unexpectedness of it. May's distress, her conviction that she had done something wrong, that the event was her fault. Nothing could dissuade her. The death of their little girl remained with her for the rest of her days. Christina looked at him with sympathy while he talked and said finally that May had told her the same story. May talked on and on about causes. She said she felt she had been marked. Chosen in some way. That what had happened to her was foreordained, a punishment for misdeeds. And that she would never bear children, that was a punishment also. May was most upset telling the story, Christina said. She did say that you were wonderful during her ordeal. Strong. I had the feeling, Christina said, that she had not sorted things out in her own mind. That there was something she was missing. Harry listened carefully and when Christina was finished he shook his head and said only, I had no idea. What misdeeds was she talking about? She didn't say, Christina said. Africa certainly was not her sphere. She was unprepared. Harry supposed that was true as far as it went. Unpreparedness was a problem generally. Christina leaned forward, gestured, opened her mouth—but said nothing. May had told her of a liaison with a careless Belgian. A night to remember, May said. Her story was incomplete and there was surely no need to speak of it now or ever. Christina knew Africa, a difficult region under any circumstances. Lately the Chinese had arrived, supposedly looking for agricultural land, and perhaps they could make headway amid the violence and disorganization but she doubted it. Confucius himself, with his affective concern for all living things, would have his hands full. The admiral rose to fetch another bottle of marc, commencing a complicated story involving corruption at the Élysée, something to do with a real-estate swindle and the subsequent—what do you Americans call it?—cover-up. The admiral went on and on about the swindle and the atmosphere at the Élysée, reminiscent of Simenon's low-rent milieu. Christina made her night-nights and went off to bed, leaving Harry, the admiral, and the bottle of marc in a suspended zone of silence.

The admiral cleared his throat and said, What have you learned, Harry?

Harry's mind was elsewhere. He said, I beg your pardon?

Your career, the admiral said. The American foreign service. Your postings, Africa and the others, Oslo. Here. So many years abroad. What have the years taught you?

Harry was quiet a moment. He said, My father's table.

The admiral smiled. I could say, I see. But that would end our interesting conversation. The fact is, I do not see. Explain your father's table. Or, if you wish, tell me to piss off. Mind my own business.

Harry was quiet once again. Then he said, I grew up in Connecticut. That's like growing up in your château country down near the Loire. Most Sundays we'd have a splendid lunch with the squires, our neighbors, a congresswoman and her husband, a professional soldier and his wife, two bankers, other locals, including a retired ambassador and various characters who had been in and out of government. The congresswoman was an excellent mimic and hilarious as she went about describing the legislative sausage machine. Brigadier General Candless was similarly superb on military science and tactics, including the Bulge in 1944. He had taken part in it. The bankers were entertaining as they went about demystifying Wall Street, or trying to. Where my mother and father fit into this company I cannot say, except they were fine hosts. They set a fine table. Everyone was fond of them. I think it's fair to say my parents established a sphere of intimacy, almost of confidentiality, at their Sunday table. No one had to say, This stays in the room among us. Everyone knew that the conversation stayed in the room, and the remarkable, or contradictory, fact was that indiscretions were rare. These were people of the wider world and sexual or financial escapades had no real interest for them unless a president, a secretary of state or defense, or the speaker of the House was implicated, whereupon the worm of malice began to crawl as at any other table. But that aside, the company rarely spoke of current events but of things of the past, the general's campaigns, the congresswoman's battles with Senator Joe McCarthy. Elections won and lost, wars won, stalemated, or lost, promises kept, promises broken. I would say also that the atmosphere was often melancholy. At my father's table failure was more instructive, more revealing, than success.

The admiral nodded thoughtfully, adding a ghost of a smile.

Thing was, Harry went on, all the stories they told had something missing. This, it seemed to me then as it does now, is common among government people. Congresswoman Finch, for example, in describing the eternal struggle over foreign aid was meticulous in her account of who said what to whom and when, the politics of it, the influence of lobbyists. But at a certain point she shrugged and changed the subject. To go beyond that certain point might have—would have—undermined faith in the system. She had realized she was addressing—I suppose the word would be civilians. Brigadier General Candless was eloquent on the progress of the Battle of the Bulge, an account drawn from a set-piece annual lecture he delivered to senior cadets at West Point. He had the names of the principal officers and their units, which performed well and which performed badly. The flow of the engagement. He had the German order of battle. He noted the weather, the terrain, and the fortifications. He quoted from diaries and after-action reports. Still, there was something between the lines where you found a hint of something else, something excruciating, beyond words, unspeakable. The hint was indistinct, a single voice in the chorus of a thousand. Brigadier General Candless was an intelligent man and knew a blank space when he saw it, and the same was true of Congresswoman Finch, even the bankers. As they were talking there would come a moment when their voices trailed off and any attentive listener would know they were deep in their memories, pondering what they were unable—not unwilling but unable—to say aloud. The missing piece. All the stories had missing pieces that spoke to motive and perhaps misprision or something very like misprision. This was something personal and inexplicable, the fact that refused to fall in line with the other facts. A black-sheep fact, important enough to make a tidy account a little less tidy. To grasp it you had to have been there. More than any other single thing you had to understand the context, what was at stake and the consequences. No civilian could know that, even the worldly civilians around the Regency table at my father's house. These were inside jobs. That was the world they lived in, Harry said, and the world I've known since I was seven years old. I was attracted to it. I still am. And then in the bat of an eye I was fifty years old and an ambassador myself, searching, as Dean Acheson put it, like a blind man in a dark room for a black cat that isn't there. And do you want to know something else? The stakes are not small. This world is filled with mischief, and more than mischief. Time retreats. Time advances. Time is discontinuous. Time is always in motion, like the waves of a great sea. And failure is more commanding than success.

The admiral leaned forward, poured wine, and softly said, *Formidable*. And what—

We will not speak of it further, Harry said in French, and the admiral barked a laugh.

* *

236

Harry turned the embassy over to his DCM when he received the news that he was reassigned back to Washington and a position in the Department Secretariat, what he knew to be his last post in government. His days now were the sheerest drudgery, packing up his files, designating some, not many, for the burn bag, others for the archives, still others for the Department files, a few for his office safe. He was distracted, his mind elsewhere. More than once he put a file in the burn bag that was meant for the archives and vice versa. Harry did retain his diaries, mostly appointment daybooks kept by his faithful secretary—the foreign minister for lunch, the DCM at four p.m., cocktails at the Portuguese embassy at seven. The small change of diplomatic life. He was surprised that there was so little that could be described as personal. Hardly anything at all. A thick file was reserved for arms deals, mostly paperwork from the Pentagon when it suited them, with an occasional query from an assistant secretary of state: Is this truly necessary? Or, depending on the politics of the administration: Why can't we do this right now? Usually the Pentagon went its own way, putting Harry in mind of the observation about nineteenth-century Prussia being not a state with an army but an army with a state. And when Harry replied that the deal was neither necessary nor desirable, it sometimes died. Not often enough. Arms deals rarely died, merely went into intensive care, only to return a few months later in excellent health, like the living dead. Harry opened his desk drawer and removed his personal phone book, bought by May at Cassegrain in Paris, organized by country—and so many of the names blacked out owing to death or disappearance. He put that in his briefcase, remembering how pleased May was with her purchase. It came with a Montblanc pen but the pen was long since lost. Harry had asked his DCM to keep his personal things in the embassy basement until he decided where he would live after his hitch at the Secretariat. He had made no firm decision concerning his retirement venue but thought that the south of France sounded about right, a domain close to the sea for sure, some quiet and anonymous property where he might from time to time hear the moo of a cow. Not so anonymous, however, that a railway station wouldn't be nearby and offer fast-train service to Paris. He would require a small car to get around. Necessary also would be an open porch with a view of the Mediterranean. An American kitchen. Bookshelves in every room. Some country place close to a village with a decent restaurant. Harry knew that something suitable would turn up. It always had before.

The most difficult task he put off until the last week. That was sorting May's clothes and arranging for them to be sent to one of the local charities. An especially pretty silk blouse and a black Gucci bag he would give to Christina Noiret. May's smell clung to the blouse. In the recesses of her bedroom closet he found a dozen albums of her photographs and the unfinished typescript of her life of Goya, another of her projects, this one begun in Washington; he couldn't remember the year, but it was post-Africa. May confided that she had run out of material and, well, she needed access to the Prado or wherever Goya's papers were kept, if there were any papers. As things stood she could not see Goya whole or even partway but wasn't that the usual thing with artists? What you had to go on was the work and not much else. Also, they tended to be liars, as smooth as a snake-oil salesman. And the Apocalypse was always near. An exception would be Van Gogh in his letters to brother Theo, always candid even when asking for money. Probably there were exceptions to the general rule. Honestly, she didn't know much about it, the sincerity issue. She loved Goya's work and when you came down to it the artist was secondary to the work. For her fortieth birthday Harry bought her a print from the "Capricios" series, the one of the blushing bride-to-be crowded by her elderly and leering suitor and her devastated family, save for her cynical papa. The dowry this time would go the other way. Goya called the piece *Qué Sacrificio!* What a sacrifice! May loved the print and hung it in their bedroom next to a photograph of her and Harry on their wedding day, at a restaurant in Montparnasse, before them a giant platter of oysters and a bottle of Perrier-Jouët in a silver bucket. May had never eaten an oyster and had to be shown the technique and the uses of the lemon and mignonette. Forget the fork and slip the oyster from the shell to your tongue and wait a moment. May was laughing and never looked lovelier.

Harry had never been in her closet. Most everything had been given away. The closet looked forlorn, with a well-worn blue robe and slippers tucked into a corner ready for the garbage bin. The closet was dusty and dark and he almost missed the two remaining items, a heavy manila envelope and her diaries. He had not known she kept a diary. He looked at them a long minute, wondering about the contents. He picked up the diaries and weighed them in his hands like a goldsmith assaying value. There were four diaries with entries written in a close-hauled script. Here and there were sentences written in a five-number code. He remembered a dinner in Africa with the station chief years ago when she asked about codes, how you went about making them and deciphering them in a way that was simple and easy to remember. The station chief was a connoisseur of codes and cryptology and went on and on about letter codes and number codes, the Vigenère Square with its keyboard, and much else besides. A classic five-number code was efficient and he explained how that was constructed. May was fascinated. She couldn't hear enough about codes. Harry riffled the pages of the diaries but did not read them. Diaries were notoriously unreliable, a furtive means of settling scores. That which the diarist did not dare to speak aloud she committed to paper, and hid the paper. These diaries were the size and weight of a short hardcover book, leather-bound, the pages ruled. Harry thought they had a sinister aspect, something forbidden. The black leather binding, the ruled pages, the five-number codes here and there, all of it composed in a dense hand.

You fox, he said aloud.

But what he saw was a hand reaching from an open grave.

Harry looked around their bedroom, the bureaus and their big bed with the red pillows and heavy duvet. Photographs on the bureaus, even one of her family sitting on the steps of their house in Slother. Their room, her arrangements. The air was close, as if he were underground. Harry scooped up the diaries and the manila envelope and moved downstairs to his office and set the diaries one by one on his desk. The manila envelope he put to one side.

The late-afternoon sun cast a dull milky glow on the figured carpet. He remembered buying the carpet in Tunisia. The rug was May's choice. She was having the time of her life bargaining with the rug man, a fat bastard with a neatly trimmed beard and merry little eyes. Harry picked up the diaries and thought about the rug man in Sfax. The hotel in Sfax was mediocre. Mediocre suite, mediocre food, and in the dining room three tables of Germans with parade-ground voices. He was ambassador in Oslo then, and he and May had taken a week in Tunisia because of the appalling Norwegian February. When the carpet arrived a month later May insisted he lay it in his office to give the room a dash of color. He scarcely remembered a thing about Tunisia except the fat bastard, the hotel, the Germans, and his aching feet. He thought about the heat and the hotel and the Germans and his feet and the rest of it, knowing that he had willed himself to stray ever so slightly off the point, holding in his hands a poison pill, diaries that would give clues to secrets held—better yet, the secrets themselves, innermost secrets, secrets that went unspoken, secrets private enough that some of them were written in code. He had never kept a confessional diary and never read one. He did not as a matter of principle read other people's mail—and then he laughed out loud because he read other people's mail all the time. The station chief walked in with a sheaf of papers, handing them over with a thin smile. Wait'll you read this, Harry! Unbelievable! They were transcripts of conversations in the presidential palace or the defense ministry, a café on the wrong side of town or a hotel room, and Harry would dig in as at a four-course meal. Not Oslo. No need to bug the friendly Norwegians. But at every other posting he had had there was a lively traffic in intercepted conversations. So principle had nothing whatever to do with a decision to read or not to read his wife's diaries except to satisfy his own curiosity, with no doubt a disturbing surprise somewhere along the line, a bitter payback from someone loved at once and forever, loved from the moment of hello and the breathless hesitation after hello, the crowded bar, Sure, I'd like to join you and your friends; and within an hour or so the friends disappeared, leaving you both in a companionable climate of silence before the conversation began and could be said to have continued until this very moment. No need to strip someone clean in order to satisfy the itch of curiosity. Something narrow-minded about it. Vulgar. Fear was in there somewhere, too, an apprehension. No good could come of this. Now was not the time. At last Harry shook his head decisively and threw the diaries into the burn bag. If he did not read them now he would never read them, so what was the point of keeping them? He had an illusion and he would remain with the illusion, the unopened door. Often enough the more you knew the less you understood. As for the diarist — the diarist had a right of privacy, even the dead, and perhaps the dead most of all.

That left the manila envelope, a government-issue envelope of heavy paper, the flap fastened by a string wound around a dime-sized cardboard wheel. In black type at the upper left were the words "United States Department of State." It looked to be years old, the paper creased and curled with handling. He placed the envelope on his desk and stepped to the sideboard and poured a glass of whiskey, adding ice and a twist of lemon. The time was six p.m.; the pale afternoon sunlight had vanished as darkness gathered. The French residence next door was ablaze with light, another reception. In the driveway the chauffeurs were gathered around an idling Mercedes smoking cigarettes. Harry watched them a moment, then switched on the desk lamp and opened the envelope. Inside were letters, dozens of them, addressed to May Huerwood, poste restante. He looked at the postmarks and discovered that the most recent date was the summer of the year before. The correspondence stopped there. Harry was in no hurry and glanced now at the stamps, Thailand and India, South Africa and Senegal, Holland and Austria, three from Canada and two from the United States, four from Russia. The smaller the country, the gaudier the stamp. There were no return addresses, unless the five-figure blocks carefully written on the back flaps were a kind of address. Harry took a few of the letters in his hand and fanned them as he would a deck of cards. The ink was blue, the writer's script a professional-quality cursive. It had a feminine look, script from a girls' boarding school of his youth, Emma Willard or Foxcroft, all loops and flourishes, loosely composed. Harry sat at his desk and looked at the contraband, settling himself before starting to read. The second thoughts he had about May's diary did not apply here. He chose a letter at random, noticing at once that some of the spellings were British. But that was consistent with the Anglophilia of American boarding schools. *I heard a rumour the other day that you and Himself are bound for Oslo. Be sure to bring your woolies . . .* Harry looked at the ceiling, pensive, and took a slow swallow of his drink, the scotch going down so smoothly he barely tasted it. But the jolt came quickly. The letter was signed "With love" and carried a signature he did not recognize. The scrawl was hard to decipher, the loops and flourishes collapsing into a long horizontal line. Harry knew right away that May's correspondent was no schoolgirl, sentences rolling on about Oslo and its phlegmatic inhabitants, not forgetting the savage winters and interminable summers, the sun setting sometime around midnight and rising thirty minutes later, an Ibsen world of nagging anxiety and gloom, nothing at all like cheerful raucous sensual sentimental ruined Africa. *Would you like to join me in Luanda?* Something about the forced cadence reminded him of a young attaché in Africa who looked after things for the Belgians. May saw him at parties. May liked him. He was young—well, they were all young, but this one was in his twenties, elfin, a good-looking boy who drove a green Karmann Ghia. He had come to the residence a few times, once at the annual Fourth of July reception where he

242

wore a goofy red-white-and-blue hat that fell around his ears. He carried a title. Count? Baron? One of the two. Very popular with women was Andres, a dilettante diplomat, here today, gone tomorrow. He was unattached, amusing, a bon vivant. Andres was usually turned out in bespoke summer suits and bench-made shoes, a Borsalino hat and a little yellow hankie in the top pocket of his jacket. Harry had taken an instant dislike to him.

May said, Oh, come on, give Andres a break.

Harry said, He's a *poseur*. Not a serious man.

Well, she said with a laugh, that's true enough.

Playboy, Harry said.

He doesn't have much to do here, May said. So he fools around.

I think he dyes his hair, Harry said.

He does not, May said.

Gotcha, Harry said, but he did notice May's quick response and the answer that followed.

Anyway, May said, he's leaving soon.

Where to?

France, May said. He's going to work for a bank, one of the French ones. The idea is, the bank wants to set up facilities in underdeveloped countries. Andres assesses the political climate, how stable it is, how reliable, and how corrupt. He calls himself a security consultant. Risk, reward. Can we give him a going-away party?

Why not, Harry said, thinking as he said it that the Belgian was on to something.

So she had another life, a long-distance life from the look of the postmarks. Harry had not suspected anything, least of all with the Belgian twit. He looked at his glass, empty, and moved to the sideboard to fill it, taking his time. There was no rush. He looked again at the letters, rereading bits and pieces of them. For the most part they were travelogues, accounts of journeys to Asia and Central America, the Middle East and Africa. Evidently he loved travel for its own sake, the hotels and airplanes, meetings with businessmen and foreign correspondents, those in the know. Andres did not have a high opinion of those in the know and on the make. He had a lavish expense account. The hotels were all of the five-star variety, and when he arrived somewhere he was always met by a driver with a limousine.

Somewhere along the line he switched jobs. Now he was working for an insurance company, assessing threats, attempting to read the future. Here and there were the five-figure codes, usually at the end of the letter. It took Harry a moment to get beyond the schoolgirl script, incongruous in the circumstances. Letters home to Mom. We just beat the pants off Foxcroft in lacrosse. Harry stacked the letters on the desk where he sat glumly in his chair drinking scotch. How could he have no idea? He blamed his incuriosity, though he had not always been incurious. That was a latter-day phenomenon that commenced roughly around the time of his sixtieth birthday, though he had never counted suspicion as a virtue. This business appeared to date from Africa after they had lost their little girl. They were both distraught, not themselves. They were careful with each other. Harry was often away but never more than a night or two, and it was one of those nights when Zoe came to his bed and remained there until dawn. When he woke up she was gone, and a week later he learned she had been transferred to the coast, Dar es Salaam. He forgot about her, but a few years later when he and May were living in Washington, Zoe called him at home. What's up? How are you doing? Can we meet sometime? Without a word he hung up the telephone, waiting a minute to see if she would call back. But she didn't, as he was certain she wouldn't. Who was that? May called from the kitchen. He said, Wrong number. And that was that, except the memory of her was with him once again. Zoe was a product of disobedient high-stress environments where the rules were made up as you went along. She was a free spirit, her good cheer infectious. Also, she was fearless, traveling without escort to the most dangerous parts of Africa. She loved her work and she loved what could come after work. She lived by the statute of no entangling alliances. She slipped out of his bed as easily as she had slipped into it. Wasn't that fun! Much later she married Axel Brown, Harry's solid and dependable aid administrator. Axel called her the Sally Bowles of the Bush. Their night together those many years before seemed to Harry a moment of no consequence, a kind of reward for them both at the end of a discouraging day, all too common in the work they were called upon to do and the place they were called upon to do it in. Still, something lingered, because when she called that night he did not say, Good to hear from you, Zoe. What's up? How are you doing? Not at all. He dropped the telephone as if it were radioactive. May knew it, too, looking at him strangely as he returned to the kitchen to toss the salad.

Wrong number? she said.

Somebody selling something, Harry replied.

From the parts of Andres's letter that he read there was no mention of a specific rendezvous. He decided to ignore the five-figure codes. May's was apparently an epistolary romance, at least after the Belgian had left Africa for his career in finance. Harry wagged his finger at her photograph on the desk, a gesture of reproach. She smiled back at him from poolside in Sfax, the water so blue, the sky pale white. Her skin was a golden tan, her hair bleached by the sun. Her mouth was parted slightly and he remembered her saying something when he snapped her picture, one of her straightforward Vermont endearments. He smiled at her and winked. She said it the instant he took her picture and then she asked for the camera and made one of him, waiting until she got the look she wanted. The photograph was in a frame in their bedroom. The colors had faded over the years, the water not so blue, his skin a washed-out white. However, the rest of him was the same, his broad shoulders and sandy hair, his capable hands, his half-smile, in the distance a minaret. He remembered the call to prayer.

All the embassy residences they had lived in came equipped with a study. This one was unfortunate, a formal space with heavy furniture and leaded-glass windows, in shadows at all times. He had never felt at home in it, using it mainly for personal correspondence and bills, now and then a nap. Sometimes May would drop by in late afternoon bearing a plate of marzipan cakes and a pot of tea, and after the marzipan and tea a leisurely tumble on the long davenport, a slow-motion tumble until slow-motion became insupportable, the conclusion raucous, May's high shriek that, he swore, only an animal could hear. Afterward he would tell her what he was up to, personnel problems, difficulties with the government, both his own and the one he was accredited to. My struggles, he said with only a little sarcasm. The last conversation they had, Harry admitted to weariness. He said to her, We have been at this so long, you and I, that I seem to meet myself coming around the corner. Different personalities, same problems. At those late-afternoon times he felt they were alone in the world, the experience so dense and private that he was loath to describe it.

He said, I'm losing interest.

She said, You'll never give it up. Never in a hundred years.

Don't be so sure, he said. There's a time for everything and maybe it's time now to think about something else.

May looked at him doubtfully and said, That time is past. It's been past for a while now.

He said, Pessimist.

The next day, she was gone before he was awake. But she was there with him now. She lingered in the dark corners of his study and in the air itself. He could smell her perfume and hear her voice, the words run together like an unfamiliar language, fluent but unintelligible, their meaning obscured. He did not know if she was smiling. Her face was turned from him. Surely she could read his thoughts, understanding that he saw himself now as a soldier on a worn-out battlefield at twilight. He thought of Othello's words at the end of his life: I have done the state some service . . .

He wished she had disposed of the diaries and letters herself. They were her responsibility. But that task had fallen to him and he decided to delay a minute more, allow his emotions to settle. He was not himself. Nor Othello. He was in the eye of an invisible storm, unable to move safely or make a decision. He made himself another whiskey, a strong one, avoiding the photograph only a few feet away. Harry sat at the big desk and looked at the letters with their colorful stamps and returned them to the manila envelope one by one, closing the flap, winding the string around the cardboard wheel. Night had closed in for keeps and he felt May's spirit withdraw from the room, leaving him alone at last. Alone and half drunk, he said to himself. He glanced at the correspondence on his desk, three letters that required his immediate attention. But they would have to wait awhile.

He knew that from time to time for the remainder of his days she would appear in the shadows, the smell of her body, the lilt of her arcane accent, a trace of the north country in every line, her wink. Harry took another swallow of whiskey and felt things go down another notch. A tap at the door caused him to pause but, listening hard, he decided the tap was imaginary, a *trompe-oreille*. He realized he had made a pun.

I made a pun, he said aloud. How do you like it?

But the audience was silent.

Harry sat a while longer, sipping whiskey and contemplating a future that refused to take shape. The tide was ebbing. He had the idea that there were rules somewhere and that if you followed the rules things would come out all right. He thought about that, wondering where fear came in, fear of the known and fear of the unknown, fear of capricious gods rolling dice for their own amusement. And without warning your world turned upside down. No logic to it. Your world was no longer familiar. Instead, he heard mysterious taps at the door, surely a warning, but of what? His desk lamp cast a wan light, shadows dim at the edges. The clock on his desk was fast. He had a meeting in the morning but could not remember what it was about. Finally, having exhausted the other possibilities, he dropped the manila envelope into the burn bag, waiting for a signal, any signal at all. But what he heard was the dull thump of the envelope as it settled. He was alone in the room and all he heard now was the heavy north wind rattling the shutters. He tried to imagine life without May Huerwood but was unsuccessful. That was Rule One. Rule Two was to press on. Even so, he could not bring the future into focus. He could not see its shape, and so he touched the CD button to summon the *German Requiem*, which did bring a measure of comfort.

In Washington, they gave him a comfortable office and he easily settled into the routine, the senior staff meeting at nine a.m. sharp, his own assistants gathering in his office at eleven. The in and out boxes were arranged just so, east and west on his desk. Read the cable traffic after lunch. He filled the bookshelves with old favorites. Miłosz was there, along with Koestler and Kennan, the poems of Poe, the five-volume life of Henry James, Bismarck's *Gedanken und Erinnerugen*, Barzun's *From Dawn to Decadence*, Fitzgerald's *The Crack-Up*, many others. During the slow afternoon hours he would take down a book and read an excerpt before dozing off to the hum of the air conditioner. All in all, Harry thought, a pleasant way to spend the day.

The Department was in a state of unease because the Secretary was contemplating a reorganization, and in any reorganization there were winners and losers, and the strategy of the senior staff was to move cautiously, leave no stone unturned until the next election when a new Secretary would take office and then—well, the stones would be passed on to the new chap, a fat filing cabinet full of stones, and so many of them too heavy to lift. In any case, the senior staff would be gone by then, into retirement or the public sector, Harry among them. He rented a row house in Georgetown within walking distance of the Department, though often enough he drove his car or took a bus, a question of his feet. Harry was in at nine and out at five unless there was a crisis that spoke to his own experience. But there was only one of those, and it was cleared up in a week. One day rolled into another and almost before he knew it he had accumulated leave time and thought he would take a break and visit his father, his first visit in more than six months. No one objected. Take as much time as you need, Harry. Everyone deserves a holiday from time to time. We'll soldier on.

Harry flew to La Guardia and rented a Chevrolet convertible to drive to Salisbury through towns familiar to him since childhood. Kent, Cornwall Bridge, West Cornwall, Lime Rock. The afternoon light fell beautifully from a clear sky. The hill towns had not changed much. The lawns were tidy, the houses middle-aged and older, well maintained behind rail fencing or low stone walls. They were comfortable houses with porches and gardens, here and there a youthful mansion, surely the object of derision from the squires. If they had wanted a Hamptons house why didn't they build it in the Hamptons? His father had told him that the mansions were popular with people in the entertainment industry, who tricked them out with tennis courts and Olympic-sized swimming pools and, in one instance, a seven-hole golf course with a resident pro. Can you believe it? The entertainment industry people were strange. They were not dangerous but they were often foulmouthed. The children were foulmouthed, too, and spoiled. Well, his father said, they were here today but they would be gone tomorrow. They were people who were always moving on, you see. Harry drove slowly as he reacquainted himself with the landscape and the small towns. There were horses everywhere in the fields and that put him in mind of May. He stopped once near Lime Rock to watch the horses cavort in the fields. A lithe equestrienne was exercising a jumper and the way she moved her head and body reminded him of May. Harry leaned against a rail fence and watched the girl, wondering all the while why he had been so against retiring to Connecticut, and then a BMW station wagon thundered by at high speed trailing loud music, a teenager at the wheel, and Harry's wondering ceased. When the girl completed one of her jumps, she raised her hand to give Harry a jaunty wave and he called back, Bravo!

When Harry arrived, his father was waiting for him in the Adirondack chair near the stone wall where the dogs were buried. He was engrossed in a book. The season was late autumn, the trees nearly bare of leaves, the weather unseasonably warm. The old man gave him a bear hug and a kiss on the cheek. He said, You look tired. Have you lost weight? He was in fine spirits and excellent health, save a little of this and a little of that: arthritis and indigestion, failing eyesight. Harry glanced at the open book next to the Adirondack chair, Philip Roth's novel *American Pastoral* in large type. The old man was full of surprises.

He had arranged Sunday lunch as in the old days. Many of the Sunday regulars were still alive, causing Harry to inquire if there was something auspicious in the Connecticut water. Of course Congresswoman Finch and her doctor husband were long gone but well remembered. Mr. Wilson had been gone for a decade. But the Candlesses were there, he with a walker, she with a cane. Despite the walker, Jimmy Candless maintained the bearing of a brigadier general. The widow Born, she of the diamond business, was still a consultant to the Fifth Avenue shop. The brothers Green had long ago sold their concern on Wall Street but continued to trade on their own account. When Harry asked if they had a strategy, they hemmed and hawed until the widow Born said, Oh, for God's sake, you two, tell him. Buy and hold, they said in one voice.

They drank cocktails for an hour and sat at table for three. His father brought out his best Bordeaux and the good glassware and china. The Regency table, one leaf less than in the old days, accommodated everyone nicely. His father carved the lamb himself. They talked American politics and, a concession to Harry, a little about foreign affairs. But the conversation always returned to Washington. What do they think in Europe of this fellow Clinton? Gives a good speech, doesn't he? His wife's a hellion. They were mostly Democrats but they had a high regard for George H. W. Bush. Harry Sr. and Horace Green had been at Yale at more or less the same time as Poppy, give or take a decade or two. Like the former president, Horace had been a member of Skull and Bones, though of course that was not mentioned. They agreed that Poppy wasn't much of a politician but that was what they liked about him, a gentleman through and through. Jimmy Candless thought the Kuwait action was superbly conceived and executed. Over the years Harry's father had lost his enthusiasm for Bob Taft, humorless man of principle. Instead, he favored Adlai Stevenson, a man of his own generation. They said Adlai dithered but that was a vicious calumny. Adlai was patient, quite another thing altogether. Whatever happened to wit in our politics? Instead of wit we got Reagan.

Harry was relaxed at his father's table, everything in the room familiar, including the roast lamb, the Bordeaux, and the conversation, the company ever so slightly dotty. Harry had the idea that this Connecticut world was a closed circle that had existed since the Continental Congress, or anyway since the first Roosevelt administration, with a way to go before the impatient God of the universe snapped His fingers and closed it down, never to be seen again. Time's up! Too much of a good thing. Harry's mind drifted as the company commenced a discussion of FDR's love life, Missy Lehand and Mrs. Suckley and others before them. Of course everyone knew but no one said anything. That was the way things were done then, in the way that news photographers never photographed Roosevelt in his wheelchair. A common courtesy. That was before the press flew out of control, putting themselves on the wrong side of common decency in their zeal to air dirty linen, bedroom stuff. Didn't you find them that way, Harry? Well, Harry said, no, not actually—and then, noticing the frowns, he knew he had to throw them a bone lest he be seen as a spoilsport. He said, Some of them are egomaniacs. Well, of course, Horace Green said, that's the fundamental problem, unchecked power. They're ghouls, you know . . . And then, distracted once again, Harry noticed that the Marsden Hartley was missing from the wall behind his father's head. Munnings's horse was there next to Homer's boat but Marsden Hartley's landscape had vanished. Harry waited until the guests had departed before he asked his father about it. The old man made a dismissive gesture.

He said, What's it to you?

What happened to it? I always liked it where it was.

Gave it to Yale, his father said.

What are they going to do with it at Yale?

Put it in the art museum, dummy.

I didn't know they had an art museum at Yale.

Of course they do. Beautiful museum. First-rate stuff.

I miss it on the wall.

You can see it at Yale, his father said.

I'm damned if I'm driving all the way to New Haven to see the Marsden Hartley.

If you want to see it, you will. Because that's where it is and it isn't going anywhere. I gave it in the name of your mother.

All right then, Harry said.

They were very appreciative, his father said.

I imagine they were, Harry said.

Harry awoke early the next morning, made a pot of coffee, and went outside to sit on the stone wall and wait for his father, still abed. The weather remained warm. He thought he had never seen a surround as benign as this one, close to an artist's conception of well-heeled country life. It had a fullness and completion not found in nature. Even the hollyhocks and roses looked sketched rather than natural, even now in late autumn. The land itself seemed to re-lax and take a breather. The oak grove had not grown but the trees were ancient when he was a boy. Harry supposed they were patient like Adlai Stevenson. And then as if on cue a doe and her two fawns appeared in the field, paused, and bounded away. The deer fam-ily looked as if they were weightless and at any moment might as-cend into the sky like Santa's reindeer. They disappeared into the mist rising from the brook beyond the oak grove. Harry turned to see his father at the kitchen window. He, too, had been watching the deer family and had not noticed Harry sitting on the stone wall. He moved away from the window and Harry thought again how the house was much too big for one solitary man, five bedrooms and four baths, a living room the size of a squash court, and of course the dining room. The kitchen was as big as any of his embassy kitchens. Better appointed, too, though the appliances were decades old and the linoleum floor was cracking. Although that was not how his father saw it.

Nonsense, he said. This is where I live, have done since before you were born . . . The old man paused then and went away somewhere, his face expressionless, his eyes fixed on some distant vista. You see, he said at last, I know where everything is. That's the point. Nothing's lost.

On the road the next day, driving at speed now, Harry decided he had had a fine time with his father, despite the moments of amnesia. They had reminisced a little and the old man had told a charming story about Harry's mother, something to do with an old flirtation, a harmless flirtation, a flirtation they could laugh about. Oh, I do miss her, he said. I almost gave it up when she died and then I decided not to. She wouldn't've liked it if I had. Pull up your socks! she would've said. There were other stories from the old days, as well worn as an old suit. Harry told a few stories of his own, about May and May's love of horseback riding, her unfinished life of Goya, her apprehension of the diplomatic life, their good times together that were cut short by the accident, god damned freak accident. Harry said to his father, Did you like her? Oh, yes, the old man said. Your mother, too. May was down-to-earth. She fit right in here, didn't she? Yes, Harry said after a moment. Yes, I think she did.

Isn't it a grand old place?

The best, Harry said.

You're welcome here anytime. Stay as long as you'd like. Move in if you want to. God knows there's room.

I've found a place in the south of France. Small village. Hospitable.

Well, good, his father said. I hope it works out. I've never liked the French myself.

You don't know the French.

I knew them in my youth.

You did?

I was there with Mother and Dad, a few years after the Great War. We sailed from New York and docked at Southampton. We took the grand tour. First class all the way. One week in London, one week in Paris, a week in Berlin, and a week in Rome. In Paris we stayed at the Meurice. We had a view of the Tuileries from our rooms.

Well, that would certainly do it.

Exactly. I've never liked them, knowing them as I do.

Harry was almost at the Connecticut Turnpike when he remembered the Marsden Hartley and decided to make a detour to New Haven. It took him some time to find the museum but there the landscape was, on the second floor, on a crowded wall of American art. His father's Marsden Hartley looked out of place among the Sloans and an especially fine Sargent. Harry wondered why this was and decided finally that its abnormality had to do only with his own familiarity with it. He looked at the Marsden Hartley and the other pictures for a while, then returned to his car, happy he had made the detour. A month later Harry resigned from the foreign service and returned to Europe, convinced the Marsden Hartley belonged on his father's dining room wall where it had lived for so many years. But, even so, it was not lost.

Ten

H E WAS OLD NOW and forgetful of things large and small, to the point where he did not venture far from his cottage on the Mediterranean coast. Somewhere in the back of his mind was the thought that he might lose himself if he strayed too far from familiar surroundings, the village up the road, the tiny port in the crease a half mile or so due south. Really, he was comfortable only in his own context, his cottage and what he could see from the porch of the cottage. Harry's world had become abbreviated, spare like an early Frost poem or one of Edward Hopper's night scenes. Yet Harry was not lonely and in fact prospered in his remote corner of Provence. The twice-weekly *femme de ménage* now came every other day, inventing fantastic excuses on arrival. The electricity failed last night and I was worried about you, and now that I am here I intend to dust the closets. Claudette pretended to dust the closets and Harry pretended irritation at being disturbed. The truth was, he liked having her around. She was talkative and devoted to him in her own way. Claudette's husband had died years ago and her children had their own lives in Avignon. She preferred Harry's house with its view of the sea to her own house in the village. She liked him, too, with his stories and observations of the diplomatic life. She thought of him as a gentleman of the old school, his chronic forgetfulness but an endearing consequence of his years as a man of the world. Often at the end of the day she would prepare a pot of tea and they would sit quietly and talk of small things. Promptly at six she would depart for the village and he would clear away the tea things and make himself a large scotch, ice, no water.

He no longer walked to the village but drove his car. Arthritic hips affected his balance and his feet were worse than ever. Still, he enjoyed the domino games and the country gossip that surrounded him in the café. At gatherings in the café after a funeral he was often asked to contribute a reminiscence. He was still called upon to settle disputes of a factual nature. Were the Bonaparte and Orléans families banished from France before the Franco-Prussian War or after it? Was it Manet or Monet who painted water lilies? In his turn, he would ask about Jacques Chirac's many mistresses. Their response was muted, ambiguous, and ever so slightly offended. The truth was, they had no idea of the president's romantic life. That was the sort of information restricted to six or seven arrondissements in the city of Paris. There was a local idiom for it: information that did not walk but slept.

He had lived in Colle St.-Jacques for almost fifteen years and could not imagine living anywhere else. The inhabitants were old and the village was very old, its church dating to medieval times. Harry went often to Sunday Mass and also during the week, sitting in a rear pew and enjoying the creaks and groans of the ancient building, alive after all these years. One of the clerestory windows above the choir was of stained glass, some biblical scene, too distant for Harry to identify. In the bright sunlight of midmorning the colors were brilliant. For years he had thought of donating a window if there were any glassmakers in the vicinity who could construct one. At the café they knew of no one who could accomplish such a task. Of course he was remembering the wretched Connecticut Window at the Église St.-Sylvestre, itself as ugly a church as he had ever seen. He imagined his window as short, not too short, and narrow. In the village they would call it the American's Window. But there were no glassmakers, so there would be no window. Probably it was just as well. The little medieval church in Colle St.-Jacques was sublime as it stood and needed no gilding. The itinerant priest who officiated at Mass would not approve in any case. Father Émile approved of very little beyond the acknowledgment of sin and a four-course meal at the café following services. Maybe he could be bought off. Harry had more money than he knew what to do with, the legacy of his father. How would you go about bribing a priest? He supposed the same way he had gone about bribing presidents and clan chiefs and army colonels and their surrogates. You would hand him the money and say it was for the glorification of God, God's stained-glass window, with something left over for the church fathers to distribute to the needy. Those were the things Harry thought about sitting alone in the pew at the rear of the church. When he got up to leave, his bones were chilled all the way through.

When his father died the year before, age one hundred and five years old, Harry briefly considered returning to Connecticut but could not face the transatlantic flight, and if he moved to Connecticut, what would he do there? He knew no one. The house was too large for him. A New England winter would be a tragedy, snow to the eaves, power outages, icy roads, gloom. He would need a full-time housekeeper and a part-time gardener and a driver to help him get around, altogether too much bother. He believed the trick of old age was simplicity, a certain elegance, meaning economy of means. American medicine was no good, focused as it was on costly surgeries rather than pharmaceuticals as the French preferred. By then he knew very well that he had his mother's genes. He was seventy-four but he looked and felt like someone much older. His mother presented the same face to the world, seventy-six when she died on the operating table after a ghastly six months of unremitting pain; that surgery was the third of three. To his last days his father had the ruddy look and physique of a polo player, beautifully turned out in gray slacks and his shabby tweed jacket, a silk ascot at his throat. He thought often of his parents, their affection for each other, their squire's life in Connecticut. The Regency table, the kilim carpet. Marsden Hartley.

Harry was sitting in his rocking chair on the porch impatiently waiting for the mailman. He was eager to read the newspaper's accounts of the presidential campaign, now in full October flower. A black man running for the presidency! Harry had lived outside the country for so long he could not fathom how such a thing could happen, yet here he was, a graduate of both Columbia University and Harvard Law, a white man's pedigree. He was a marvelous speaker and an even better writer. The last time a writer had occupied the White House was the time of the Civil War, and what a writer he was. Teddy Roosevelt wrote, too, but not very well; and nothing at all from that time to this, except for Wilson and Jimmy Carter. Some caution warranted there. Probably a writer's temperament would not fit well in the modern White House, too much time given over to the shape and music of sentences while all around him clamored for action. A writer required repose, moments of stillness wherein an angel might speak. However, angels did not always bring benevolent thoughts, and they were not always angels. Sometimes they arrived in disguise. One look at Lincoln's ruined face as the war drew to a close was the evidence on offer. Harry remembered FDR at the end of his life, only sixty-three years old, his face ashen, eyes dull, hands trembling. Photographs concealed much but they did not conceal everything. A Washington friend of his father's reported the trembling hands and the wandering speech, to his father's shocked dismay: My God, what will we do without him? Harry sat in his rocking chair on the porch of his French cottage and thought about his father's dismay and his abrupt turn to face Harry. You're not to breathe a word of this, son. This news stays here in this room, between us.

Two letters arrived along with the American newspaper. He put them aside while he looked at page one, two articles on the campaign, two on Iraq. A movie star was dead. A scientist won a prize. The Dow was down owing to the financial crisis, banks broken, panic in the air, the government rushing to the rescue. Harry turned to the campaigns, reading carefully, beginning with the Democrats. He skimmed Iraq, skimmed the financial crisis, read the baseball standings, looked at a piece on men's winter fashions, and let the newspaper slip to the floor. He had been away from America for so long he did not trust his instincts. He could no longer read between the lines. Harry looked across his field to the road and the crease-port beyond, a sailing ship entering the harbor, spinnaker full, a thrilling sight in the morning brightness. He watched it a moment, thinking that he had but the vaguest purchase on American politics. He could not recall the name of the present governor of Connecticut and he had known personally three of the previous ones. He himself did not vote and hadn't for years. What he read in the newspapers and saw on French television resembled a half-remembered movie from his youth, everyone so young, the faces familiar but mostly nameless. This election was important but he wasn't sure he could get up to speed for it. He was unable to assess its meaning. America was a parallax universe, powerful, hypnotic in its way, quarrelsome and petulant, and irrelevant to him. His birth country had become a thing of curiosity; the farther away you were from it the more dangerous it seemed. A matter of optics. Up close the nation could appear harmless enough, almost buffoonish. He thought then that his various postings clung to him like a wardrobe of old suits. Each posting added another layer of distance, the picture indistinct, undeniably fabulous but foundering also. In the café his friends had stopped asking his opinion on this or that American problem. His answers were vague and off the point, his manner grudging—and then someone would ask about his war, and he was able to reply in complete sentences as if the war were only yesterday instead of decades past. But there were not very many questions about the war, another dark episode in the French version of the twentieth century. All in all, Harry preferred to watch the sailing ship, an object of vast tranquility. Tranquility was what he sought and seemed now to have found.

Harry rose heavily from his rocking chair and stepped inside the house to fetch his binoculars. When he raised them to his eyes, taking a minute or more to achieve sharp focus, he watched the spinnaker fall, followed by the mainsail. The vessel lost way, gliding toward the buoy, and in a moment or two made fast, her crew scrambling about the deck gathering lines, furling the sails. He thought of burly monkeys in miniature swinging from one tree branch to another. At last the docking chores were completed and the crew disappeared into the cabin, leaving the helmsman alone at the wheel. Harry focused closely now. The skipper appeared to be a man of about his own age, but he was fit, trim, long-muscled, a full head of snow-white hair. The skipper lit a fat cigar and sat back in his swivel chair inspecting his surroundings, an anchorage as snug as any in the Mediterranean. Harry noticed that he was deeply tanned, the color of mahogany or the Havana in his mouth. Then from the interior of the cabin a woman's slender hand ascended holding a bottle of beer. The skipper seized the beer, kissed the woman's hand, and resumed his scrutiny of the harbor as his boat rocked gently on the wavelets of the incoming tide.

Harry put his binoculars away and looked at the letters, an offer from American Express and the electric bill, then picked up the newspaper at his feet. He turned to the weather page and noted that the day would be clear. Tomorrow, too. The sun was full and behind him now. He sat in soft shade. The breeze died until it was dead still. Harry yawned deeply and closed his eyes. He thought that after a nap he would drive into town for a late lunch and a game of dominoes, perhaps take a glass of wine with his moules marinière. He felt a surge of well-being, a kind of gravitational pull. He felt as good as he had felt in ages and wondered now if a weekend trip to Paris might be in order. Drive to Marseilles, take the fast train. Stay at the good hotel near the Musée d'Orsay, spend an afternoon looking at pictures. He thought they had one, perhaps two, Marsden Hartleys. He opened his eyes and looked again at the port and the sea beyond it, a Cézanne blue that seemed to go on forever. Harry focused his binoculars and took a last look at the sailing ship, high-masted, not an inch shorter than sixty feet long, a white hull, teak decks, a spacious salon on the afterdeck. He watched the crew gather aft, a sudden bustle, the monkeys and the woman, visible at last, nicely turned out in a pale blue sundress and a floppy hat. The skipper remained in his swivel chair drinking beer. He turned to say something and the woman laughed. What a fine thing it would be to roam the Mediterranean in a sailing ship, no particular destination. Harry yawned deeply once again and then, passing into sleep, he thought of the expression on the skipper's face, a look of the most open contentment, no doubt pleased at his seamanship, pleased at his anchorage, and looking forward to the bright afternoon to come.

The cook rowed Sieglinde to the dock. He went to visit the fishmonger and she stepped into the bar-restaurant, already full at noon. But she was the only customer in a sundress and a floppy hat. The men inside were rough-looking, and the women, too, in cutoffs and T-shirts. Sieglinde asked the bartender if he could spare a moment, she was looking for someone, an American who was said to live in the village, Colle St.-Jacques. The bartender said there were no Americans in the village, though two English had a summer villa on the far side of town. Sieglinde shook her head and added some detail. The man she was looking for was an older man. He would be in his seventies now. Perhaps someone like that nearby? Her French was slang French but fluent. The bartender shook his head and turned his back to draw a beer. She said the American was a very old friend from years past. They had met in French Indochina! The bartender shook his head again. Sieglinde said that her old friend was called Harry Sanders. He had been in the American foreign service, retired now. She had an approximate address from the Department of

State. Took her years to get one and now she was here and unlikely to return and she would consider it a great courtesy if someone had an idea where her friend lived. The bartender had returned to his glassware but Sieglinde's voice rose sharply as she spoke so that everyone in the bar-restaurant could hear. The bartender said he was sorry but the people in the port and in the village above tended to keep to themselves as a matter of course, and so, alas, he was unable to help. Sieglinde looked around her, trying and failing to smile. She turned away and stepped outside, looking at the steep rise of the road to the plateau above. One of the older women in the café brushed by her and murmured in a voice so low that Sieglinde had to strain to hear, The cottage at the top of the hill. I do not know his name but I believe he is American. Sieglinde did not move but whispered back her profound thanks. You are very kind, madame. The woman said *Bonne chance* and went on, and Sieglinde stepped to the edge of the dock, looking out at the sailing ship. Her friend Samuel had left the bridge. She waited a moment. She did not wish to appear rushed, and in fact she was not rushed, only amused at the clannishness and suspicion of those in the bar-restaurant on the quay. Probably they thought Harry was a fugitive, someone on the run and therefore one to be protected. She smiled to herself. She had been looking for Harry a long time and could afford to wait a few minutes more. She looked past the ship to the open sea, feeling the breeze freshen, ruffling her hair, loose under the floppy hat. The years, what she had done with them, had treated her kindly. Everyone told her she had beautiful skin and radiant blue eyes.

Three times she tried to write him, three times she didn't. Of course she did not possess a specific address. One night she told the story to Samuel, who listened with apparent sympathy and excused himself to make a telephone call and in five minutes returned with an address. He thrust a piece of paper at her and said, Here. Samuel knew people who knew other people and it wasn't so hard after all. She waited awhile, about one year, before venturing forth. She did not know what to make of her indecision. She was not an indecisive person. Instead, she was impetuous. Perhaps it was this. Sieglinde had made her own way in the world. She distrusted return engagements, obeying her hard-won history. However, she found Harry a constant visitor to her memory. He refused to leave it. He went from visitor to guest to consort, and over time Sieglinde became accustomed to his ghostly presence. And so, as she rarely did, Sieglinde changed her mind.

She began the slow slog up the hill, pausing often. Her espadrilles were not equal to the task. Twice laboring trucks passed her but did not stop, not a matter of discourtesy but the difficulty of the road. Halfway up, Sieglinde turned to look back at the port. No one was visible on the deck of Samuel's boat. No doubt they had all gone down for a siesta. She labored on until at last she reached the crest of the crease, the land leveling abruptly, the fields golden in the sun. Nothing moved in the afternoon stillness, not even a bird. A peaceable place, Sieglinde thought. There were three houses in sight, and a kilometer or so down the road the village of Colle St.-Jacques. Some local authority had had the good sense to install a bench at the side of the road, and Sieglinde sat, breathing hard. She was sweating in the heat, scanning the land as she removed her floppy hat. What she saw brought to mind an Impressionist masterpiece on the white walls of a spacious museum. She smiled when she heard the distressed moo of a cow. So despite appearances, not entirely deserted. Sieglinde looked carefully at the closest house, a mailbox at the foot of the driveway, a small Citroën parked near the house. The porch was in deep shade. That was the house she wanted, she was sure of it. If it was not, she would return to the boat in the harbor. Samuel said he was up-sails at five p.m.

She walked slowly along the driveway and saw the man asleep in his chair on the porch. He was snoring softly. His newspaper had spilled to the floor. His head was in shadows and she could not make out his features. She took a step forward with an uneasy sense that she was trespassing and wondered for an instant if all this was a mistake, a kind of provocation. She stood irresolute, then looked once again. He had a long face, worn around the edges, closely shaven. She moved closer to him, and as she did he seemed to retreat before her. His hands rested formally on the arms of the chair, giving him the appearance of a bashful used-up pharaoh. His hands were an old man's hands, freckled, big-knuckled, a gold wedding ring on his left hand. That caused Sieglinde to take a step back, irresolute once more. She decided to ignore the ring, an unexpected, not to say unwanted, complication. Either he was married or he wasn't married, and if he was there was nothing she could do about it. She was looking at an old man, not Harry, someone like Harry, an older brother of Harry. He was barefoot and when she looked at his feet she saw the scars on his insteps and ankles and drew back, startled. Her heart turned over. She did know it was him, but a different him, not her idea of him, not the him she had known and loved and then thought about for forty years, wondering where he was and who he was with, conjuring a biography. This is what had become of him. As she watched, he opened his eyes and closed them at once, his whistle-snore softer. Sieglinde had come to Colle St.-Jacques because she wanted to know how his life had turned out and how much he remembered of their time together in the war. Did he remember Chopin? Surely he would not forget the silk-string hammock. He was not the only love of her life but he was the first, an episode cut short. She could not for the life of her explain her sudden departure on the hospital ship. What was in her mind? He had gotten under her skin. But why was she frightened? Was it because she was so young and had not formed an idea of a life for herself and was fearful of his life, the pull of it, the undertow? She thought it was that.

Harry seemed to have left few traces of himself. He had made himself hard to find, but she had found him. And what she saw in front of her eyes was scarcely recognizable. Had his life been unlucky? Sieglinde looked again at his feet, the heavy scar-ridges, the missing toenails, old wounds, life's undertow. She noticed the cane propped against the porch railing, perhaps a cane made from an elephant's tusk. What did he do with himself in a place so remote? Harry was so companionable. He had energy to burn. She herself had led an adventurous life. She had lived far afield, this place and that on one continent or another. She avoided Southeast Asia and northern Europe. She had no further use for those places. And him? Personal appearance was a superficial thing. She would not judge him from scarred feet and a long face. Sieglinde touched his arm but he did not stir. Very well, she would wait. She sat down to wait, her floppy hat in her hands. Near and far nothing moved, the surroundings stuck fast, all but defenseless in the heavy heat of midday. She heard crickets and moved a little closer to Harry. She thought, What a pretty, pretty place.

When he came to life at last Harry gave her a luminous smile and said, You.

Me, she answered.